Jen

"A delight to read from start to finish!"

—Mixing Reality with Fiction on
It Started with Christmas

"A wonderful and wholesome read that definitely leaves you with that warm tingly glow."

—By the Letter Book Reviews on
It Started with Christmas

"It's a tender treat that can be savored in any season."

—*Publishers Weekly* on *Christmas Wishes and Mistletoe Kisses*

"*Christmas Wishes and Mistletoe Kisses* is a wonderful, delightful, emotional read perfect for everyone."

—This Chick Reads on *Christmas Wishes and Mistletoe Kisses*

"Jenny Hale has outdone herself once again by creating raw, emotional, and extremely thought-provoking situations, all of which were surrounded by the serenity of the beach house."

—The Writing Garnet on *The Summer House*

"North Carolina's beautiful Outer Banks are the perfect setting for this sweet, poignant romance, and authentic characters and a riveting story make it a keeper worth savoring."

—*Publishers Weekly* on *Christmas Wishes and Mistletoe Kisses*

it
started
.with
Christmas

ALSO BY JENNY HALE

it
started
with
Christmas

JENNY HALE

FOREVER

New York   Boston

Copyright © 2018 by Jenny Hale

Cover illustration and design by Ami Smithson. Cover copyright © 2019 by Hachette Book Group, Inc.

Forever
Hachette Book Group
1290 Avenue of the Americas, New York, NY 10104
read-forever.com
twitter.com/readforeverpub

Originally published in 2018 by Bookouture, an imprint of StoryFire Ltd.

First Forever Edition: September 2019

Forever is an imprint of Grand Central Publishing. The Forever name and logo are trademarks of Hachette Book Group, Inc.

The publisher is not responsible for websites (or their content) that are not owned by the publisher.

The Hachette Speakers Bureau provides a wide range of authors for speaking events. To find out more, go to www.hachettespeakersbureau.com or call (866) 376-6591.

ISBN 978-1-5387-1644-1 (mass market)

Printed in the United States of America

OPM

10 9 8 7 6 5 4 3 2 1

it
started
with
Christmas

Chapter One

"I want to spend Christmas at the cabin." Nana's voice came from the dark stairway, startling Holly McAdams and making her jump as she walked in the front door, the warmth of the little house a stark contrast to the icy cold outside.

"You want to what?" Holly asked gently, seeing Nana standing on the top step of the staircase, and understanding fully the weight of her grandmother's statement.

Holly dropped her heavy handbag with a thud against the wall, glad to have finished her last night of waitressing for the holiday. With the Christmas crowds, the restaurant where she worked had been slam-packed from opening to closing. One of their best employees, she had requested this holiday off to be with Nana and was thrilled when she actually got the okay from management. Her boss needed convincing, given the busy season, but knowing how hard she worked for him, even putting in late hours beyond her duties, he let her have the days. Her head pounded, her feet ached, and she wanted to climb into her warm bed, but Nana was finally opening up, and this was what Holly had been hoping for.

"I've been thinking how things just aren't the same," Nana said, coming down the stairs and walking past Holly, the request she'd made hanging in the air between them.

"That's for sure…" Holly said. Her voice trailed off with her memories. Things hadn't been the same since Holly's grandfather died.

Holly turned around to view her grandmother's tiny living room, clicking on a lamp on the small table in the hallway as she trailed behind Nana, and then two more on either side of the sofa when Nana lowered herself down onto the center cushion and wrapped herself in the throw they had for chilly nights. The space was cloaked in a buttery glow. Holly pressed the button under the Christmas tree to turn it on and it sparkled in the corner, the white lights shimmering off the baubles they'd hung together during one of Nana's rare moments of contentment. Bright red ribbons snaked through the mantel greenery, drawing attention to two stockings made of thickly knit material, each one embroidered with their initials in a snowy white.

Holly stared at Nana, sensing how difficult this decision was.

"I couldn't sleep," Nana said.

Holly faced her.

"The idea kept going around in my head—restless, unable

to be denied the way I usually can talk myself out of it. So I think I'm ready."

Holly leaned on the window ledge and took in a deep breath, the memory of Papa hitting hard tonight. The view of the Nashville skyline was full of high-rise buildings all outlined in lights for the holiday season.

Arthur McAdams, or Papa as Holly called her grandfather, had been a musician, writing songs and singing in local bars. He'd never gotten The Big Deal, as he'd called it, but he'd actually played at the historic Tootsies once. He'd teased her that his life was complete because of that. But, really, his life had been complete because he'd been able to support his family by adapting parts of his songs as poems for greeting cards, selling others, and occasionally renting out his old family cabin in the Tennessee hills to tourists who wanted to be close enough to the gritty bars of Nashville's Honky Tonk Row but be able to spend their evenings secluded.

"I've never worked a day in my life," he'd said with a grin once as he tapped a loose nail on the front porch floorboards of the cabin. Even everyday chores there seemed like a labor of love to him. Papa had managed what many people hadn't: while his friends went off to their workday, he could make his money by doing what he loved.

Holly had lived in Nana's house in Music City for the last

year. The neighborhood on the outskirts of Nashville had been quaint when her grandparents bought the bungalow back in the fifties. They'd lived in that little house downtown and paid it off over the years, and neither Papa nor Nana cared one bit about moving. But as the city had grown, and the homes had aged, that small area had gone into decline, and it wasn't a great place for Nana to live all alone. Not to mention that when Papa had passed away, Nana had drifted into a distant, quiet state: she needed a companion. So Holly had moved in with her, canceling her enrollment in a local design class and taking a waitressing job at one of the upscale steakhouses in Nashville.

Nana hadn't been to Papa's cabin since before he'd passed away two years ago. She'd refused to set foot in it without him. In fact, the only time Holly had been there in recent years was when she had renovated the place. They hadn't known until his death, but he'd written songs and sold them in Nashville under a pen name. When he passed, he left them quite an inheritance. As part of the money Papa left her, she received directions from him to remodel the old cabin so they could rent it out full-time. Papa thought, with Holly's decorating help, that the cabin could pull in a sizeable income in vacation rentals to supplement Nana's retirement and give her a nice nest egg to see her through the rest of her life. He told them so in a letter accompanying his will.

Holly had always had an eye for design. She often thought that was how Papa's artistic gene had manifested itself in her. Planning things, organizing, and decorating came naturally to her. Her friends all asked her to go shopping with them when they'd move into their apartments, and she couldn't remember how many of her friends' weddings she'd lent a helping hand to. She'd planned to do something with her talent, but life seemed to have other plans.

Realizing she was lost in thought, Holly turned back to Nana. "Isn't the cabin rented for the holiday?" she asked. After she'd redone the interior, and put the new photos online, they could barely keep up with the number of rental requests.

Nana shook her head. "Like I said, I've been thinking about it for a while. I cleared the schedule starting this week, just in case I had the courage to go."

"But the snow…"

This December had been a record-breaking month, with icy temperatures plummeting, sending more snow than this area had seen in decades. There were road closures everywhere, and Holly knew that driving in the hills would be a nightmare. But even though Nana and Papa had lived here in the city, their hearts had always been at the cabin. Nana married Papa there and she spent her honeymoon there. And they always had big family Christmases there.

Should they go? The time at the cabin might do Nana some good, and it would also give Holly a chance to go through the old barn that was piled with the original furniture and things from the house that she still had to tag and either sell or give to charity.

The alternative was to sit in this house for the next week, Nana spending another holiday, thinking about how they weren't at the cabin like they'd always been, and about how Papa wasn't there with her.

Nope. Holly wasn't going to let that happen.

"You know what?" she said before Nana had answered her. "If you want to go, then that's what we'll do. We'll pack up all the gifts, take down the tree, tie it to the top of my car, and put it up at the cabin. We'll make hot chocolate, and climb under blankets, and binge-watch movies until we fall asleep. We'll read all the books we've been wanting to finish, make oven pizzas, and never put anything on our feet but fuzzy socks."

She grabbed Nana's hands, pulling her off the sofa gently, the blanket falling to a lump on the floor. "We'll dance to Christmas carols and when we get tired of that we'll visit Otis and Buddy! We can take them cookies like we used to do."

She twirled Nana around, and that little scowl she'd gotten so good at faltered just slightly.

"Even with the snow, we can drive there in less than an hour. Let's pack!"

"Right now?" Nana pressed her lips together to suppress her smile.

"Why not?" She pushed through her exhaustion for Nana's sake. "It's late, yes, but I can have that tree down and be ready to leave in a couple of hours. If we stay up till midnight, we can sleep in the next morning! I put extra thick, feather duvets on the beds, with one thousand thread-count sheets."

Nana's eyes grew round.

"Remember, Papa said, and I quote, to 'do it up right' and if I didn't, I'd have to answer to him when we saw each other next."

That made her smile.

"Let's do it," Holly said. She put her arms around Nana and squeezed her excitedly, making Nana laugh—the best sound in the world. Things were going to be great again— she could feel it—and Holly knew it would all start with Christmas.

Chapter Two

It took a few hours to pack up the ornaments and the lights, pull down the stockings, drag the small tree and mantel greenery outside, get it all secured in and on the car, pack their gifts and bags, and make the drive. The cabin was just up a winding road from a small hillside town called Leiper's Fork, known for its southern, boot-wearing hospitality, warm buttermilk biscuits, occasional famous musician sightings, and local art galleries.

On their way there the roads were treacherous. The weather forecast announcement on the radio said things were going to get worse before they got better and to be prepared to spend Christmas at home, warning that many of the roads wouldn't be passable. Holly certainly believed it. She was jittery from maneuvering the car as it slid all over the place. She prayed silently that nothing would happen to them at such a late hour on the dark and snowy route to the cabin.

It was after midnight when they pulled into the ice-covered drive. When she finally came to a stop and cut off the engine, the keys to the cabin now in her hand, she exhaled, unsure how long she'd been holding her breath. Her shoulders were tense from the events of the night, and she couldn't wait to get into the cozy warmth that awaited them.

"Stay here," she said, opening her door. "I'll come get you."

It was pitch black. Holly turned on the little light on her phone so she could see where she was walking, her boots sinking into the fluffy snow. What started out as ice billowed down after making, she noticed, the whole place look like a winter wonderland, once her eyes adjusted to the darkness. But with no porch light on it was still difficult to see, so she shined her phone toward Nana's car door and pulled the handle.

"Let's get inside and then we can think about what we want to do with the tree. I should probably get it in as soon as we can, since the snow is still falling."

Nana nodded, taking her hand and carefully exiting the car. They walked together to the porch, every step labored and careful. The last thing Nana needed was to fall way out there, in a snowstorm.

By the time they got to the distinctive red front door that always made Holly feel like Christmas, Holly was shivering so much that she could hardly slide the key into the lock, but she got it in and, with a click, she turned the knob and hit the lights.

"I'll get our bags," she said as Nana looked around at the new interior.

That sadness that had been in Nana's eyes when they pulled up remained; she didn't seem at all impressed with the updates. It was easy to see that she missed the old, familiar surroundings. Her gaze settled on a glass guitar sculpture Holly had bought from a local art dealer, thrilled that she'd been able to afford it.

Growing up, the old cabin always had a special place in Holly's heart. It was a place to lay her head after long days outside hiking, fishing, or sitting around the bonfire with friends. And in the winters, they played board games, strung popcorn garlands on the Christmas tree, and Papa hid presents all over the cabin for everyone to find.

It was simply decorated with very basic furniture—no frills. But Holly had changed that. She'd painted the interior, updated the lighting, added stainless steel appliances with a double oven feature and new cabinetry, hardwood floors and crown molding. Then she'd completely refreshed the space with creamy furniture, soft lighting, and lots of references to Nashville and its surrounding areas. She'd covered the blank walls with local artwork, and the whole place had a very southern feel to it when she'd finished—the perfect retreat to bring in the tourists.

Holly understood Nana's feelings, though. It was the

same way she'd felt the day she'd first come in to make the changes. It was the place where Papa's memory was the strongest. She remembered how he sat her on his lap whenever he retired in one of the old rocking chairs on the front porch at sunset. She'd lean back against him as he rocked to the sound of the crickets when they started their song in the woods each evening. She'd felt completely safe, like nothing bad could ever happen to her when she was sitting with him.

"Why don't you relax on the sofa?" Holly suggested.

Nana tore her eyes from the sculpture to acknowledge her granddaughter, but when she made eye contact, there was uncertainty in her face. She turned around and toddled over to the cream leather sofa, her legs stiff from the journey, and ran her weathered hand along its surface before she took a seat on the edge of it.

Pulling her coat up around her chin to keep the icy cold from assaulting her, Holly went outside again and tugged their suitcases from the backseat, shutting the car door with her foot. She brought them up the porch stairs, the weight of them making her winded, and carried them down the hallway to the bedroom. She noticed that Nana was still on the edge of the sofa, her hands on her knees, that scowl clear as day. Perhaps she was just tired. Holly would get her things into the bedroom as quickly as possible so she could have some rest. It had been a big night. Dropping the luggage at her feet, unable to drag them a step farther, she opened the bedroom door and turned on the light.

To Holly's complete surprise her eyes flew to the center of the room where a man sat straight up in bed like a bolt of lightning, before jumping to his feet, shocked out of sleep, causing her to shriek in panic. He froze, clearly taking stock of her, his gaze bouncing from her face to her bags. When it was clear to both of them that the other meant no harm, the man ran his hands through his hair in sleep-deprived confusion.

Only then did she take in the square of his jaw, the shadow of stubble, the darkness of his eyes, and his thick, jet-black, perfectly cut hair. He looked like a magazine model. Apart from the fact that he was wearing ridiculous silver striped pajamas. But even those he could manage quite well.

"I'm sorry…Are you renting here this week?" he asked.

Holly shook her head, having difficulty finding the words while those eyes bore into her. They seemed restless and curious. She cleared her throat and tried to focus on something else so she could get a coherent thought, but all she could see was the print of his body on the sheets, making it harder to concentrate. She'd stepped into this man's personal space, awakened him from sleep, and her cheeks were burning in embarrassment. "My grandmother said no one was renting this week," she managed. "We own the cabin."

He blinked excessively, and she wasn't sure if he was processing something or still trying to wake up. Then, finally, he said, "So...Are you cleaning between guests or something? At one in the morning? In a snowstorm?"

"What's going on here?" Nana said from behind Holly, taking her by surprise. "I heard a scream."

"Joseph Barnes," he said, introducing himself to Nana.

Nana's gaze pierced right through him. "We're spending Christmas here."

"I was renting last week, and I'd planned to call you, but my cell phone service has been spotty. The airport is closed and my flight was canceled."

Oh yes. Holly remembered helping Nana with the reservation. He was there on his own—a bigwig corporate financial advisor or something from New York.

"Where's your car?" Holly asked, it suddenly dawning on her that there was nothing in the driveway to alert them that they had a guest.

"I caught a cab from the airport."

Joseph took a step toward them, causing Holly to back up, stumbling over her bags. He caught her with one strong arm.

Rattled, she busied herself with moving the suitcases against the wall.

"I'd planned to pay you the extra rent. I'm so sorry if I've imposed on your family time."

Nana took in an exasperated breath. "Well, Holly and I are not leaving. There's no way in the world that I will get back into a car in this weather, so we'll have to make the best of this for a few days."

"It'll be fine," Holly said, not sure how she'd manage her movie binge-watching with a stranger lurking around. "Nana, you and I can share the other bedroom and Joseph can have the one he's in."

Nana's frown deepened as she turned around and headed for the spare room. "I'm exhausted," she said. "So let's get a move on and unpack our things."

Holly went to pick up the suitcases, but Joseph leaned forward, grabbing them first. "Please," he said. "Allow me. I'm so terribly sorry. It's the least I can do." She was impressed by his gesture. How thoughtful.

They both followed behind Nana, who had already made it into the room and was standing with her hands on her hips. "What in the world is all this?"

The room was full of cardboard boxes. Joseph moved past Nana, tidying them up, consolidating cartons, and pushing things to the side of the room. "These are all my things," he said.

When they'd gotten the bags into the room and Nana was in the en suite bathroom getting ready for bed, Joseph turned to Holly and said, "I'm sorry again. I feel just awful…"

"What could you do?" Holly said with a consoling smile. "It wasn't your fault."

"Is there anything else you need before I turn in? Any more luggage?"

She thought about the snow falling outside and the tree tied to the top of her car and bit her lip. After a full day of work and then the drive, she barely had enough energy to get the rest of the bags, let alone a giant spruce. Dare she ask him?

Joseph noticed her deliberation. "What is it? I don't mind. Ask away."

"Feel like getting a Christmas tree off my car?"

The request clearly surprised him, making him smile, the natural amusement on his face only solidifying her opinion of his good looks. Suddenly, she'd forgotten all about how tired she was.

Chapter Three

"How's that?" Joseph said from under the Christmas tree where he was holding the trunk into the stand before he twisted the bolts to secure it. He'd changed into a sweater and jeans, put his hiking boots on, and insisted that Holly stay put inside while he got the tree off her car. Now, with his coat and scarf draped on the chair in the corner, he was lying on the floor, arms stretched under the tree, wriggling it back and forth. "Is it straight?"

"It's perfect."

While he got the tree up, Holly made them a cup of coffee to combat the exhaustion that they both felt. She'd been so excited to get out of Nashville and take Nana to the cabin that she hadn't thought about the unpacking part, and it was now quarter to two in the morning. But if they'd left the tree on her car, it would've been buried in snow by the next day, and a mess when they'd brought it inside.

Once he saw their gifts and the countless ornaments and decorations, Joseph promised to bring them all in tonight. He said it was the least he could do for disrupting their plans.

Nana had gone on to bed, and Holly told her that she'd turn in too in just a bit, once they brought everything in.

Holly didn't mind the late hour, though. It was nice to have someone around her age to talk to. When she wasn't working, she spent all her time with Nana. And Joseph seemed like a good guy. He really didn't have to do all this for them, and it was clear that he was trying to make up for the miscommunication.

When he got it all secured, Joseph came over to her at the kitchen counter and took a seat on one of the iron barstools she'd found on sale downtown. She handed him a mug with a faded printed picture of a guitar on it that read "Music City" underneath in neon pink block letters. He took it, inspecting the front discreetly, but she caught him. Without thinking, she'd used Papa's stash of mugs she'd hidden at the bottom of the cabinet instead of the stone-fired, multi-glazed ones she bought to match the new dishes. On Christmas with Papa she always used his mugs for hot chocolate, and they topped them with whipped cream and candy canes.

"I didn't know how you take your coffee," she said. "I put a little cream and sugar in it. I hope that's okay."

"It's fine," he said. "Thank you." He took the mug from her and lifted it to his lips. He looked different in his sweater. It was dark navy blue and brought out the slight olive tone in his face and his dark eyes. And it was much more stylish than those pajamas he'd had on. As he sat there beside her, trying to hide his fatigue, there was no denying that he was strikingly handsome.

"Have you enjoyed your stay?"

"Yes, quite a lot, thank you." Joseph set his mug down on the counter and looked around. "This place is great. Very relaxing."

She smiled, happy that she'd pulled off what she'd intended with the remodel. "I'm so glad."

"It's definitely different from New York," he said with a chuckle.

Holly laughed a little too loudly and tried to suck it back in. The image of Joseph and his silver pajamas popping into her head, amusing her. Maybe they were a New York fashion statement—definitely not anything like what her papa would've worn in the cabin on Christmas. And they had to be cold in this weather. Joseph needed some good plaid flannel.

"Did I say something funny?" he asked, interested.

Her smile lingering, she shook her head. "No, it just reminded me of my papa. He was definitely a southern soul, very much like this place. I remember when we spent summers here, he used to sit out on the porch, wearing his dirty work boots from helping his buddies plow the fields," she digressed. "He'd always have a drink on the table and a guitar in his hands. I think he'd have sat out on that porch all day and night if my nana had let him."

Suddenly, it occurred to her that she'd been going on about strangers Joseph didn't know, which she worried might bore him. But it was as if her story had entranced him. He was smiling, looking into her eyes. She liked how he did that.

His gaze shifted upward as he surveyed the room. "Your papa lived *here*?"

Holly's story probably didn't fit with the new décor. "I've remodeled since he passed away. When I came as a kid, it was more...rustic."

"Mmm." Joseph continued looking around. "*You* did this?"

She nodded.

"It's really current and professionally done. So you're a decorator?"

Holly shrugged and shook her head, uncertainty taking over. She wasn't ashamed of what she did for a living but by the fact that she wasn't busy pursuing what she really wanted to do in life. The problem was that she just wasn't willing to be away from Nana, and doing decorating jobs or starting her own full-scale business would mean she'd be working all hours to get a company started. Just the remodel of the cabin had consumed a huge amount of her time. "I'm a server at a steakhouse in Nashville."

"Really?" He seemed perplexed by her answer, but he worked to straighten out his expression. "It seems like you could undoubtedly be an interior decorator."

"Yeah, it comes easily for me. I really love event-planning too—anything creative, really. But I could never do that full-time."

He held his mug, his strong hands nearly covering the surface entirely, making it look much smaller than it had previously. "Why?" he asked.

It might be simple for him to just start a career from scratch with whatever millions he probably had, but she had bills to pay and Nana to care for. And even if she tried to find a job in that realm, who would hire her when she had no experience whatsoever?

"I'm happy waitressing," Holly said, just to stop the conversation. She could tell by his face that he didn't agree, so she cut it off before he could try to convince her otherwise. She didn't need some guy filling her head with grand ideas that would fall flat and waste her time and money she could be spending to give Nana a great life. Waitressing was safe; it gave her a steady income and regular hours.

"I'm a lot like my papa: I have that creative bug, but I'm content just making a regular living." She didn't need anything fancy. Papa had stuck to those ideals and he'd saved enough to leave his family with quite a nice inheritance. Where would his money have gone if he'd run around trying to do something grand?

When Holly twisted toward Joseph to get comfortable, she ignored the disbelieving look in his eyes. "Your papa sounds like a fun guy," he said, and she was happy he'd let her off the hook.

"He was."

Just mentioning Papa made her relax. He had that effect on people, which was probably why Nana had been uptight ever since his passing. He'd been her sunshine, and when he was gone, she just didn't have a reason to smile anymore. But Holly was going to do her very best to change that.

"I naturally gravitated to my papa, so my parents let me spend every summer with him and Nana here at the cabin, and I was always with him on holidays. I can't imagine a childhood with anyone other than Papa." She hadn't chatted this much to anyone in ages. "I guess all dads and granddads are like that, though. What's your granddad like?"

Joseph pursed his lips, his eyebrows raised. "Uhh…" He seemed a little frazzled, but he was obviously good at keeping himself together. "I never knew either of my grandparents. They both passed away before I was born."

"Oh, that's really sad," she said, feeling terrible for having glorified her childhood with her own grandfather. She hadn't meant to seem insensitive. "What about your dad? What was he like?"

"I don't...speak to my father."

"You don't?" Holly couldn't fathom not talking to her own dad. "Why don't you talk to him?" She probably shouldn't have asked him such a personal question but her curiosity overpowered her sense of restraint.

"I don't think he's a very nice person." Joseph took his mug over to the coffeepot, topped it off, and then reached out for hers.

She handed the mug over, noticing the exhaustion in his face as he grabbed the cream and sugar. "Why not?" she asked while he filled up her mug. Holly reached for the spoon, and he slid the sugar over. They made coffee together while talking like old friends, which didn't happen often when she met someone.

After he set the coffees at their places, he stretched his shoulders back and relaxed them as if releasing pent-up tension. "It's just a hunch I have. I never knew him." He turned toward the buttery light coming in from the other room before those dark eyes came back toward her. "Enough about me, though. I don't want to dampen your spirits. It's Christmas." He smiled that million-dollar smile, and as she looked at it this time, she wondered if it was authentic or just well practiced.

Holly held her mug with both hands to keep her warm. The old heater was working overtime in this cold, and even though the rooms were heated, it was as if a winter current still slinked through them, penetrating down to her bones. She considered digging her big wooly socks from her suitcase but didn't want to wake Nana. Instead, she just hovered over her mug that was covered in mini posters of bars from downtown with Tootsies at the center.

She'd enjoyed herself tonight, and, even in the cold, Joseph made her feel warmer. Conversation with him was effortless, and she liked the way it felt to have his attention on her. "I didn't expect you to stay up half the night, putting up the tree with me," she said. "But thank you."

"It's no problem. I don't sleep a whole lot anyway these days."

"I need lots of sleep," she said with a smile. "Tonight will set me back a whole week. I'll be out by suppertime tomorrow, just wait and see." She was just making conversation so they could stay up longer, but she didn't think she'd be tired at all with him around.

When she mentioned supper, her mind went to the idea of sharing a meal with him. They could tell stories, maybe she'd be lucky enough to make him laugh—the look he'd given her a few times could melt the ice outside it was so warmhearted and sincere. This unexpected visitor had already brought so much fresh air into the house that Holly couldn't help but be hopeful that the snow would keep falling.

She didn't have to worry, though, she decided. She'd definitely have more time with him, unless the county could get the streets cleared by some miracle. No one had been prepared for the precipitation they were getting, so it seemed they'd all have to stay right where they were.

"Speaking of dinner," he said, "we're really low on food. I was going to try to walk into town and find a market."

"I brought a little bit, but, yes, let's see if we can get to the main road tomorrow." Holly was being positive, but she wasn't hopeful about it, even on foot. She'd hardly gotten here tonight the roads were so bad; businesses were closed everywhere; the news on the car radio was full of accidents on both I-65 and tons of the country back roads.

Reflecting on it, Holly had been stupid to even try to drive in such a mess, but Nana hadn't seemed this hopeful in years. Holly wondered if, subconsciously, Nana had just wanted to be close to Papa this Christmas. But now, as she looked around, she realized there wasn't anything left of him here except his request to redo the place that lingered on every surface. Not only could she and Nana no longer get home, but now they'd been thrown together with Joseph Barnes. While *she* didn't mind at all, Holly wondered how Nana would react in the morning.

Holly took a drink from her mug, realizing her tummy had started to feel empty. "I've been up so long and the mention of food…" She turned to him. "…I'm starting to get hungry."

Joseph glanced toward the kitchen pantry, thoughtful. "I have a few slices left from a sweet potato pie I bought while I was here. We could have some."

Holly couldn't help the grin that crawled across her face at the idea that Joseph had bought himself a pie. "You have sweet potato pie? How very southern of you."

He gave her that inquiring look she'd seen him do before. "I'd never had it before, and it sounded good."

"It *is* good! It's my favorite, actually. I'd eat sweet potato pie instead of cake. Just put a candle in it and pipe my name on the top for my birthday."

He laughed. "Well, then, we *must* have some with our coffees."

"I can't possibly argue with that suggestion."

He opened the pantry door and retrieved a box with a window-lid revealing two-thirds of a pie that looked divine. As he turned away and grabbed a pie cutter from the drawer, Holly considered the inconvenience this storm may be causing *him* as well. He'd been so worried about them, but he, too, was trapped here with strangers, unable to return home.

"Joseph?" she said to get his attention.

He swiveled around, those dark eyes landing on her, a quick thought passing over them before he addressed her. "Please, call me Joe. Everybody does."

Had their moment of sharing tonight made them no longer seem like strangers to him? She liked that idea. "Joe." She tried the new name on her lips. "I'm sorry you're stuck here with us," she said. "I'm sure you'd like to be home for Christmas."

There was a shift in his expression and then he nodded and turned back to the pie, without answering, making her wonder if she'd said something too personal. But he'd just shared a little about not speaking to his dad earlier... Did he not have anyone to return to for Christmas? Surely he had a family to see.

"Here you go," he said, sliding a piece toward her, the sweet cinnamon smell of it absolute perfection. Joe took his own and sat down next to her. "I'm glad I could share this. I wasn't sure how I was going to eat it all." He turned his plate, admiring the golden piece of sugary deliciousness. "Although, I was certainly going to try."

Holly laughed. "I could definitely eat a whole sweet potato pie if I let myself." She scraped a forkful, took a bite, and swallowed. "The flavor of this takes me back to my childhood. Nana would make up stacks of pies for the homeless shelters and we'd deliver them together." Holly had forgotten about it until now. "She hasn't done that in quite a while."

"That's a kind gesture," Joe said, the point of his pie already gone. He cut another bite.

"It might be nice to get her involved in something like that again. She's been depressed since my papa passed away a couple of years ago. That's why we're here: to give her a change of scenery and hopefully, with the Christmas atmosphere, lift her mood."

Joe nodded, contemplative.

The two of them sat in silence for a bit and then Joe looked over at her, his face full of heavy thoughts, she could tell. She felt an instant connection with Joe, wanting to ask him what it was she saw in his eyes. Her rational mind told her it was ridiculous—maybe the lack of sleep had made her delirious. Holly picked up her fork and dragged it along the surface of the pie, making a heart.

That heaviness lifted when she did that, and Joe studied the drawing she'd made. Then with his own fork, he made a little doodle on his pie.

"What did you draw?" she asked, leaning over it.

"You can't tell?"

He turned the plate in her direction and Holly noticed how close his arm was to hers, giving her goose bumps. She caught sight of the masculinity of his wrist, the way his watch sat on his skin, the stillness in his fingers, and, over the aroma of the pie, she could make out the tiniest hint of his spicy, sandalwood scent mixed with clean cotton. It was all so delicious.

"Is it a house?" She tried to keep her focus on the pie.

"Ha! No." He squinted as if he were trying to make out the house she'd seen. "It's not obvious?" When he tipped his head to the side to make eye contact their faces were close, that natural grin making her forget all about her hunger.

"A pencil?"

Little huffs of laughter escaped him, and he shook his head.

"Tell me," she said, completely stumped.

"How could you not guess it? It's a Christmas tree! It's a perfect representation, if you ask me."

The late hour and the sugar were making her punchy, and she laughed out loud. "Sorry. I should've guessed," she said, looking down at his pencil-slash-house. "I totally see a tree now," she lied. Holly leaned in to look at it again, his fingers resting close enough that she could brush them with her own. She wanted to.

Without warning, he stood up, clearly pulling away and taking the moment with him. Holly mentally scrambled to figure out if she'd said or done anything to cause the abrupt change. She searched his face for an answer, but he didn't give her any.

"We'll never get to sleep if we don't finish decorating that tree." Joe kept talking as he paced into the living room.

It was only then that she realized she'd been keeping him up. Perhaps he had things to do tomorrow—she hadn't even asked.

"Please," he said. "Finish your pie. I'll start unwinding more lights."

Holly looked down at the heart she'd made, suddenly wondering why she'd drawn it. It stared back at her like a little ray of sunshine from behind the clouds. She had been surprised at every turn tonight, and after it all, she could swear she felt a little Christmas magic in the air.

Chapter Four

Ah hem.

The sound came filtering through Holly's dreamlike state, and she couldn't open her eyes no matter how hard she tried because she was *so* comfortable. She'd stayed up entirely too late. It felt like it must still be the middle of the night; there was no way it could be morning yet.

Ah hem!

It was definitely Nana clearing her throat the way she did when she wanted Holly to look at something important, but she was trying to be subtle. Holly attempted to wake up to find out what she needed, but her eyelids wouldn't budge. Her limbs were dead weight. She was so exhausted that her brain couldn't even locate the nerves in them; all she could feel was their heaviness. She just wanted to stay in bed a little longer…

But then, as her mind began to work, she struggled to recall the moments when she'd brushed her teeth, changed into her pajamas, and climbed into bed with Nana. The last thing she could remember was decorating the tree. Joe had dropped down onto the sofa, facing it, and patted the cushion beside him. With the room completely dark except the white twinkling Christmas lights, they'd stopped to admire their work, daylight only a few hours away. But no matter how hard Holly tried, she couldn't get her memory to move past that point.

Suddenly, she was aware of an arm behind her head, supporting her neck, a strong leg entwined with hers, soft, even breathing at her cheek. This was not Nana.

Holly willed her eyes to open, using every ounce of strength she had. When she'd finally been able to get her lids to move, it took her a minute, but as the image became clear, she saw Joe's gorgeous face right in front of her, his eyes closed, his peaceful expression, and behind him, out of focus, was Nana, standing in the center of the living room. She had her arms crossed, her lips pressed together, but Holly couldn't budge.

She shifted just slightly to make eye contact with Nana and was immediately met with her disapproving glare. Holly knew what it looked like: Joe was handsome and kind. He was just the sort of guy Holly would flirt with, given the chance. But she'd done no such thing; she'd been a complete lady, and Nana should know that. Holly wouldn't mention the fact that she'd moved beyond the flirting stage anyway. Last night, she'd had real, honest conversations with Joe and she liked him.

The idea that Nana would think negatively about either

of them made her feel tense, and she wanted to spring right up from the sofa to explain, but exhaustion and fear kept her rooted where she was. She didn't know what to do because she was sure that the complete mortification of falling asleep together and then cuddling all night would immediately descend upon them both the minute he woke up.

Joe changed positions as he snuggled down into her neck, sending a fiery sensation through her face. This looked so bad… Holly didn't want Nana to think that she'd shacked up with some guy on their first night in Leiper's Fork. This holiday was about family, and making Nana feel comfortable.

Joe inhaled, relaxed and contented. He opened his eyes and then, when the situation obviously registered, he rolled backward onto the floor with a thump.

While he struggled to stand and regain composure, he regarded Holly with wide-eyed shock. "I'm so sorry," he said quickly, his breaths short and tense. She willed herself not to look at the chest she'd been so comfortable against only seconds ago.

Holly stood up to face him, nervous energy shooting through her veins and making the movements easier than they should be after such little sleep. "No," she said anxiously. "It's totally fine." Her last statement came out as almost a squeak and she coughed to try to cover it up. *It's totally fine?* What in the world had she meant by *that?* Curling up with him on the sofa the first night she'd met him was totally fine? She didn't want him to think this was a common occurrence for her. What a stupid thing to say.

"The tree looks nice." Nana's words held no emotion. She followed Joe's every movement with disdain before finally padding to the other side of the room and walking into the kitchen, only the bar separating them in the open floor plan. "Anyone want me to make breakfast?" she asked, opening a cabinet door and then nearly slamming it shut, the sound of it rattling Holly more. "I'm assuming coffee is in order." She opened another cabinet door and it smacked against the frame as she shut it.

"Please, Ms...." Joe said, striding over with purpose, his face flaming red.

"McAdams," Nana spit the word at him.

"Ms. McAdams..."

While he was clearly trying to be adult about the situation, the look on Joe's face gave away his embarrassment. Holly could see the same look he might have had as a child when he'd eaten the last cookie that his mother had been saving and he hadn't wanted her to find out.

"Allow me to make everyone coffee," he said. "It's the least I could do."

Joe was still blinking, stifling a yawn, and not making

any further attempts to look over at Holly. She was glad for that because she'd never been so mortified in her life. She dragged her fingertips through the tangles in her long brown hair, wishing she could run a comb through it. She didn't even want to think about whether she had mascara down her face or not. But more than that, she knew, without a doubt, that if Joe met her eyes, he'd be able to see the effect he had on her.

Nana squinted at him. "The least you could do?" she said slowly. "That sounds like you're guilty of something. Is there anything for which you need to make amends?"

His eyes finally fluttered over to Holly again, sending her pulse into a panic. Why was he looking at her when Nana mentioned the word "guilty"? A tiny fizzle of a thought swelled in her mind: had he felt just as comfortable next to her? Or was it something else? Perhaps he felt guilty making Holly blush the way she was.

Suddenly, Holly realized she should intervene here. She knew Nana best, and she should be the one on the other end of this conversation. "Nana," she said, walking over and stepping up next to him, "Joe didn't mean a thing by his offer, I'm sure."

"Joe?" Nana turned away from them and started rooting in the cabinets again. "The last I heard he'd introduced himself as Joseph. Are you two on a nickname basis already?"

"I always introduce myself as Joseph . . . but I usually go by just Joe. Since I was helping Holly for a considerable amount of time with the decorations last night, I suggested she call me Joe. You can too."

"Nana's name is Jean," Holly said to try to steer the conversation to a lighter thought. Papa had always called Nana Jean except when he needed her help with something. Then he'd call in a sing-songy voice, "Jeany-Lou!"

"Well, you can call me Ms. McAdams. Where is the coffee?" she asked with frustration as she opened another cabinet. *Bang!* It slammed shut.

"I moved it to the corner." Holly came up behind her and reached around Nana, opening the cabinet and pulling out the bag of coffee grounds. She'd noticed last night that it was nearly untouched after the week and only now in the reality of morning did she consider that Joe might not have coffee on a regular basis.

"Are you a regular coffee drinker?" Holly asked Joe, so relieved to have a complete change in the conversation. She pulled her eyes from him, not waiting for a response, his smile making her unexpectedly nervy, last night feeling like a dream. She filled the carafe with water and scooped out the coffee, dumping it into the machine.

Out of the corner of her eye, she saw Joe sit down on one of the barstools. "I usually don't drink it. I don't sleep well as it is, remember? The last thing I need is coffee to keep me awake, but I'll make an exception this morning. I'm beat."

"Seems to me that you sleep just fine," Nana said, her gaze dancing over to Holly, sending her brain on a loop like an old movie, clips from last night running over and over.

She kept thinking about the warmth of his body, the way he fit against her, how absolutely perfect it had felt, his scent filling her lungs with every breath. It was intoxicating in the very best way. Holly met tons of people every night at work and in the city, and she'd never come across someone whom she felt so comfortable with so quickly. It was just a sort of feeling she got from him—their reactions to each other were so natural. He relaxed her without even trying. She knew it was too fast, her feelings getting away from her too quickly, but she couldn't stop it.

Nana leaned down and peered under the cabinet. "You've moved the pans as well?"

"Yes. Sorry. They're over by the stove. I reorganized everything based on proximity to the appliances. It just made sense."

Nana gave an exasperated huff. Perhaps it was the bright light of day reflected off all the snow coming through the windows, but Nana looked so much older right now than she'd appeared even days before. It was so obvious that it worried Holly. Nana looked tired, the laugh lines at her eyes now turned down, those lips set in the scowl that had seemed to be there more these days than the smile that Holly had loved so much as a girl.

"Or," Nana said in a clipped tone, as she retrieved a pan and set it on the burner of the stove, "the renters could simply learn where everything is in about five minutes and use it where it has always been." She threw open the refrigerator and grabbed the eggs.

It was pretty evident that Nana was not in good spirits. Today she was particularly irritable. Holly had only been trying to help by bringing her here—after all, it had been Nana who'd suggested it. Neither of them could've foreseen what had happened when they'd arrived, but they had to make the best of it.

Holly also worried about what Joe thought of Nana. She didn't want him to think that Nana was anything other than wonderful, because she *was* wonderful.

Before Papa died, she'd been full of life. She'd bopped through the house, playing music on the old record player they had, while she cooked. She constantly had something cooking: stews in the winter, seafood in the summer, and always a sweet treat. Holly's favorite was her apple pie. She'd get her apples from the local orchard in the fall. They made the most delicious pies with just the right amount of tart. And no one could do the braided crust like Nana. She'd cut a big wedge of pie with that golden, flaky crust and place it on a plate next to a scoop of homemade vanilla ice cream. Some of Holly's favorite memories were those times she sat around the table with Papa and Nana, laughing and telling stories over that pie.

Holly noticed the rigidity in Nana's arms and the tension in her shoulders as she whisked the eggs in a bowl, her face set in that unhappy position. She was focused on stirring, but Holly wondered what was going on in that mind of hers. She missed the Nana she'd had while Papa was alive. The one who would hum the lullaby Papa had written himself while she washed dishes, the one who would tuck her in at night and ask her which voice she should use for her bedtime stories—sometimes she'd read whole books in a cowboy voice if Holly asked her to. The sparkle that had been in Nana's eyes was absent now, her spirit suppressed. Holly wanted so badly to bring her out of the depression she was in, but she feared that the only thing that could do that was bringing Papa back.

"Do we have any milk?" Nana barked, breaking Holly's train of thought.

Joe got off his stool and headed for the refrigerator when Nana whirled around, the bowl still pressed in her bosom. "Sit!" she thundered. "Down." She ground her teeth and then said more quietly but still just as upset, "I can get it. I was just making sure we had some." She opened the refrigerator and retrieved the carton, shaking it back and forth, the sound of the tiny bit left in the bottom revealing they were nearly out. "We need to get to the market," Nana said. "If we can't get the car out, try to call Buddy. He might be able to come get you on the tractor."

Buddy Lane was a good friend of Papa's and he'd spent many a night on the porch with the rest of them. He had a small farm a few miles down the road. Holly knew Buddy would probably do his best to come out and pick them up, but it was freezing out there. They couldn't drive all the way into town in the cab of that tractor—they'd be frostbitten by the time they arrived. She didn't share any of this with Nana, though. Holly just nodded and slid the cream and sugar, still on the counter from last night, over to Joe where she took a seat beside him.

"Toast will have to suffice until I can get enough milk for my biscuits," Nana said, turning the heat on the eggs down so they could finish cooking, and locating the toaster.

"Nana makes the best buttermilk biscuits," Holly told Joe, hoping to lift Nana's mood. What was wrong with her grandmother this morning? "I've never had another biscuit top hers." She looked over at Nana, but she was unmoved. Nana clearly wasn't happy at all with the situation she'd found herself in. Had she actually made things worse by bringing Nana here?

Chapter Five

Holly peered out the window, getting warmer by the minute. Nana had the fire going, and the fur hood was up on Holly's winter coat, a stocking cap underneath it. She had on a scarf, her gloves, layered with a pair of mittens overtop, the yoga pants she'd brought, thinking she could get a TV workout or two in every morning, jeans, two pairs of socks, and her snow boots. Bundled like she was, she'd die of heatstroke if she didn't get outside soon, but just the thought of being out in that cold made her want to forget the whole thing.

"You're going to have to walk to the bottom of the hill, Holly," Nana said. "Buddy won't get his tractor up the drive with the ice on the ground."

Holly knew that Nana was right. Trudging down the drive that stretched at a steep incline to the road would be no easy task. The car had barely made it last night; she'd feared that she would have to get out and push it. She was so happy when the tires caught the snow and ground their way to the top. And now, having snowed another six inches overnight, it seemed a daunting task to make it down. She could see the street through the trees and there was no sign of a snowplow. No salt had been put on the roads. They'd be lucky if they saw anyone at all out in this mess.

Buddy had been delighted to help them get to Puckett's to buy some groceries to make it through the next few days, but Holly did worry that the stores would all be closed. They didn't usually get snow like this and they weren't prepared for it. Everything shut down when they had even an inch, let alone this type of blizzard. A front had moved in and the conditions were perfect for the kind of white Christmas that the Nashville area had rarely ever encountered. The closest they'd come to snow of this magnitude on Christmas had been all the way back in 1963. Holly had never seen it in her lifetime. Until now.

Joe came out of his room, donning a flawlessly tailored navy trench coat with a matching scarf and black leather gloves. His thick crop of dark hair was perfectly combed and he'd shaved. He looked like he was ready to walk the streets of Manhattan with the exception of the heavy-treaded snow boots he was wearing peeking out from his jeans.

"Will you be warm enough?" she asked, her concern manifesting itself in the form of a question.

"I'll be just fine," he said reassuringly. His eyes moved from the top of her head to her feet. "I'm acclimated to this sort of weather."

That might be true, but he'd never had to make a journey in Buddy's tractor. Holly had fuzzy memories of it as a girl, and that was when it was a much younger machine. She'd been in it one summer in the fields. It was drafty and loud, the heat pouring in, making the wisps of hair that had escaped her ponytail stick to the perspiration on her neck. She could only imagine that heat turned ice cold, and it gave her a shiver just thinking about it.

"Shall we walk down to the road to meet him like your grandmother advised?" Joe asked.

Reluctantly, she nodded. Holly had suggested going shopping alone. After barging in on him last night, she didn't want to disrupt him any further. But he insisted on taking care of the grocery bill, since he'd inconvenienced them, and he said there were a few things he wanted to pick up from the store too, so they both ended up getting ready, and Nana called Buddy to pick them up.

Joe opened the door for them just as a gust of frosty air blew in, turning Holly's nose to ice before she'd even stepped foot onto the porch. Wincing, she walked into it, Joe following without even a flinch. Although, *she* sure flinched when he placed his hand on her back to keep her steady down the frozen steps. It gave her a tingle all the way down her spine.

"Sorry," he said, but he didn't remove his hand. She could

tell by his expression, though, that he knew why she'd jumped, and she thought perhaps their unexpected night on the sofa and easy conversation had been just as significant to him. Her mind whirred with the thought of it…

When they got to the bottom, the cabin caught her eye. "Oh!" Holly said. "I've never seen it like this." The two dormer windows that jutted out from the snow-covered tin roof were draped in a blanket of white, every railing on the long country porch outlined in fluffy, billowing snow. Drifts of powder stuck to the stone chimney, the red door, and the logs that formed the exterior walls. "It's so beautiful."

Joe smiled, but his eyes were on her rather than the house. The way he was looking at her, he probably thought she'd never seen snow before—which was somewhat true, as she'd never seen snow like this, here in Tennessee.

Holly turned around to look at the woods obscuring the road down the hill below. The only way she could see the driveway was by the tiny strip of white that meandered between the trees. She hadn't gotten around to changing that yet, but it was on her renovations list. The pathway was still just the way Papa had originally dug it. The trees looked like dark pencil sketches against the white sky, their barren branches holding up the snow that had settled on them. Holly stumbled but caught herself. It was steep and, even in her snow boots, she was struggling to get traction.

Joe slowed down to keep pace with her and she lost her footing again. Her boots were no match for this amount of snow, the bottoms slipping as they made contact with the earth at every step. She turned sideways and marched, but that didn't seem to help much, so she turned back around.

Holly only got a few more paces before she unintentionally stepped into a small hole that was covered with snow. Suddenly, she felt herself falling, the ground coming toward her face faster than she could process what to do, and the shooting pain in her ankle was clouding everything. She reached out for the ground to stop her fall but never felt it because Joe had scooped her up in a flash. She held on to him, putting her weight on her good ankle and trying to clear her mind enough to realize what was happening, but it was difficult with that spicy scent of his wafting toward her, his arms around her, keeping her from falling again.

"I guess my boots aren't that great," she said.

Joe was inspecting the path, and she remembered exactly what it was she'd stepped in: the little area just under the trees, where the rain had made its own trail across the drive on its way down the hill, carving out a large chunk of earth. After the first year of interior remodeling, she'd saved enough of Papa's renovation money to hire someone to install a drainage pipe, fill it all in, and pave that enormous drive. She knew she should've done it sooner but she was focused on the inside. Now, she'd have to wait for warmer weather. Thank goodness no one else had fallen there or she'd be looking down the barrel of a lawsuit. Nana certainly didn't need to deal with something like that.

Still holding one of Joe's arms, Holly tried to take a step, the pain zipping up her leg, making her whimper before she could suck it back in.

Joe turned with concern. "What's the matter?"

"Nothing," she lied.

With another step, the pain made her knee buckle. She bit her lip to keep from yelling out in anguish.

Joe looked back at the house, but they were about halfway, and she knew what he was thinking: they needed food for the week and if they had gotten this far, they might as well keep going.

They'd be in Buddy's tractor soon and she could sit down and rest her ankle.

"I'll take you up to the house and go alone," he suggested, his brows pulling together as he glanced down at her foot. "Why don't I give you a piggyback ride?"

"Because we'll fall backward and tumble headfirst until we're nothing but a giant snowball, hurling our way down to the bottom." She took another few excruciating steps and faltered again, lurching forward. Joe caught her. "And I'm not going back up to the house. I'll get Nana's groceries for her; I know what she likes, and she's particular." She smiled up at him, but it didn't seem to lighten his apprehension.

"We'll just go very slowly then," he said, taking her arm carefully.

Holly let him, feeling secure in the fact that he wouldn't let her fall.

When they got down the drive, her cheeks were numb, her ears cold inside her stocking cap, and she was sure that her nose would be a dark shade of purple by now with the frostbite that must be setting in. And if she didn't sit down, she might pass out from the ache in her ankle.

The growl of Buddy's engine filled the air as it pulled up just in time, the old green tractor still alive and well. What little heat it might have was a beacon of hope. Buddy waved from inside the cab, and Holly relished the familiarity of his weatherworn face. He was always so kind when she visited Papa. While Papa's other friends talked football and the disconcerting state of the world, Buddy would ask her how her day was and he'd clap when she showed him her one-handed cartwheels.

Buddy reached over and unlatched the door, the thin metal swinging open with a rattle as the engine shook it on its hinges.

"Good grief!" Buddy said, his eyes sweeping over her. "You're a spittin' image of your mama!" He had an old

Budweiser baseball cap on and a thick brown coat with snaps as worn as the old planks from the warped barn wood her papa piled up for firewood after he had to replace it. Buddy was grinning from ear to ear, deep lines across his face showing how often he smiled, which warmed her.

Holly crawled in first on her good foot, taking Joe's hand as he helped her up. She was immediately disappointed that the interior temperature wasn't much better than outside, but the relief on her ankle made it all fine. Joe slid in after her and shut the door.

"You all right?" Buddy asked in his thick southern accent, glancing down at her foot.

"I'm okay, Buddy. I just twisted my ankle, but I've got a ton of snow to put on it once we get home." She shifted uncomfortably. "How are *you*?"

"I'm just fine, Miss Holly. I heard you was down here sprucin' the place up. Your papa always thought he could rent to those fancy folk." Buddy offered a wink in her direction before his gaze settled on Joe. One good look at him and Buddy fell silent, clearly realizing that they were in the presence of one of those fancy customers right now. He cleared his throat and put the tractor into gear. "Y'all headed to Puckett's?"

She nodded.

"I went past it earlier. It's open, which says somethin', dunnit?"

Joe peered over at him questioningly.

"People 'round here watch out for each other. Things need to be open if they can be. We ain't used to all this weather. I'll bet there's not a soul in Leiper's Fork that has enough buttermilk to get 'em through."

Holly caught Joe smiling out of her peripheral vision. He was enjoying himself.

"I don't mean any harm in asking this," Joe said. "I'm quite interested. I know Holly's grandmother makes biscuits with it, but what else would you use buttermilk for?"

Buddy's tractor swerved slightly when he gave Joe a look like he'd just lost his mind. He offered a consoling smile right before a disbelieving chuckle. "Holly, your nana's got some cookin' to do for this one!" He leaned forward just a little bit, both calloused hands still on the wheel as they bumped along down the snow-covered road, passing old barns, their burgundy painted wood and large spruce Christmas wreaths in the center peaks contrasting against the white hills.

"My wife, Freda, uses buttermilk for lots of things: corn-bread, pancakes, marinade for her fried chicken, mashed potatoes, muffins, salad dressing…But I'll let you know what it's best for and you can tell all your friends this secret."

Holly knew exactly what he was going to say because he'd told her before.

"One cup at bedtime makes you healthy as an ox and sleep like a rock—it takes all your stress away. It'll do you right!"

"Really?" Joe said, showing interest.

Buddy nodded definitively. "It's how old geezers like me live so long."

He pulled onto Old Hillsboro Road, the main thoroughfare in Leiper's Fork.

"Ah," Buddy said as they approached the handful of buildings that lined the narrow lane before it stretched back out into countryside. "Civilization." He changed gears on the tractor to slow down. "But don't blink. You'll miss it." Then he laughed at his own joke.

The tiny slip of road was something out of a small-town storybook. Little clapboard cottages, their natural wood painted in varying colors, their roofs topped with snow, were the only color on the street. Each one had its own Christmas wreath on the door and rocking chairs outside for visitors. The old porch paddle fans, which did nothing more in the summers than push the hot air around, were stilled today in the silence of winter. The local art gallery, framed by the bare branches of old oak trees, had a pile of frosty wood outside and a fire going in the fire pit with a few skewers and a glass jar of marshmallows on offer for anyone who could get out in this mess. Holly caught Joe's inquisitiveness as he eyed them.

Buddy pulled the tractor to a stop outside Puckett's, the

parking area indistinguishable from the road. The only way she could tell where the patio began were by the barbeque pit and the snow-covered Christmas trees that protruded from the mass of white. Both men got out and helped lift Holly down onto the snow.

Buddy threw up a hand to the young lady working the front register as she opened the door to greet them. Holly broke out in the biggest grin when she saw who it was. The woman was waving, her long, blond hair in a single braid down her back, dropping from under her Puckett's baseball cap. "Hey there, Tammy!" Buddy called. "Been busy at all today?"

"No, not a soul till y'all stopped by." She waved like crazy at Holly. "Hey, Holly! Ain't seen you in a month of Sundays! Y'all come on in! I'm offerin' free coffee."

"I got one needs a chair," Buddy said, his thumb pointed at Holly.

"We've got plenty of those too." She held the door open for them as they came in, the heat wrapping its way around Holly, causing her to shiver. "Girl, what have you done to your foot?"

"I stepped in a hole," Holly said, giving Tammy a hug. They'd spent many summers together growing up, running through the fields, climbing trees, and catching caterpillars on the side of Johnson's bridge.

"It's been too long…I haven't seen you since we planned my wedding! You did such a beautiful job—made me feel like a princess." Tammy ran her long thin fingers down her braid before putting her hand on her hips. "Who you got here?"

"Hello. I'm Joseph Barnes," Joe said with a friendly nod, taking a step forward. He held out a hand in greeting, but Tammy grabbed it and yanked him toward her. She threw her arms around him, pulling him in for a hug as she gave an excited look to Holly over his shoulder.

Tammy pulled back. "Well, Joey, glad you're here for Christmas with Holly! That's so cute! Joey and Holly…"

Holly tried to tell Tammy with her facial expression that she was mistaken about the situation, but her face was heating up from embarrassment and she turned away. When she finally got herself under control, she tried to clarify for Tammy. "Actually, it's—"

"It's nothin' but adorable!" Tammy said, finishing her sentence. That wasn't what she was planning to say. Tammy started dragging chairs over to one of the tables. "Y'all get your things and I'll make us all some coffee."

Puckett's was a concept as unique as Leiper's Fork itself. At the front was a stage, with four microphones and a drum kit that sat empty today. But every Thursday at six p.m. was open mic night, and the place would be standing room only, apart from the group that gathered in a circle of chairs around the fire pit outside. An American flag, a bunch of memorabilia, and a few guitars covered the old wooden walls, painted the same barn red and nearly camouflaging the vintage Coca-Cola sign just next to a large wooden plank of wood with the original lettering faded and slightly yellowed that said: "Puckett's Bros." At the back, behind the mass of mix-and-matched tables and chairs, next to an olive-green jukebox featuring the likes of B.B. King, Elvis Presley, and Hank Williams, was a small grocery. And using the word "small" was being generous. It was three aisles, about as long as Holly was tall.

While Tammy filled four white foam cups of coffee at the spot along the counter that usually had all the hot food like scrambled eggs, fried potatoes, and biscuits, Holly pulled the crumpled list Nana had made from her pocket and hobbled to the back, shooing off Joe's protective gestures to have her sit. She grabbed a bag of flour, brown sugar, a container of oatmeal, and a couple cans of vegetables. At the back, next to the beer, she pulled a jug of milk and a second container of buttermilk from the refrigerators. Joe, who was setting Holly's things on the counter in front of Tammy as she pulled each one off the shelf, came back to look around, clearly unsure what to get.

He leaned toward one of the bags on display. "Old

South Fish Fry Meal," he said, his brows pulling together. A small smile played at his lips, and she couldn't help but think again how he seemed to be enjoying himself.

"What's making you smile?" she asked as they browsed.

He looked up from a can of beans he had in his hand as if he'd been caught in the act of something. "Oh, I don't know."

"It's okay to smile, you know."

He set the can back on the shelf. "I suppose this is so different from anything at home that I find it . . . fun."

"Fun."

Joe gave her that grin of his, this time not hiding a thing about how he felt in that moment. "For instance, do you use this?" He grabbed the fish fry meal.

Holly laughed. "When I'm not watching my calories. You roll your fish in it and fry it. The summers we used to go to the river, we'd fish for catfish and bring it home. Papa would filet it, clean it all up, and we'd roll it in that before we cooked it in an old iron skillet on a bonfire out back. I can still remember the smell of the oil as it heated up."

That curiosity had returned, but he didn't say anything.

"Don't you just love those kinds of memories from childhood? A whole season of spending all day barefoot, swinging on old tire swings, and staying out until the mosquitoes got so bad you had to go in?"

Joe pursed his lips and slowly shook his head, the absence of understanding in his eyes. "I went to a year-round board-ing school. Very strict rules."

"Y'all come on over and drink your coffee before it gets cold," Tammy called. She'd sat down at one of the tables with Buddy, her eye on Joe as she patted the seat next to her.

Joe gave a playfully wary look to Holly, making her laugh. The music was on low—country music. Tim McGraw was playing quietly above them, and it occurred to Holly that the normal things about her life weren't so normal to Joe. She was willing to bet his life was a world away from hers.

Chapter Six

"You can't pull me and all the groceries up this hill," Holly said with uncertainty as she sat on the old crate panel Buddy had loaded into his tractor at Puckett's.

She had her legs stretched out straight, with the grocery bags piled in her lap, while plopped down on part of a giant produce crate that Puckett's had put aside for trash. Tammy and Buddy had had the brilliant idea to break off the side of the crate and tie a rope to it so that Buddy and Joe could pull Holly up the drive when they got home, giving her sore ankle a rest. It was starting to swell now and she wondered how she'd get her boot off.

Before he left, Buddy parked the tractor and helped set up the makeshift sled, but Joe had insisted that he could do it and sent Buddy and his tractor back down the road with a friendly handshake and a sincere thank-you. So Joe stood in his trench coat, the rope wound around his leather-gloved hands. His cheeks were pink from cold, but the temperature didn't seem to bother him.

"You don't have faith in me?" he asked, clearly amused.

Holly suppressed an eye-roll. Even though she liked his lighthearted banter, she didn't want to be the girl who batted her eyelashes while he saved her. She considered trying to get up and walk, but her ankle was aching so badly, she knew she'd never make it.

"It's not against the law to let someone help," he said as if he'd read her mind. "If it were Buddy on that sled, I know you'd pull him, right? It wouldn't make Buddy weak by any standard if he'd hurt his ankle and needed a ride, would it? You're not giving up any control."

Holly hadn't had the opportunity to meet a great guy in a long time. Working all hours and hanging out with Nana didn't give her many occasions for meeting people, and even when she did get the chance to go out, she'd never found anyone like Joe. He was someone with whom she could picture herself having long conversations, moving from one topic to another with ease, not realizing they had talked long into the wee hours of the morning—like they'd done last night. She didn't have to pretend with him; she could already be herself, and he seemed to enjoy being with her. His curiosity made her feel interesting, and she was just as curious about him.

"Hold on," Joe said, walking around behind her, just as she felt a huge jolt under her bottom, sending her arms frantically grasping for the bags of food.

Holly hugged the groceries to her as they started to

make their way toward the cabin. So she wouldn't roll off, her back was to him, her eyes on the track they were making in the newly fallen snow behind the sled. She kept looking over her shoulder at Joe, as his muscles worked to move her. She'd only just met him and without a word he'd personally pulled her up this hill—who does that for someone they'd just met? He could've easily let Buddy do most of it. She could feel the kindness seeping out from every choice he made, and she was excited to spend more time with him. The prospect of being snowed in wasn't so uncomfortable anymore. Not with Joe.

"We made it," he said when they reached the cabin, the sled coming to a stop.

Joe was clearly winded, his chest rising and falling with his breath. He walked around and took the bags off Holly's lap, setting them on the step of the cabin before he offered a hand to help her get up from the sled. She planted her good foot firmly in the snow and used Joe's strength to stand, her bad ankle hovering over the ground.

"Thank you," she said, truly grateful.

He smiled down at her, his chocolate-colored eyes dazzling and creasing at the corners. "You're welcome."

The door opened before they could get to the top of the steps, Nana pouting in the open doorway.

"Good grief, child. What have you done?" Nana's gaze

moved from Joe's arm that was around Holly, as he lifted her up each step, to her bent knee and down to her boot. Nana moved to the side to allow them to enter.

"I stepped in a hole and twisted my ankle."

Joe took Holly in through the door and helped her to sit on the sofa. Then he bent down to assist her with her boot. Nana's eyes, drilling into them, were making Holly uneasy.

"I've got it, thanks," she said kindly to him, reaching down to her good foot. She slipped off the boot and set it beside her, leaving a clump of snow on the new shag rug. As she untied her other one, her ankle throbbed with pain, and she had to hold her breath to pull the boot off her foot.

Joe, who'd popped back outside to get the groceries from the steps, set them on the kitchen counter and then came over to take a look at her ankle. He kneeled in front of her again and lifted her foot gingerly onto his knee, slowly sliding down her fuzzy sock with his finger, his touch making her heart patter. She swallowed and tried not to notice how gentle his hands were. It was easy to focus on something else, however, with Nana hunched over his shoulder.

"It needs ice to bring the swelling down," Nana said. "We've got a bag of peas in the freezer that someone left. I'll grab them." Then she clamped her eyes on Joe. "I think she'll be just fine," she said quietly, through clenched teeth. "You can go on about your business of taking care of all that wedding stuff in the bedroom." She glared at him as if she could actually say "back off" with her eyes.

Wedding?

Holly had a view of Nana's bed across the room, through the short hallway. Her suitcases were emptied and sat off to one side. She could see Joe's boxes more clearly now that she had a moment to pay attention to them. It seemed as though Nana had attempted to move them, which wasn't unusual. She was famous for rearranging a room to suit her needs. The boxes were open with tissue paper spewing from them, crates of gifts, it seemed like, different types of champagne in various-sized bottles, chocolates, and what seemed to be party favors in more silver and white.

Holly wondered if Joe was some sort of event planner in his spare time, which was right up her alley. She'd have lots to chat about. Planning events was one of her favorite things to do.

"What *is* all that stuff in Nana's room?"

Joe sat beside her and intertwined his fingers, turning them outward and straightening his arms, a clear attempt to pull the stress out of his shoulders, then cleared his throat, his gaze moving over to Nana before answering.

"It's..." He swallowed and then turned toward Holly. "...for my wedding."

If this had been a movie, there would've been a record

screech. Nana sent a scowl over her shoulder as she left the living area and grabbed the bag of peas from the freezer in the kitchen. She brought it to Holly. "I'll make you some coffee to warm you up." Then she stomped away again.

Holly felt as though she'd just been hit by a ton of bricks, a new and unforeseen reality now weaving its way around her. She leaned away from Joe casually, all of a sudden keenly aware of their proximity. His answer surprised her in more ways than one: while she hadn't been expecting him to say that, she was also stunned by the disappointment that she knew had slid down her face involuntarily. She forced her lips into a pleasant expression.

Now his lack of response to her comment about being home for Christmas made sense. He was probably terribly worried, having to be away from his fiancée for the holiday, and he'd rather not discuss it with someone he'd never met before. Why wasn't the bride-to-be here with him right now? He'd been visiting for two weeks, planning their wedding it seemed . . . That had to be the source of his anxiety.

"Sorry, I didn't know," she said, not certain what to actually say, but nearly sure that hadn't come out right at all. Why was she sorry he was getting married? She wasn't. She was sorry she'd pried by asking about the boxes and sorry for finding him so attractive and enjoyable to be around.

He smiled at her. "It isn't a secret or anything. I'm

allowed to tell people," he said. He rubbed the back of his neck. Had he slept wrong or was it the stress of having woken up beside Holly?

The weight of guilt settled upon her, considering what his fiancée might think about all this. They'd only met last night, so she shouldn't feel any shame... She hadn't asked just as much as he hadn't told her. It's not something he'd say upon meeting her: "Oh, hello. I'm Joseph Barnes, getting married shortly..." But the guilt came back. The error wasn't his at all, but, rather, *her* assumption. She had let her feelings get away from her.

Holly shifted the peas, the cold making the pain worse and causing her to grimace. Joe's gaze went to her ankle in concern, but she changed the subject.

"When is your wedding?" she asked, clumsily trying to fill the silence that was now slithering between them. The subject felt odd, and she noticed her back had started to ache just a little like it did on busy nights at the restaurant when she was flying around at a hundred miles an hour and stressed out. She consciously relaxed her muscles.

"Just after New Year's, January second." His voice was flat as he said it.

Nana slammed two mugs down on the coffee table in front of them, Holly's splashing over the rim, creating a ring on the glass.

"So are you organizing the wedding or something?" she asked, still watching Nana who had turned her back to them again and was heading toward the kitchen.

He took in a deep breath. "No. I was here to see the venue because Katharine couldn't leave work that long. She's trying a high-profile case..." He looked down at his coffee, not drinking it. "She's a lawyer. My fiancée. Her name is Katharine." The words came out strained and Holly feared she was making him uneasy with all her questions. But then he looked over at her and smiled, changing her mind. He was difficult to read, for sure.

"Are you getting married in town then?" Just the idea of a Leiper's Fork wedding sounded dreamy: a barn with old wooden floors, whiskey barrels for tables, the entire ceiling full of rafters draped in white lights and tulle, enormous plumes of magnolias and roses, candles dripping wax in jars on the thick windowsills, a satin runner down the middle of the barn with rows of chairs on either side, the edges draped in greenery and winter-red bows...

"We're having it at a private estate in Brentwood." While Holly was still swimming out of her faux wedding, he added, "It made sense, since Katharine was going to be researching a case in Nashville that week and it's just outside."

Romantic.

Having worked at a high-end restaurant, Holly knew

Brentwood well; she'd served many people who lived there. It was full of Nashville's famous and those who created a life around work with the famous: producers, record label executives, artists. Brentwood was one of the wealthiest cities in America. Its rolling hills just outside Nashville were dotted with enormous homes—the kinds that had wings bigger than apartment buildings, gated driveways and staff to work them, and manicured lawns that stretched for miles. While it wasn't her dreamy country wedding, Holly was sure that an estate ceremony in Brentwood would be nothing less than spectacular.

"Katharine sent me those items in the box to go through. She's been too busy to take care of the details, so I've been helping the best that I can. She sent all of it out here before the snow, for me to choose what I like." He took in another breath, and Holly wondered if having to decide on those things overwhelmed him. "Maybe you could look at some of it today to give me your opinion? At the very least, we could open the champagne, since I can't take it in my carry-on." Joe gave her a smile, but his eyes looked tired, reminding her of last night.

Holly tried to view him differently than she had before, but she didn't know why, because it wasn't like she'd consciously created an opinion of him prior to knowing about a fiancée. He was still the kind person he'd been when he'd helped her—that's all. But she found herself pushing a little farther away from him inconspicuously out of respect for Katharine.

"To be stranded in the snow, things aren't so bad. We might not have food, but at least we'll have champagne," he teased, clearly trying to lighten the mood.

They were gonna need it.

Chapter Seven

Holly glanced down the hallway toward Joe's bedroom. Joe had barely eaten any breakfast this morning with Nana's lack of hospitality. Then, only a little while after they'd returned from Puckett's, he'd gone to his room. The door had been closed for hours and she knew that, unless he was eating the Jordan almonds that she'd seen in that wedding box, he hadn't had lunch either. Her tummy was starting to growl, so she worried he might be hungry too.

Nana was sitting in the corner chair with her knitting. It looked like she was making a red-and-white striped scarf that had fringe on the finished end. She glanced up over the top of her reading glasses after finishing a stitch, but then went back to her yarn, her hands moving effortlessly to steer the knitting needles. Holly had been trying to read her book while she elevated her ankle, but she kept fretting about Joe. She felt terrible keeping him closed in his bedroom all day. Nana's response to him had been less than warm, and Holly worried he was trying to give them space.

"You're restless," Nana said from behind her glasses. She took them off and set them in her lap with her knitting.

"I'm hungry," Holly said.

"Well, we keep our food in the kitchen, not down the hallway." With a frustrated breath, Nana hoisted herself out of the chair and set her things on the side table. "I can heat up that Christmas ham we've got sliced—did you pack that?"

"Yes," Holly said, thinking. "Nana, why are you so irritated by Joe?" she whispered.

Nana turned to Holly. "I don't like him," she whispered.

"Why?" Holly asked in a hushed tone, baffled. Joe had been nothing but helpful since they'd arrived.

"I watched him pull you up that hill. Why didn't he let Buddy do it? He's cozying up with you on the sofa, running errands with you... You two just met! Not to mention he's practically a married man. He should be ashamed of himself." She sent a fuming glance down the hallway.

"You're reading into things," Holly said quietly. "When you found us on the sofa together, we'd been awake the entire night, putting the tree up, and we both passed out from exhaustion. And the reason Joe pulled me up the hill was because he was being kind to Buddy—he's getting on in age. That amount of exertion could give Buddy a heart attack," she heard herself say, her pulse rising in frustration, unsure why Nana's assessment of Joe was bothering her so much.

"We needed food and he offered to pay because he's intruding on our Christmas, which is due to the awful weather, and not his fault. And did you want him to just ignore my ankle?" She moved to get comfortable, trying to calm down, pain still present. It wasn't like her to be so direct with Nana.

Nana didn't look any more convinced as she stared at Holly. "Well."

That was what Nana always said when her opinion couldn't be altered. So Holly guessed the conversation was finished. Nana was not going to be persuaded, so she might as well drop the topic for now. Papa used to say, "There are two things in life that cannot be changed: the weather and your nana's mind once she's decided something." He was right about that.

Holly closed her book around her bookmark and sat forward to see if she could put weight on her ankle and get up to invite Joe to join her for a bite to eat, but thought better of it and leaned back against the cushion. He was a grown man—if he needed something, he'd come out and get it.

Instead, Holly decided to just grab a sandwich and the labeling stickers that she'd brought with her and hobble out to the barn to figure out what to do with all the things in there. It was freezing outside, and the snow was thick and powdery underfoot, but anything was better than staying in the cabin with her ankle up on pillows. And she felt better if she stayed away from Joe. Nana didn't need any more to worry about than she already had.

The doors creaked on their hinges as she pushed them open, the thick wood rough under her gloves.

During the renovations, she'd put all her attention on the cabin just as Papa had asked, setting aside the remnants of her childhood for later. Those old things lingered in the back of her mind, giving her an overwhelming need to take care of them. With a deep breath of that familiar musty air, she scanned Papa's belongings at the back, not sure if she was ready to see them yet. It had been the same when she'd put the furniture out there: she'd focused on the pull of her muscles as she dragged the pieces, the heat of the summer day, anything to avoid processing what was in the barn.

Now that the dust had settled with the renovations, and she could actually think about things, she still didn't have the strength to go through his personal items, but having Papa's furniture all piled up out there made her uncomfortable. Most of the pieces were old and worn, not of any monetary worth, but the sentimental value was overwhelming. It just seemed so desolate and cold in the space that she couldn't sit around with it out there.

She stepped onto the worn wooden floor, putting her weight on her good ankle, and ran her glove across the kitchen table that had sat in the cabin for so many years. It

had held the food for countless Christmas dinners, birth-
days, anniversaries, and even those not-so-big days when
a young Holly would toddle out in her pajamas, her hair
a mess at the back, and Nana would slide a bowl of her
favorite cereal in front of her. She couldn't have imagined
then that this barn would be where that table would spend
its final days before it was donated to a local charity shop.

Holly unwrapped her sandwich and reached into her
pocket, pulling out a wad of colored stickers, little dots
in yellow, green, and orange. The yellow dots would go
on charity items, green would mark the few things they'd
want to save for family, and the orange was trash. Holly set
her sandwich down on the paper towel she'd wrapped it
in, removed her gloves, and began to place a small yellow
charity sticker on the table.

But she couldn't do it. Redesigning the cabin was easy,
but sifting through the things that marked her life was a bit
harder. She placed the sticker back on its paper and chewed
on her lip. She couldn't possibly keep it all. It was useless
sitting out here. But at the same time, she couldn't just
abandon it either.

"It's not easy to let go, is it?"

Holly faced Nana, who'd come in quietly behind her
and shook her head. Nana stepped inside, the grit on the
old floors making a scratching sound with her steps. She

stood in front of the pile of things, touching them gently and clearly thinking of all the memories they brought.

Holly wanted to be strong, knowing how emotional seeing all this could make her grandmother, but even Holly couldn't pretend it wasn't difficult.

"It's old, but it could be made new again with some fresh paint," Nana suggested. "Maybe another family will fix it up…"

Holly nodded, unable to speak for fear that she'd start to tear up.

"It *will* make someone very happy, I'm sure. Every piece will hold its own story and make new ones as it sits in another house, while time moves on around it."

Without a word, Holly wrapped her arms around her grandmother and gave her a hug. Not because Nana needed it, but because Holly did. All she wanted was to make things okay for Nana, and the pressure of that was more than she could manage. "I love you" was all she could say. What more was there?

When they finally pulled away and an air of regularity had filtered between them again, Nana said, "I've put some soup on the stove. Why don't you come inside? You need more than just a sandwich." Nana looked out through the open barn door toward Joe's window, seemingly annoyed by the act of having to look toward it at all. But then her face softened just a little. "It's a *large* pot of soup." She rubbed her hands together as if kneading the pain out of them, her thoughts noticeably distant again.

Holly wondered if Nana was thinking about the last time she'd made a big pot of soup during the Christmas season, when it wasn't just the two of them, about five years ago, before Holly's older sister, Alicia, moved all the way to Seattle. Alicia, her husband, Carlos, and their adorable little girl, Emma, took the family Labradoodle and all their things and relocated for Carlos's job. Alicia was a college professor. She got a job right away at the University of Washington teaching economics, while Carlos climbed the corporate ladder in the engineering department at Boeing.

Holly couldn't fault her sister for moving so far away—it was a great opportunity. But what always stuck with her was that her parents had moved to Seattle as well to be nearer to Emma, leaving Holly and Nana back in Nashville. But they returned once a year and had big Christmases together at the cabin, the whole family crammed into it. There were people on sofas and the sink was always full of dishes, but it was happy and festive and Holly couldn't imagine anything better.

After Papa passed, when Nana started regularly renting the cabin where they usually spent family holidays, Holly's parents planned big trips for Christmas instead of staying in Nashville—last year it was Paris, and this year they were all going to Playa del Carmen in Mexico. While she'd been invited to go, Holly didn't want to admit that she thought being away from home wasn't very Christmassy, and she felt like she'd lost something important when they stopped getting together at the cabin.

Last year Holly made the excuse that Nana was still too emotionally fragile and Holly needed to stay in Nashville. This year, she'd blamed work. Nana made it easy, too, because she'd been indignant at the thought of spending Christmas anywhere but Nashville. So they settled for a family Christmas Day call as their new tradition.

"I suppose we shouldn't let Joseph starve…" Nana said, bringing Holly back to the present.

"Joe," Holly corrected her.

Nana threw her gaze to the rafters, pinching those lips together. She cleared her throat and headed into the house. Holly left the stickers, grabbed her sandwich, and followed Nana inside.

"I'll go check on him," Holly said, once she got into the cabin. "I should probably keep moving around anyway or my ankle will get stiff."

She limped down the hallway and lifted her hand to rap on Joe's door, but stopped when she heard his voice from the other side. It sounded like he was on a phone call.

"I don't know, Katharine," he said softly. "Could you do the gold and gray?"

Holly stretched out her fingers, looking down at her nails and tried not to listen, instead considering how walking around was helping her sore ankle. While it was still throbbing, it was definitely better, which was good, because they couldn't get to a doctor if they tried. She'd just give Joe a minute to get off the phone...

"Yes, but what do *you* like?" she heard. "Why are you letting Brea decide?"

Holly casually rested against the wall, pondering what she'd say if he opened the door. Perhaps she should just come back.

"I'm still thinking," Joe said, drawing her attention to the door again.

He was silent then, and Holly wondered what his fiancée was telling him. She leaned toward the door quietly, something making her curious about their conversation, but knowing she shouldn't eavesdrop. What kinds of things did they talk about? Did he make her laugh? When he looked at Katharine did his lips turn up in that way she'd seen them do? Had he explained to Katharine about her and Nana yet?

"I'm trying," he said, his voice tense.

Holly held her breath.

"I don't know," he said and then, "All right. Well, just keep me in the loop, I guess."

When she heard him end the call, she knocked.

"Come in," he said.

Holly pushed the door open, and she found the bed was made, drawing her eyes to it, which sent her mind into a rewind to when she'd first encountered him. Joe was now at the small desk in the room, tapping on his laptop, his back to her, his phone resting beside the computer. He finished whatever he was typing and swiveled around in his chair.

"Nana's making some soup and we have ham sandwiches. Are you hungry?"

"That's very generous of you to offer," he said, that smile of his now slightly more reserved. "I'd love some, but you two need to have a bit of space, I'm sure. I'll just eat in here, if you'd be so kind as to let me know when it's ready."

Holly took a step inside and shut the door a little to keep her voice from traveling down to the kitchen. "Please don't feel like you have to spend the whole time in your room. You're more than welcome to have lunch with us."

There was a ping on his computer and his head twisted back around to view it. "I should probably just stay in here and work. My hot spot finally has a signal and I've got a ton of things piling up from when I was out looking at the venue for the wedding. It set me back." He stretched.

"And I'm supposed to make a decision soon on the wedding items Katharine sent me. I'm terrible about that sort of thing." He eyed Holly for a second. "Perhaps we could take a look at it all at some point? It would be helpful to have your perspective."

Talking wedding details with Joe would be too hard. "Didn't Katharine give you her thoughts on them?" she said, stalling, not wanting to tell him "no" outright.

"No. She offered the options, but she's in the middle of a pretty heated case right now, and she asked me to finalize these things. She said if I can't decide, it would default to our wedding planner, Brea." He was facing away from her again, turning off his computer, and a current of excitement zinged through her chest. Was he coming out to eat with them?

He stood up.

"If I leave it to Brea, we'll end up paying millions for things we'd never have chosen, so if Katharine can't decide, I suppose I should."

Katharine was a soon-to-be bride—this was supposed to be the day she'd dreamed about since childhood. Didn't all brides have a pretty clear vision of what they wanted for their wedding? And if not, wouldn't she want to explore the choices herself? Or with Joe, as a couple?

"Please don't make me have to call Brea." He walked

toward the door, his coming to lunch obviously a plea for help with the wedding. "You know, she goes by just Brea. Like Cher or Madonna."

Holly giggled. But in all seriousness, she didn't even want to think about how lavish this wedding would be. Joe had said the word "millions." Plural. As in more than one million. The wedding was in Brentwood, the land of mansions. The wedding planner had only one name…Holly jumped as he put his hand on her shoulder and waved his other arm to usher her out of the room.

"Tammy said you were her wedding planner, right?" he asked as they started walking.

"I helped her plan the wedding, yes. But it was more of a backyard barbeque with white paper tablecloths and a tall cake."

He stopped and faced her, making her turn mid-stride. They were super close in that tight hallway and her heart rate sped up from the proximity.

"It was casual," he said, "because that's what she probably wanted. I've seen your work right here in the cabin. I know you have great taste and an incredible eye for detail. That backyard barbeque was probably the most elegant barbeque in history."

They fell back into silence as they walked into the living room, and all Holly could think about was how easy it would be to make those wedding decisions for him. She'd know in seconds what Katharine should have, as long as their tastes lined up. Even if they didn't, however, all Holly had to see was the venue and the dress and she could guess pretty accurately.

The entire cabin brimmed with the aroma of Nana's famous vegetable chowder. The savory, cheesy smell of it made Holly aware of her hunger. The Christmas tree lights were on, and, even with her aching ankle, Holly had managed to keep the fire going in the fireplace most of the day.

It was so cozy in the living room that she decided to set the coffee table with dishes, grabbing some from the kitchen cabinets. She placed them on the table and then scattered a few large throw pillows on the floor, an extra one for her foot, and an afghan on the sofa for Nana, who was in the kitchen, giving the soup one last stir. The glow around the room from the fire and the lights, the greenery and stockings on the mantel, and the delicious scent of holiday cooking filled Holly with nostalgia.

She noticed Joe was watching her.

"I thought we could eat in here."

"That sounds great," he said, but she wondered if he found it unusual.

Nana came in and quietly settled on the sofa.

"Please," Holly said, "make yourself comfortable and

I'll get our soup. How does everyone take their ham sandwiches? Nana, cheese and mayo?"

Nana allowed a little smile. "That's right."

"How about you, Joe?"

"Let me help you," he offered. "You don't need to be doing all that with your ankle."

"Thank you," she said, happy he offered.

Nana eyed him suspiciously, fiddling with her napkin, while Holly went into the kitchen to prepare their sandwiches. She couldn't help but wonder about Katharine, that phone call still on her mind.

She'd have to kick into waitress mode. She was great at it. She knew just how to ask questions to get the customers talking but not seeming like she was prying. She had tricks for remembering the little details and she was an ace at knowing just when to slip them into conversation later. She did it a hundred times in a night, her mind shut off, but her smile bright and her people skills going like a well-oiled machine. That same tactic could work with Joe: she could ask him about the wedding, since he seemed to be okay with sharing that information. After all, he'd asked for help in decision-making. That would be a good place to start.

Then maybe she wouldn't feel so awkward around Joe all the time.

Chapter Eight

Holly handed Nana her bowl of soup and glass of iced tea first, setting her sandwich on the table. She'd been a little wobbly carrying it all in, so Joe insisted on bringing in her lunch, asking her to sit and rest. With Joe in the room, Nana was not the picture of enthusiasm. She looked like she'd rather eat out in the snow than have to endure sitting with him. Holly wasn't sure how she was going to persuade her to enjoy this.

"It smells delicious," he said, placing Holly's plate and glass down onto the table in front of her and heading back toward the kitchen.

"I assure you, it tastes as good as it smells. Nana's famous for her cooking."

Joe smiled over his shoulder, his interest apparent.

Nana didn't look up from her soup, but Holly did catch a small smile twitch at her lips. Holly knew it wasn't due to the comment, however; Nana loved cooking, and she was truly great at it. Regardless of the reason, Holly was relieved to get even the tiniest indication of anything less than hostility.

"She won first prize in the Leiper's Fork Farmer's Market

pie contest one year with her cherry cobbler," Holly added, her voice carrying lightly across the room. She was trying to capitalize on Nana's slight hint of happiness. "And her ginger snaps are to die for."

This made Nana look up, that pout relenting. She dipped her spoon into her bowl and took another bite.

Joe came back with the last few things from the kitchen and sat down beside Holly, his clean scent wafting toward her. She held her breath so as not to smell it, as he leaned closer momentarily, trying to get comfortable on the pillow. There was a slightly awkward silence when the three of them began to eat. Time for waitress mode. Her head was buzzing for some reason and she wasn't on her game like she was at the restaurant. *Talk about the wedding*, she told herself.

"So, Joe's fiancée, Katharine," she said to Nana, "she's a lawyer in New York, is that right, Joe?"

"Uh, yes."

He seemed a bit startled. Maybe she should've talked more about the ginger snaps. They were a safer topic, weren't they? Too late now, though. She'd have to press on. Her mind raced for a springboard from her last comment. She thought about weddings. Weddings…Proposals usually happen. She wondered about Joe's proposal, that gentle voice of his sailing back into her memory. Had it been romantic? Had he shopped for months to find the perfect ring just for

Katharine? Had he whisked her away to a secluded place, or had he proposed in front of masses?

"Holly." Nana's voice cut through her thoughts and Holly met her eyes.

"I just asked Joe about the boxes of things I encountered in my room."

Holly took a large drink of her iced tea and let the cold wake up her realistic side, now completely focused on Nana.

"I told her you and I were going to go through them together," Joe said, those dark eyes sending her that information as a question.

"Yes! And I'm sure Nana could help us too. She's great at that sort of thing." She wasn't sure if Nana was great at wedding planning or not, but at least the subject got them all talking.

"Perfect," Joe said.

He smiled at her, making her feel like her lunch had swelled in her stomach. Holly was one of the best waitresses in the business. She nailed every single job interview with her charismatic banter and pulled tips that made the other wait-staff envious. But she'd become a pile of mush today, spacing out, not able to form coherent sentences...

"I think I'll leave you two to the wedding choices, although I'm wondering why your fiancée isn't having those conversations with you, rather than my granddaughter."

"Mm," Joe said, clearly understanding Nana's apprehension. "Katharine is very practical, and whether flowers are red or yellow is of no concern to her. She finds them all beautiful in their own way. However," he raised his eyebrows addressing Nana, "we've had talks about this very thing, and she says that she's more interested in being married than she is in the wedding, but we have around a thousand people who'd like to celebrate it with us, so she's going along with it all."

Joe's phone rang in his pocket, drawing Holly's attention to it. "Sorry." He glanced quickly at his watch. "Katharine is supposed to be in the courtroom right now, in the middle of a trial and she's calling. Mind if I get this?" he asked.

Holly shook her head.

He slid his finger across the screen to take the call, sending an apologetic glance to both Holly and Nana.

"Hello?" he said, placing his napkin beside the soup bowl and standing up. "Slow down. I can't understand you." He started to walk out of the room but stopped, whatever she was saying keeping him fixed in one place. "It's okay." He regarded Holly quickly and then looked away. "Katharine…"

Joe started to slowly stride back and forth through the room. Questioning, Holly tried to catch his eye again, but he was too busy listening.

"Don't panic."

That was when Katharine got so loud Holly could hear her coming through the phone: *Don't panic? Brea just quit on me! She has an emergency conflict out in LA! Something went wrong with the wedding after ours and it's a "high-profile" issue, she said! Why didn't she plan for this sort of thing? That's her job! This is completely unacceptable! I don't have time to finish planning a wedding, Joseph!*

"Slow down," he said calmly, clearly grasping for answers himself. "It's almost finished. We could make the last few decisions ourselves—"

Katharine sent through an inaudible couple of sentences and Joe pulled the phone away from his ear as if he were saving his eardrum, pacing back over toward Holly. When he neared her, it looked like something occurred to him. He took a large breath. "I might have a wedding planner." Joe stared at Holly as if she had the answer.

Why was he looking at her? Holly didn't know any million-dollar-wedding planners. Did he want her to start searching for them online? Was there a list in one of his wedding boxes—what?

"She does it on the side," he continued, attempting to soothe Katharine, still looking at Holly, "so I'll have to check her availability. She's here in the Nashville area."

He was tapping his hand nervously against his leg. "Yes. She planned a wedding in Leiper's Fork, in fact."

Nana's head slowly turned toward Holly, complete disbelief on her face.

That was when it hit Holly. *What?* Was Joe really suggesting that she finish this wedding? She had zero experience in this *and* she was taking over from a professional! There was no way she could compete with that. *Oh, no. No, no, no...* Holly wobbled her way to a standing position and stuck her face in front of his. "I can't plan your wedding," she mouthed to him.

"She's really good, yes." He turned away from her. "She has an eye for design." He peered over his shoulder briefly but wouldn't look Holly in the eyes this time, to avoid her objections.

Her mouth bone dry, Holly grabbed her iced tea off the table, wishing there was a shot of whiskey in it. But as she looked back at Joe, she could see he was scrambling to help his fiancée. He was trying to fix this, and the gesture was so sweet that she couldn't say no. She realized right then that maybe she and Joe could be friends after this. He was so kindhearted that she *wanted* to be friends, to have someone like him in her life.

"What does she do for her full-time job? She's a wait—"

Holly tugged his sleeve and shook her head, fearing her choice of career wouldn't make her seem versed in the ins and outs of the wedding industry.

"She works with high-end clientele, in...sales."

Holly started to cough, the tea stinging her nose as she choked. The minute they met, Katharine would see right through this, Holly was certain. She'd never planned anything on such a big scale in her life! How would she take care of Nana and complete the final details of a wedding like this? Her heart was pounding, her mind racing, and she was caught between the total horror of taking this on and the absolute excitement that filled her at the thought of it.

Joe put his hand over the phone and whispered, "It won't be much work, I promise. We're almost finished—it's just a few things. I'll help—you'll have my cell, Katharine's cell, and all the information you'll need on my computer. But if you don't want to, I'll tell her you were already busy, and we'll start looking for someone." He stood there as if he were waiting for an answer right now, while Katharine kept talking.

Holly turned and searched Nana's face for her reaction, but for the first time in her life, Nana had a neutral expression: she wasn't upset, but she didn't look overly excited either. It was completely up to Holly to decide this.

"What do you say?" Joe whispered, a tiny bit of happiness reaching his eyes. He seemed to like the idea.

That look of his could make Holly say yes to almost anything. It was only the final details...She found herself warming to the suggestion. Why? What in the world was going on? Could she actually use her skills to her advantage and turn her passions into work? Or was she in over her head? She was off from the restaurant until after New Year's, which should give her just enough time…She peered back up at Joe, her hands trembling just slightly. With a nervous grin, before she could talk herself out of it, she nodded.

"I'll get her to call you, Katharine. It'll be just fine," he spoke into the phone. He huffed out a little laugh at something she said, causing Holly to turn back to her sandwich. She sat down and picked at the crust. "Don't worry, we've got this," he said to his fiancée. "Okay, bye."

So much for parting ways when the snow melted. What had she just agreed to?

Chapter Nine

Nana went to lie down after lunch, and Holly hoped she'd wake up in a better mood. She'd never seen Nana as agitated as she'd been since they arrived at the cabin. While it was just Joe and Holly, Joe carried the boxes of wedding items that he'd retrieved earlier into the living room and set them in the empty space on the floor in front of the Christmas tree. Holly grabbed a pad of paper and her pen to take notes while Joe went to the kitchen. When he returned, he placed five bottles of champagne on the table.

"Now that you're our wedding planner, we'll need to decide which of these would be great for the toast at the rehearsal, and then choose the bottle that we'll offer the guests at the reception."

"What made you think I'd be good for this job?" she asked, seriously wondering if he'd hit his head when she wasn't around or something.

"You said you planned a wedding before, and I'm blown away by the interior of this cabin—you did that, right?"

He was smiling at her when he said it, as if her question

was funny or cute in some way. Well, it wasn't. She was being serious. She peered down at the champagne choices to avoid looking at him.

"I told you the wedding was very informal and small-scale. Nothing like what you're talking about. We didn't even have champagne. We had beer in the can..."

Holly pulled a bottle toward her. She'd seen one of these labels before in the restaurant where she worked. It was easily a seven-hundred-dollar bottle of champagne and had its own special location, under lock and key. She picked it up and ran her hand over the label.

"It's cold," she noted, her surprise causing her to abandon the original conversation for a moment.

"Yes," he said, leaning over her and viewing the one she'd chosen. "I put them in the fridge this morning. I figured even if you didn't help me decide, I'd rather have cold champagne to make the choice myself."

Holly's shoulders relaxed when he moved away from her to dig around in all the wedding items. He pulled out a large, rectangular gift box and untied the white satin ribbon, retrieving from inside a champagne flute. It had silver around the rim, cut edges through the glass that made the whole thing look like diamonds, and two silver rings with tiny white rhinestones encircling the stem. He set it down with a thud, the way Nana would've set a Tupperware cup, its beauty clearly lost on him, and reached back into the box. One after another, he set up flutes, each its own work of art. After the sixth glass had been unwrapped, he sat back and scrutinized them.

"We're drinking from one of these for the rehearsal and we need another for when we toast after cake cutting. I think that's what Katharine told me. Does that sound right?"

Holly was so blown away by their loveliness that she almost missed what Joe said and forgot to answer him. She pictured each one in Katharine's hands, guessing Katharine would probably have long, thin fingers with a perfect pearl-colored manicure wrapped around the flute, the bubbling and fizzing gold liquid shimmering in the cuts of glass under the evening lights. She set the bottle down and picked up the flute with the silver rings.

"Katharine told me they all look just as exquisite to her, so we can pick whichever one we like for each night. I have to agree with her—any of them would be fine with me. Do you think there's one that's better suited for each event? Let's put the champagne in them and see if that helps to make the decision."

He picked up the seven-hundred-dollar bottle and unwound the casing on the top. Holly jumped at the hollow pop as Joe pushed the cork free. Gently, he took the glass from her hands and filled it, handing it back to her.

Holly stared down at it, the roaring fire behind her making the glass appear blazing orange.

"A toast," Joe said, causing her focus to move from her flute. He'd filled another glass—this one more substantial with less embellishment. "To chance meetings and perfect timing." He held up his champagne. "You saved our wedding," he said.

Holly raised her own glass and tapped it to his, wondering if she was going to wake up in Nana's house back in Nashville and realize that this was just some sort of stress dream. Was this really happening?

She tipped the champagne glass against her lips and let the liquid slide into her mouth, using restraint not to down it like a shot. She needed a nice drink right about now. The champagne was smooth and fizzing against her tongue, the most delicious champagne she'd ever had.

"Wow," she said, despite herself. "This is really good."

"Okay, it's a contender then." Joe popped the cork off another bottle, filling two more glasses and handing her one.

Holly had to force herself to put the one she was drinking down, deciding she'd come back to it and finish it off. It was too good not to. She took a drink of the next glass, this one even better than the other. "That's amazing!"

He laughed. "It ought to be. It's a thousand dollars a bottle."

"Oh!" She snapped her mouth shut, surprise taking over.

Joe laughed again. "It's fine. Just let me know which one tastes the best once we've tried them all."

After they'd opened every bottle, Holly had glasses lined up in front of her, all with half-finished champagne in them. She kept going back and forth, trying each one, attempting to choose, but every one was so delicious that she couldn't decide. Her shoulders were relaxed now, she'd forgotten about the dull pain in her ankle, and she had to keep blinking to keep her vision clear. Joe was on the sofa across from her, reclined, his arm outstretched along the back with a champagne flute dangling from his fingers. He'd refilled his flute a few times. His features were relaxed and content as he looked at her.

"Have you made a choice yet?" he asked.

"Do *you* have one that stands out above the others?" She set her flute down and tried to read the labels of each one again, still undecided.

"I like this one," he said, leaning forward and taking one of the bottles into his hand. He added more to his glass.

"Me too."

He topped hers off. "Rehearsal or reception? Or both?"

"How expensive is it? If it's outrageous, then I'd say rehearsal. If it's moderately priced, then both."

"It's somewhere in the middle," he said. "So let's go with this one for both the rehearsal and the reception."

Holly lifted the bottle and jotted down the name of the champagne on her pad of paper.

Joe took another drink from his glass, the now dwindling fire and the alcohol making his cheeks flush in a way that made him even more attractive. He got up and moved closer to Holly, sitting down on the floor beside her. Her pulse rose, making her wonder if the alcohol was affecting her heartbeat. She tried to move away, but he leaned toward her, and she held her breath, nearly spilling her champagne. Before she could process anything, he'd stuck his hand in the box behind her and pulled out a tin.

"On to wedding favors," he said, holding it up. "This is the first option: a tiny tin of mints." He pursed his lips, clearly thinking it over as he set it on the coffee table.

"It's *mint* green," she said, amusement surfacing. "Mint green mints." She laughed quietly.

His eyes were on her and it seemed that he found it just as funny. He held her gaze, making her stomach feel fluttery. Suddenly, she worried that if she tried to form a sentence, it would come out jumbled.

Holly decided to switch to a non-alcoholic drink. She'd have thought she hadn't been in the presence of a man before. Why did he fluster her so badly? It must have been the champagne—how strong was it?

"I think I need some water before we start this round."

She went to get up, but he'd placed his hand on her arm, stopping her cold.

"Wait . . ." He pulled out a water bottle that said, "Joseph and Katharine" in curly script the same mint green as the tin and placed it in front of her with a grin.

She laughed. "Water bottles as wedding favors?"

He offered a mock serious expression. "You think it's funny?" Then he dug back into the box. "I'll show you funny." He turned around, wearing the most ridiculous pair of black sunglasses she'd ever seen with "Joseph and Katharine" in green script on the side. The sight of it made her burst into laughter.

"What?" he said from behind them as if there was nothing wrong, only succeeding in making her laugh more.

He handed Holly a pair and she slipped them on, the two of them still sitting on the floor, the fire now just a flicker of blue light.

Without taking them off, he said, "How many weddings have you been to?"

"I don't know." She pushed her sunglasses up on the bridge of her nose.

"Actually try to count. Three? Seven? Twenty-five? What?" He reached over and grabbed his glass of champagne off the table, taking a sip.

"Uh." Holly shook her head and adjusted her glasses

again, mentally counting. "Seven, I think. Eight! Yes, eight."

"And how many of those eight wedding favors do you still own?"

"Mmm. One. I have a beer koozie."

"And when you drink a can of beer, do you use it?"

"No. I prefer the one I got in Florida on vacation."

"Exactly." He set out a carton of golf tees, a hand-painted drink coaster, a box of matches, a tiny packet of cookies, a sachet of chocolates, and a few other items. "These are all fine party favors—people give them all the time. But how am I supposed to pick one of these when I just don't see the purpose in them?"

He was right. None of the items were hitting the mark for her either. They needed something, though—it was customary to send guests home with a token to remember the day. She grabbed her own champagne, abandoning the bottle of water, and turned toward the window. The light came in off the snow in a shade of blue through her sunglasses. She needed something useful but also beautiful... "What if we could find little crystal snowflakes? We could tie mint green ribbons to them, and they could be used as Christmas ornaments the next year."

"You are a genius!" he said. "That's amazing. Do you think we can find some?"

"I'm sure we can! But if not, we always have the sunglasses to fall back on."

They both grinned at each other.

"You call this work?" Nana's voice came sailing across to them from the doorway. She marched into the center of the room and put her hands on her hips. "With those glasses on, you two look like you're about to be in a Tom Cruise movie."

Joe must've had just enough champagne to loosen up, because he rummaged around in the box and stood with a third pair of glasses. "Don't worry," he said, opening them up, his lips set in an affectionate smile. "We've got a pair for you."

Nana batted them away, but the corners of her mouth were twitching upward ever so slightly, and Holly knew Joe had said just the right thing. That was the sort of thing Papa would've said, and in that moment it made Holly a little sentimental. She wished for more great times, more laughter, more happiness. That was how Christmas should be.

Chapter Ten

Holly was still working on the wedding ideas this morning, and she'd been going strong for the last few hours, considering Katharine's choice of mint green as the accent color for January, trying to quickly come up with a winter color scheme to complement it. Maybe she could add dark red rose bouquets with trailing deep red ribbons from the handles—she'd have to check with the florist...

Last night, Joe went back to his room to get some work done, leaving Holly to familiarize herself with the wedding plans, while Nana stayed busy in the kitchen, cleaning up and finding everything she needed for making a few batches of cookies. With everyone having gone their separate ways, Nana decided to wait and make them today. The room was awash in Nana's baking preparations—something with sugar and molasses.

Joe and Katharine were about to spend the rest of their lives together. The idea of this made Holly think about Papa and Nana. She couldn't imagine one without the other. Would Holly ever find love that could stand the test of time? She hadn't been looking before now, but meeting Joe had made her think about it. She hadn't known that guys like Joe even existed. He'd definitely raised the bar.

The fire had been going all morning and was now completely out. Holly went to the door to get more logs, a blast of icy air assaulting her, making her shiver as she stepped onto the front porch. She wriggled one of the heavy logs, the giant piece of wood teetering precariously on the top of the dwindling pile as Holly worked to steady it, her weight on her strongest ankle.

"Are you trying to heat the outside?" Nana said from the doorway, while drying her hands on a kitchen towel.

Her question caused Holly to turn, the log slamming down onto the porch. "I was getting more wood for the fire, but it's super heavy." She made a mental note that she might need to chop the pieces smaller for the winter renters from now on. Papa had always lifted the logs with ease, and she felt his absence as she bent down to retrieve the cumbersome piece of wood, struggling with her icy cold hands.

Joe poked his head out from behind Nana. Holly had barely seen him this morning.

"I heard a slam." He leaned outside and zeroed in on the log that was still mere inches from Holly's foot. "Let me help." He came outside, his dark navy sweater contrasting against the blanket of white around him, and lifted the log from the porch easily, carrying it inside.

Holly followed.

"I emailed Katharine about the snowflake ornaments," he said, turning around to address Holly before dumping the log into the fire. It popped and sizzled in protest. "She said that sounded wonderful."

"Great."

Nana was back at the kitchen counter, cracking eggs into a large bowl. She turned the mixer on, the squeal slicing through their conversation. Holly kept her focus on Joe.

"I also realized I should go over your fees with you to be sure we're all on the same page. Katharine had asked about it and I told her I'd pay you what I'd planned to pay Brea—I hope that's okay."

Holly plopped down on the sofa and Joe faced her, clapping his hands together to rid them of any dirt from the log and then sliding them into the pockets of his jeans in an adorably casual way. "What's the going rate for a wedding planner these days?" she asked.

"At five hours per weekday, over a holiday, Brea would charge us around ten thousand dollars from here on out to work until the wedding."

Nana dropped a spoon and it clattered to the floor. She picked it up, her eyes round with surprise as she looked at

Holly through the large opening between the rooms. She straightened her expression and pulled out the silverware drawer for another utensil.

Joe's attention moved to the kitchen briefly before returning to Holly. "Every additional hour after the five each week would cost us one hundred and seventy-five dollars. Would that be sufficient?"

There were actual people in the world that got paid ten grand for a few weeks of choosing wedding décor and making a couple of phone calls? She was bursting with excitement for a few seconds before something hit her: this wasn't Papa's cabin in the woods or Tammy's backyard wedding. This was a mansion, a thousand guests... She needed elegance like she'd never created before, grandeur up to her eyeballs. This was big. It was *huge*.

Nana came in and set a warm plate of ginger snaps in front of them. "I've got more cooking in the oven," she said, lingering there.

"You'll have a full team. There are people to set up and take down both the wedding and the reception; you'll have cleaning crews, decorators who can carry out your plans, carpenters if you need them; once you get the wedding party down the aisle, there will be coordinators for the estate that will take over from there. Brea wasn't planning to stay—she had another engagement in LA after ours—but she had an agreement with Katharine to start the wedding. The team at the estate would do this, but Katharine wanted her own private coordinator to get everyone down the aisle, since that part involves pairing up the wedding party, timing of the march in the processional, and placement of everyone for the ceremony. She'd rather trust Brea with that than event staff, so Brea had agreed to stay to begin the ceremony. But then the team will take over, and all you have to do is tell them what you want."

Holly gazed into those dark eyes, the fire causing little flecks of gold to dance in them. Even though this was the first time she'd ever done anything like this, and she could fail miserably, she knew it was the chance of a lifetime and she was ready.

With her eyes still clamped on Joe, Nana cut in once more. "Holly, when you and Joe finish this conversation, I need to see you in the kitchen, please." She pushed the plate of cookies toward them and, before Holly could get a read on her, she shuffled out of the room with purpose.

"If you pull this off for us, I'll even wear the Joseph-and-Katharine sunglasses if you want me to," he teased.

"If you mention them again, I'm going to assume you want them and you're just too scared to admit it." She snagged a ginger snap before getting up and walking over to the mantel, where she'd left her pair. "I mean, you're the one who pulled them out of the box." She peered down at the green writing on the side, reading it again—*Joseph and*

Katharine—and she looked up at him. "Why don't these say '*Joe* and Katharine' since that's what everyone calls you?"

He leaned over to the coffee table and grabbed a cookie, but didn't take a bite. With a deep breath, he said, "Katharine prefers to call me Joseph."

"Shouldn't your wife be the *least* formal of all your acquaintances?" Holly hadn't meant to verbalize the thought, but it came racing out of her mouth, the idea that Katharine wouldn't call him by his nickname completely baffling her.

"Yes, but she has a very interesting way of looking at the world. That's what drew me to her. One of her quirks is that she dislikes nicknames. She finds them insignificant and annoying, thinking that we should be called the name that was intended for us because that's who we really are. She started calling me Joseph because of this and it became a term of endearment."

"Well, *Joey*, better not get her around Tammy."

He laughed out loud, the memory of Tammy's meeting clearly coming to mind. Once the initial amusement was over, he opened his mouth, as if he wanted to say something, but then he didn't. He just smiled and took a bite of his cookie.

❆

"I'm worried for you," Nana said quietly under the Christmas music she had playing, her petite hands wrapped around a cup of steaming coffee. Joe had gone into his room, so he couldn't hear, but she was clearly trying to be discreet. Nana stood across from more cookies she had set out on one of the holiday platters she'd asked Holly to pack.

"What are you worried about, Nana?" Holly pulled the barstool out next to her and took a seat. In all the years she'd been with Nana, her grandmother had never expressed concern about her.

"Have you asked Joe why he's here?"

"I don't need to." Holly grabbed a cookie. "I already know. He's here to see the wedding venue in Brentwood."

"Holly, he'd booked the cabin for two weeks. That's an awfully long time to spend viewing a venue. Why is he by himself? He's spent more time with us than he has on the phone with his fiancée. I'm worried by being so friendly that you're playing with fire here."

Holly's cheeks heated up, but she didn't know why. She hadn't done anything wrong. "I think you're jumping to conclusions when there's nothing to worry about. Katharine's working on a big case—he said so himself."

Nana set her mug down solidly on the counter as if for emphasis. "When I met your papa, he was the only man I wanted to spend time with. He was the person that filled my thoughts the moment I awakened in the morning and as I lay my head down to sleep at night. We spent our days laughing, holding each other, dancing, being together, because being apart just wasn't an option for us. When I said his name, I could feel my whole face light up. I haven't seen that in Joe's eyes when he speaks of Katharine. It isn't my place to judge, but where it *is* my place is when it involves my family."

"I'm just doing him a favor, and it'll make me money in the process. Maybe we can use it to see Mom and Dad next Christmas. I think they want to go to Aspen."

Nana tutted. "Why don't they just have normal Christmases like everyone else? Wouldn't they like some sort of tradition for Emma? How is she supposed to know what Christmas is like with her family if they keep traipsing all over the planet every year?" As the words came out of Nana's mouth, Holly could see her dissecting them, and she wondered if Nana realized that they hadn't had tradition since they stopped coming to the cabin for the holiday.

"You know…We could all come back here for Christmas again like we used to."

Nana's face dropped, and she took in a deep breath. Her eyes filled with tears as she formulated an answer to Holly's suggestion—yes or no, it would certainly be accompanied by an explanation. After a quiet moment between them, she said, "It's difficult to even face the day since Papa isn't here to share this life anymore. Every morning that I fill my lungs with air is one more day alone. I'm tired. Being away from him is exhausting." Her pout began to tremble. "And now I look around this cabin and there's nothing left of him. Life has moved on. There isn't a shred of him here for me. I might as well be out in that barn with all the furniture." Nana ran her fingers around her mug. "I feel like I'm left behind. I should be with Papa and I couldn't have everyone come and not have him with us, no matter where we are."

Holly tried to swallow down the lump in her throat. "Please don't talk like that," she said, wiping a tear that had slipped down her cheek. "I miss Papa too and I can only imagine how you feel. I've never loved someone like that."

The skin between Nana's eyes wrinkled in concern as she blinked away her sadness. "Holly, you are only at the very beginning of this life. Which is why I want you to be careful and not fall for the wrong person. When you love someone like that and you lose it, you might not ever recover."

❄

Holly was staring out the window at the snow, her heart heavy. The precipitation had finally relented, what was left sparkling in the bit of light that escaped through the parting clouds every so often. Temperatures remained well below freezing however, so it wasn't going anywhere for a while, and neither were they.

Joe startled her when he came up behind her.

"Sorry," he said, holding his laptop under his arm. "You okay?"

His face was friendly and concerned, like he could read her worry over Nana perfectly, and when he sat down beside her, his mere presence felt supportive. Holly wanted to shrug it off and say that she was fine, but the truth of the matter was that she wasn't fine at all. Papa had told her to take care of Nana in the same letter where he'd asked Holly to redo the cabin. And she'd failed. She wasn't taking care of Nana at all. Because if she were, Nana would be happy. Now, even after all she'd done bringing Nana to the cabin, she was certain that Nana would not have a good holiday. It made her feel defeated and concerned for her grandmother.

"You're not okay."

She was afraid to let her thoughts leave her lips for fear she might start crying. The last thing Joe needed was a sniveling, sobbing wedding planner.

"Did it have anything to do with the conversation you just had with your grandmother?"

"You heard?"

"No." He set his laptop on the side table and twisted toward her. "But your face gave away the sentiment."

Holly rubbed her neck to relieve the ache that was building where she held all her stress. "I thought I could make this the best Christmas for Nana. I wanted to see her laugh like she used to. I wanted to dance and make cookies, and I'd even brought along new knitting yarn that I bought in secret. I was going to leave it for her as if Santa had been here, just for fun like Papa used to do. I have glitter and ornament-making kits—tons of stuff. But now, I don't think she'll be in the mood for all that." Holly closed her eyes. "I don't know how to make her happy anymore," she said, her voice breaking. "Because the only person who made her happy was Papa."

Joe sat, thoughtful, his gaze on something above her and moving around the room, until it finally rested on her. "I don't know if there's any coming back from something so tragic," he said. "Her feelings are her own, and we can't change them." A soft smile formed on his lips. "But we can try. We shouldn't give up simply because she isn't in the mood for Christmas. We just have to be gentler in our approach."

Holly liked that he'd said "we"; it made her feel unified with someone for the first time in her life. She'd always done everything by herself, and she'd gotten quite good at it, but there was something calming about knowing that a person had her back. The lump that had been stuck in her throat was subsiding a little.

Chapter Eleven

Joe had just opened his laptop when Holly heard the doorbell buzz. Who could be stopping by at nearly suppertime in all this snow? Joe, clearly thinking the same thing, set the computer aside and stood up behind her.

"Hey, y'all!" a smiling Tammy said from across the threshold when Holly opened the door. She lived within walking distance but her face still looked as cold as if she'd made a four-mile trek. With her mitten-clad hands, she thrust a takeout box into Joe's chest, forcing him to grab it. "We had leftovers at the restaurant tonight so I brought you some." She offered a wink in Joe's direction.

He opened the lid.

"Brought you your southern meat and three! That's country-fried steak, potatoes, green beans, and macaroni and cheese."

Holly thanked her.

"What's this?" Joe asked. "It looks delicious. Is it corn-bread?"

"It is!" Tammy said, shuffling in and shutting the door, trailing snow onto the foyer rug.

"Wouldn't that be a meat and four then?"

Tammy burst into laughter, throwing a hand on his arm, making him almost fumble the box. "You're funny!" She grinned up at him.

Joe just stared at her like she'd flown in from another planet, clearly not understanding that meat and three without cornbread or biscuits was like an apple pie sans apples: it just didn't make sense. So, clearly, bread wouldn't count as a meal option. It was mandatory.

"I can't stay," Tammy said. "I just stopped by because… Remember how Otis Rigley redid his barn?" She addressed Joe to explain further. "He finished the inside of it for big family reunions his daughter plans every Christmas. She flies in once or twice a year, along with the whole family— they're scattered all over the country."

Holly remembered the barn well. Otis had a talent for construction and he'd outfitted the entire barn as an enormous party area with a stage, a bar, tables, and a dusty wooden floor just for dancing.

"Airport cancelations kept 'em all home this year, so Otis decided to open it up tomorrow for us so we could get together while we're stuck here in this snow. I thought I'd let y'all know about it." Her eyebrows bounced. "There are even porch heaters inside—no one knows where he got 'em. You know Otis . . . Always doin' somethin'."

In the evenings, Papa drank beer or moonshine whiskey, preferring whiskey. Never too much, but just enough to get his cheeks rosy. While whiskey had risen in popularity, giving prominence to Southerners who drank it in trendy downtown bars, all of them trying the newest in mixers, Papa always had his "plain and simple," as he'd called it. He got it from Otis Rigley, who lived down the road from the cabin. He made it in his barn with corn from his field. Otis's possession of a distilled spirits permit was always questionable, but no one said a word, because he only made enough for him, Papa, and their couple of friends. They used to sit on his front porch, drinking it on ice in mason jars, and it always looked just like iced tea until Holly had gotten close enough to smell it.

"Thank you for the invite," Holly said, wondering if she could get Nana to go.

"It should be real fun! We're bringing all the food, but Otis is in charge of drinks." Tammy offered a mischievous grin the way she did whenever she had some sort of insider scoop. Local gossip was Tammy's specialty; she considered it part of her duty as a resident to keep everyone informed. "And Rhett's setting up in the barn loft to play for us. He's in town."

That last sentence was like a cold wet smack to Holly's face. A wave of uncertainty slid down her spine and her breath became shallow. "Rhett's in town?"

Tammy nodded slowly. "Mmm. Hmm. He sure is. He's home to have Christmas with his mama."

Rhett Burton, a singer-songwriter, was the darling of Leiper's Fork, having grown up his whole life in the small town. He'd had his first brush with fame when his single "Take Me Home" hit number one on the country charts a few years back. He'd sold out every show since.

Holly remembered those lyrics as they left his lips for the first time, the two of them under the old oak tree out back of the cabin, a pencil in his hand and that tattered notebook he scribbled in sitting on his lap: *Take me home, where the pines know my name, where the world is the same, and I still have you.* That was when he'd, ironically, moved downtown to a condo near Music Row in Nashville, although he rarely lived there, traveling the world, playing large venues year-round. He'd left everyone to follow his dream. Even Holly.

"Please say you'll come."

When Holly surfaced from her fog of panic, she noticed Joe studying her. She pushed a smile across her face, making the decision right then that she wasn't going to let Rhett keep her from enjoying herself. It was water under the bridge, anyway. He'd had to go.

"I'd love to come. I'll clear it with Nana when she wakes up from her nap and if she isn't up for it tomorrow, I'll stop by for little while."

"Buddy's comin' around with the tractor if y'all need a lift. Just let him know. He smartened up and put the plow on, so he can probably clear this driveway if he comes through the field out back and hits the brakes all the way down the hill."

Holly nodded, worried already about how Nana would manage in Buddy's tractor. But if she could, it would be really great to get her around old friends.

"We're startin' about seven." Tammy turned the knob on the door and pulled it open, a surge of frigid air taking Holly's breath away. "I'm off! Got more people to invite!" Then she turned to Joe. "I didn't bring everybody food, you know. Y'all are just special, that's all." She batted her eyelashes at him lightheartedly. "Hope you like it, Joey!"

As Tammy left, she leaned into Holly and whispered, "He's a keeper, girl! So cute!" Before Holly could say anything in return, she'd gone.

Holly took the box of food from Joe. "I'll put this in the fridge for now and we can heat it up later." Noticing the wary look on his face, she added, "You know, you don't have to go tomorrow if you don't want to." She'd only meant to let him off the hook, but the way he looked at her, it was as if her words had come off differently. Those wheels were turning and she suddenly wondered if Joe thought she didn't want him there. "I mean I'd love you to go..." She'd *love* him to go? Now she was being too forward! All the cold air from the snow must have done a number on her brain.

"You'll need someone to help you get your grandmother in and out of Buddy's tractor." As if he were unbothered, which was contradictory to the look he'd just given her, he walked over to the sofa, grabbing his laptop on the way. "It'll be nice to get out before cabin fever completely sets in." He sat down and opened his computer. "Once you get the meat and four in the fridge, I'll show you the wedding spreadsheet."

Meat and *four.* That made her smile.

Chapter Twelve

Holly found herself inside the barn again the next morning.

Nana had said she'd like to rest up for tonight, opting to stay in her room, and Joe was working most of the morning, so Holly decided that it would be the perfect time to brainstorm ideas for what to do with everything—she just couldn't get her mind around lumping it all in a charity shop. There had to be something better.

Staying in the front of the barn, she maneuvered around the pile of old lighting she'd sorted and pulled two of the kitchen chairs over to the side, near where she'd scooted the table to make room in the center of the floor. Then she surveyed the pieces, working her mind for ideas. There was the old sofa where they'd watched movies and eaten popcorn, a smattering of side tables, a ton of bedroom furniture, but the dresser from the room where she'd slept caught her eye. She went over to it and fiddled with the brass pulls that had discolored with time, noting how thin its coat of paint was.

Nana had been right. All this needed was a good sand

and new color. The wood was substantial, and there wasn't a blemish on it. If Papa were here, he'd have set in right away, restoring it. Holly felt like she owed it to him to try.

She was willing to bet Papa had an electric sander out there, and she mustered the will to look around, feeling his silent encouragement. This was his place, the spot he liked to spend his evenings. He'd built handmade boxes for all his fishing gear and shelves. Anything, really, that allowed him to use his hands. Nana had teased him about that. She'd said his fingers would get restless when he didn't give them a guitar, so he'd had to find other uses for them.

Holly skimmed the shelving near the woodpile Papa kept to replenish the load on the porch to see if she could find a sander, delighted and emotional when she spotted it. Gently, as if it would break, she took it down and grabbed the extension cord, plugging it into an outlet. Then she wrapped her fingers around the handle, trying not to think about the fact that Papa had been the last one to touch it. He'd want her to use it, she told herself. She'd just test a spot at the back to see if it would be easy to get the old paint off.

The sander came to life with a hissing buzz, and Holly pressed it against the back of the dresser. Just as she'd thought, the paint seemed to disappear under the pressure of the machine. While the drawers would be a bit more work, the unit itself would be easy to sand. With gentle motions, just like she'd seen Papa do, she moved the sander over the entire back, revealing the grain of the wood beneath.

She was so engrossed in sanding that she didn't notice Nana until she waved a hand in front of Holly, her eyes glassy. Through the light dust in the air, her grandmother surveyed the dresser.

"That sound," she said, still concentrating on the furniture. "I could hear the sander through the panes of my bedroom window and if I closed my eyes, it took me back to a different time." She cleared her throat, putting her hand on the dresser as if she needed support. "I knew it was you, but I just had to see." She gave Holly an unsteady smile. "I wanted to make sure Papa hadn't managed some of that Christmas magic he always rattled on about." Nana walked around the dresser. "What are you planning to do?"

Holly took in a breath, still trying to get past the reaction she'd caused in Nana with the sander. She hadn't meant to bring back any uncomfortable memories for her. Perhaps she should focus on the present so they both didn't fall apart. "I thought I might try to paint this and spruce it up."

"Mm." Nana bent over to see the area she'd sanded. "It's pretty under all that paint."

"I thought so too. I wondered if I might sand it down

and then keep it sort of rustic—just use a sealer or something. Maybe some southern drawer pulls with a bit of character…"

Nana smiled. "I think you know what you're doing, so I'll leave you to it."

As Nana left, Holly felt an overpowering need to take care of every piece of furniture that Papa had so lovingly put into the cabin.

※

Nana grimaced when Holly helped her onto the front porch. She had a long coat, buttoned all the way up around her matching wool scarf, her hat pulled down over her white hair and her gloved hands in her pockets.

"How many heaters did Otis say he had?" Nana asked. She had called Otis earlier to find out more about the gathering before making a final decision. She'd allowed a little smile when Otis said it didn't matter who came, because if Nana was the only one there, that would be just fine with him, and he'd delight in reminiscing about the old times.

"A whole town's worth," Holly answered.

She was so happy Nana had decided to go with them. Nana had protested at first, worried about moving around so many people all night, but it was Joe that had convinced her, telling her he needed her to protect him from Tammy at all times. He said at some point Holly would have to get them all drinks and he wasn't sure he could handle Tammy alone. With Nana's lips struggling to keep their frown, she got up and combed her hair.

Just like Tammy said, Buddy's tractor came clattering around from behind the cabin, the plow clearing the land as it went. Joe offered Nana one arm and Holly the other. Only because of her still-sore ankle did Holly take it. The three of them stepped slowly down each stair until they reached flat ground. Buddy slung open the door.

His weathered face emerged as they neared him.

"Jeany, you comin' too? Don't make me get you out on that dance floor."

Nana rolled her eyes, but she didn't look overly bothered by Buddy. After all, she'd known him since they were kids. "I haven't gone by Jeany since I was about twelve. Are you trying to wind me up, Buddy?"

"Always!"

"Well, I'm not doing any dancing on a barn floor."

"You sure? Rhett's gonna play."

Nana's gaze flew over to Holly protectively, but there was also an excitement there that made Holly feel like she'd been punched in the stomach. Holly smiled uneasily, not wanting to cause a lot of drama in front of Joe. But she was kicking herself now for not warning Nana that Rhett would be there. By the look on Nana's face, she missed Rhett a whole lot more than she'd let on over the years.

"Who's Rhett?" Joe asked, addressing Buddy first and then Holly when Buddy didn't answer.

"Just a guy who used to live here." Holly made eye contact with neither Nana nor Buddy when she said it, knowing that her answer wasn't at all sufficient to describe who Rhett really was, but what could she say?

That night on Papa's porch, Rhett said he was going on tour, and then he just disappeared, without even a phone call. He said he'd call, but Holly reckoned that he'd gotten busy and the days escaped him. Rhett lived in the moment and, while he hadn't spoken to them, she knew that he'd pick up right where he left off the minute they were together again. That was just how he was. He was like family, and she cared about him whether he called or not, but the fact that he didn't tore her heart out. Especially when Rhett hadn't called when Papa died. It took Holly quite a while to get over it. However, she had, and she'd just assumed Nana had too. They'd moved on without him. So why in the world would Nana care one bit whether he was there tonight or not?

Holly noticed Joe still studying her, and it was clear that he could read the heat in her cheeks and the slight buzz of electricity in her veins. He didn't believe her answer one bit.

"If Rhett's got his guitar," Nana said to Buddy, "then I might let you give me a spin or two on that floor." She let go of Joe's arm and wrapped her gloved hand around the support bar of the tractor. "Holly, help me up into this thing."

Joe and Holly gingerly lifted Nana inside and then climbed into the cab themselves. Joe closed the door, the four of them packed in a line on the icy cold bench of the tractor like sardines.

"Hold on!" Buddy said, putting it into gear, the engine groaning in protest. "It's gonna be a bumpy ride!"

As he started down the steep drive, Holly couldn't help but think about exactly how bumpy things could get...

Chapter Thirteen

"Oh, no," Joe said under his breath, just loud enough for Holly to hear, when they pulled up in front of the barn. He nodded toward the open doorway where Tammy was waving madly, an enormous smile on her face.

"She likes to dance too..." Holly said, teasing him, and Joe chuckled. Seeing him smile gave her a punch of happiness. Joe had this way about him sometimes that was a little sad or anxious—she didn't know him well enough to really label it—but then he'd smile and the mood just lifted in this glorious way.

Joe opened the tractor door and the twangs of guitar over the amplifiers sailed toward Holly right through the barn walls—she knew it was Rhett. Her shoulders tensed up, and an unexpected stabbing sensation formed at her left temple. She stared at the large red barn, the paint a little faded but still vibrant against the snow, memories now sliding into her consciousness faster than she could push them away. She tried to focus on something else. Through the open doors, it looked like twinkle lights had been hung inside, and she could see the yellow flicker of the propane patio heaters.

The sound of a throat clearing brought her back to herself, and she comprehended finally that it was Joe, his hand outstretched as he stood in the snow, looking at her questioningly. Holly realized she'd lost time for a second, and just now noticed that Tammy had already reached them, her arm around Nana, having taken her up to the door, and was leading her inside.

"You okay?" Joe asked.

Holly nodded and held his hand, his grip tight, keeping her steady in the slippery snow as she stepped down, and turned back to Buddy. "Thank you for coming to get us," she said.

"Yes, ma'am!" Buddy returned as if it had been his duty. "I've got a few more folks to pick up and then I'll be inside to tease Jeany a little more."

Holly laughed. "I'm sure Nana will look forward to it." She noticed as she spoke that the guitar sounds had gone quiet. Just the idea of Rhett walking around, in close proximity, made her heart rate speed up. She didn't welcome any awkward conversations tonight. She just wanted to enjoy herself and have a little fun.

Buddy's tractor started down the field toward the road as Joe and Holly made their way to the party.

"How's your ankle?" he asked, looking down at her.

"It's okay. I can walk on it now and I don't need to limp, so that's a good sign, but it's still sore. I think I just twisted it really badly."

"I did notice you were walking better. Glad to see it." He got that sparkle in his eye the way he did just before he made a joke—she was starting to learn it. "Tammy's going to need someone to keep her busy on the dance floor..."

"Aw, you know you'd like to practice some good ol' line dancing."

Joe's eyes bulged. "Will they be doing that?"

"If they drink enough of Otis's iced tea, they might." She laughed. "If anyone offers you a mason jar that Otis poured, run in the other direction."

"Okay. Anything else I need to know before we enter?"

Holly wasn't able to respond because Tammy had already pushed herself between them and locked arms with them both. "I got your nana inside. She's sitting at one of the tables."

"Thank you," Holly said, already feeling festive as the warmth of the heaters hit her.

The barn was full of tables and chairs, and piles of hay surrounded those that didn't have chairs for sitting. There were tea candles in old jelly jars everywhere and white Christmas lights strung on all the surfaces. A spindly spruce tree, held up by bricks and adorned with red and green plaid bows, filled the space in the corner. Holly's eyes followed the lights and, as they settled on the loft, an icy chill swallowed her when she saw that familiar guitar in its stand behind the microphone.

Holly kept her gaze on it, because she was too afraid to look around and find Rhett.

The pain over his absence made her want to run for the hills right now. She'd finally become comfortable again, without him. It had taken quite a while, but she'd managed, and now it didn't seem odd not to have him with her anymore. Not until now.

"If you're looking for the musician," Joe's voice came into her ear, giving her a shiver, "he's talking to your grandmother."

Holly tore her stare from the guitar and slowly turned to find Nana—smiling as she talked to Rhett. He looked… healthy and happy. He'd grown some stubble on his face, and his hair was actually styled a little in the front now, made to have that messy look. His fingers were hooked on the back pockets of his jeans, his crooked grin evident as he shook his head at something Nana was saying. A surge of anger bubbled in the pit of Holly's stomach. Rhett had waltzed right in and managed to make Nana smile first try.

In mid-sentence, Rhett caught sight of Holly and stopped talking altogether. Nana looked her way too. Holly wasn't sure what came over her—maybe it was her sore ankle, maybe it was an attempt not to fall over at the sight of Rhett—but, as Rhett left Nana and began to walk toward them, Holly grabbed Joe's arm and held on to him, making Rhett stop, his attention moving to Joe.

Before they could speak, Tammy sloshed a mason jar in between the three of them. "Who wants some of Otis's iced tea?" She turned her face to Holly's and under her breath said, "Girl, you'd better have the first one."

Holly took the jar with her free hand, the sour alcohol smell filling the air in front of her nose. How did Papa ever drink this stuff? She leaned in and took a large swig, the fiery liquid sliding down her throat and instantly warming her. Joe's arm tightened under her grip and she could feel his concern without even looking at him.

"Hey, Holly," Rhett said. There was cautiousness in his voice. "You look good."

"Thanks," she said, the hurt she felt coming through in that one word. And he read it perfectly; she could tell by the brief shift in his gaze to the floor.

The thing was, Holly wasn't angry with him for leaving to follow his dream; she was angry that her best friend had just left and never looked back, not once. She could've texted him, but she didn't. She was hoping that he would reach out to her and tell her he missed her. But that message never came.

Tammy handed both Rhett and Joe a jar of whiskey. Then she disappeared like a bolt of lightning, clearly feeling the buzz in the air between Holly and Rhett, and probably off to have a chat about it with innocent third parties.

"Whatcha been up to?" he asked as if he'd only been away from her a matter of days, not years.

She wanted to scream at him. She wanted to grab him and shake him. Papa had been like a grandfather to him. Nana needed an extra shoulder to cry on after Papa died. Holly remembered the first day without Papa: she turned on the television and found Rhett playing on some morning show, the anguish of losing Papa and not having Rhett to support her when she felt like falling to the ground every second washing over her like a fiery flood.

"Perhaps I should check on your grandmother," Joe said, looking down at Holly for answers, clearly giving her an opportunity to speak to Rhett alone, but she squeezed his arm.

She didn't know why, but she felt stronger holding on to Joe. Even still, it was difficult to mask the pain on her face when she looked at Rhett. But she wouldn't give Rhett the satisfaction of seeing her weakness over it, so she stared angrily at him and tightened her grasp on Joe's arm.

The barn was filling up with people, their chatter heavy in the air, but it was muted in Holly's ears as she ruminated over the ache Rhett had left in her heart. And now, he was asking her what she was doing as if nothing were wrong. He had to know what he'd done. He'd been her best friend and he'd left without even so much as a glance over his shoulder.

Rhett and Papa had a unique connection with music,

both of them immediately understanding each other. It was as if they had a silent language all their own, set to melody. But that wasn't all they shared. Papa was the first person to take Rhett fishing when Rhett and Holly were six years old, he taught Rhett how to drive a tractor, he held on to the seat of his bike when he taught Rhett to ride. He filled every moment he could with joy after Rhett's father's death in a car crash when Rhett was five.

Rhett left Holly and he left Nana, but the worst thing was that he let Papa down. Because, in the face of death, Papa had stepped up for Rhett, and when the tables were turned, Rhett failed to do the same. Rhett had only been gone a few months when Papa died. He'd been in Europe during Papa's funeral.

"Rhett!" Tammy called from the loft, interrupting Holly's thoughts and keeping her from replying. Tammy was holding Rhett's guitar, grinning. "You gonna play tonight or what? Not often do we have a superstar here for Christmas!"

Rhett's focus moved to Holly's hand on Joe's arm before awkwardly lifting his eyes to Holly. "Tammy's calling," he said as if she hadn't heard. "So...I guess I'll see ya later." Rhett turned and walked toward the stage, his whiskey in his hand. He took a large drink before bounding up the steps to the stage.

She bit her lip to keep the anger inside. Then she, too,

tipped up Otis's whiskey and let the liquid blaze down her throat before the tears came.

"Want to talk about it?" Joe said gently into her ear.

Holly then noticed she was still holding his arm, and she let go. "There's nothing to talk about," she lied, knowing that, one, if she tried to explain it, she'd only succeed in dragging Joe into a night of drama, and two, she'd probably end up sobbing, which she'd rather not make him endure. When she met his eyes, he was studying her face with that inquisitive look he had a lot.

The small crowd had gathered around the loft as Rhett slipped his guitar strap over his head. With the whiskey now sitting next to an old wooden stool on stage, he reached into the pocket of his jacket—like he always did—to get his pick. With his left hand wrapped around the neck of the instrument, his fingers finding their way to the opening chord, he strummed the first note of his hit song "A Girl Like You."

Holly swallowed another drink of her whiskey concoction to settle her nerves. She recognized the song right away.

"This one's for Holly," she heard through the speakers, a few heads turning her way.

Did Rhett really think that waltzing in after all this time and playing her a song would erase the frustration she felt by his absence?

There's light in the dark tonight... Rhett's familiar voice floated through the air, the lyrics soft as if he were whispering them, like he had when they sat together while he wrote them. *I can't tell wrong from right...*

While Rhett continued, she turned away from the loft and headed over to Nana. When she reached the table, Joe pulled out a chair and offered it to Holly, sitting down beside her. Nana was holding a cup of coffee, her expression slightly lifted in response to Rhett's singing only annoying Holly more. She wanted to ask Nana why she wasn't angry with him, but it was the first time Nana had actually looked happy, so Holly stayed quiet.

"Jeany!" Buddy said from behind them just before two arms flopped onto Holly's shoulders. "You ready for that dance?" He patted the tops of Holly's arms and walked around next to Nana.

"You haven't even had a drink yet, Buddy, and you're already pestering me," Nana teased him. But, to Holly's complete surprise, she was wriggling in her chair to stand up.

"Are you going to dance with Buddy?" Holly asked, her disbelief evident in her tone. She hadn't meant it to sound like it had; she just hadn't seen so much life in Nana since before Papa passed away.

Nana took her coffee from the table and stood by Buddy. "If he minds his manners, I might, but right now, I'm going to find a chair closer to the stage so I can hear

Rhett sing. Holly, you ought to join me. It's been a while since we've had a chance to hear our boy play."

Our boy.

He certainly wasn't Holly's boy in any way. Not anymore. She ran her finger along the rim of her glass, focused on her breathing to help herself calm down. It wasn't like Nana to be so star-struck that she'd forgotten what he'd done. Why wasn't she as furious as Holly? As Nana and Buddy made their way toward a row of chairs by the Christmas tree, Holly shook her head, aware of the whooshing feeling from the alcohol. She'd better slow down.

"You two must have quite a history," Joe said, his drink in front of him but untouched. Those eyes consumed her, his ability to decipher her emotions evident.

"Yes," she finally relented. "His name is Rhett Burton. I've known him since we were kids."

"Rhett Burton," Joe said, searching the air as if there were information floating around him.

Just hearing someone else say his whole name made her head start to ache again. It was as if Joe had just put it in bright, flashing lights above her.

"Isn't he on the radio?"

Holly nodded, concentrating on the kindness in Joe's face to help her relax.

"That must be pretty cool, to know someone famous."

Clearly, Joe was trying to lighten the mood, and Holly felt awful for not showing him a better time. She'd gotten derailed by Rhett, and only now was able to get herself together enough to realize she'd left poor Joe out of the loop.

But then, bringing her out of her state for a moment, it occurred to her… "Did you just say 'cool'?" She finally allowed herself to smile. The word had sounded too informal on his lips. Was he starting to relax in this environment?

Joe, obviously grabbing on to the slight boost in mood, playfully drew back a little. "What? I use the word 'cool.'"

"It doesn't sound like a word you'd say." Her headache started to fade just by talking to him.

"What word would I use instead then?"

Holly pressed her lips together and leaned on her hands to think. "Mmm…Maybe…'fascinating'?"

"I wouldn't say 'fascinating' for that!" He laughed, that flutter hitting her in full force. Perhaps she just enjoyed the cheerful atmosphere that Joe could create. Even when he was serious, he always made her feel more festive—the way she was supposed to feel at Christmas, the way it felt seeing family she hadn't seen in a long time…

"What else have you ever called 'cool' in your life?" she challenged him.

He raised his glass and took a sip of Otis's concoction,

obviously muscling it down. He swallowed. "I can't think of anything right off the bat."

"Because you don't say it!" she ventured with a giggle, taking another drink from her glass. "Wanna see cool?" She stood up, her ankle perfectly fine under the spell of the whiskey. "Get your coat. Let's get out of here for a little while."

Joe's expression revealed uncertainty as he contemplated this, and she wasn't quite sure why, because she hadn't asked him to drive or anything. They were just taking a walk. But he stood up. While he gathered their coats, Holly ran over to Nana and told her she'd be back in a bit and to text her if she needed anything. Nana responded with a frown, but Holly knew it was just her apprehension over Joe, and Nana had nothing to worry about. Holly would never overstep the mark.

"Buddy, do you have a lighter?"

Buddy reached into his pocket and pulled out a silver-and-red cigarette lighter. He always carried one.

"Thanks!" She took it and slid it into the back pocket of her jeans. Then she went over to Joe to get her coat and he held it out for her so she could put her arms into it. As they walked toward the door, she allowed herself one last glance at the stage. Rhett was still singing, but his eyes were on her, watching her leave.

Chapter Fourteen

"I'm surprised you don't mind missing the concert," Joe said.

It took Holly a minute to realize that Rhett playing guitar in a barn was a concert for someone like Joe. She hadn't stopped to think about the fact that strangers paid money to see him strum his guitar and sing out his poetry. It was odd, since she'd seen him do it as long as she'd known him—every day.

"I've been around his music my whole life, so, for me, it's not a big deal."

The clouds had finally moved out, and the sky was an inky black, the stars like twinkle lights above them. Holly's breath dissipated in front of her as she looked up to view them, the reality of having Rhett so close causing her to feel the weight of the world on her shoulders.

She stepped over the edge of the walk into the snow, deciding she should probably fill Joe in just a little, although she was leaving Otis's barn to get her mind off Rhett. "When Rhett got famous, he left, without a trace. That made me angry because no matter how big he got, I felt like he should remember where he came from and the fact that there are people here who loved him before he was a headliner on some stage."

"Mmm," Joe said in agreement, but it seemed as though he were thinking about something more. He took another one of his deep breaths and Holly wondered if it was his way of clearing his mind—he did it a lot. "I like how welcoming everyone is here. You seem to have closer relationships with your friends than I do with my own family."

That was saying something, since Holly hadn't even seen these people in quite a while. But she had a history with them all, and that united them. "I suppose you're right: they *are* like family. It's as if each one of them is a favorite cousin, but you never get to see them. You could go years and then just pick up where you left off."

She saw a slight wrinkle form between his eyes and then disappear. Perhaps he couldn't just pick up where he left off with his family. Then she remembered something he'd said. "Did you mention that you don't talk to your dad?"

His body immediately tensed up and he looked out ahead of them. "Yeah... Where are we headed?" he asked, changing the subject, his navy coat making his dark eyes look incredible in the low light.

"Behind the barn. There's something I want to show you."

He seemed cautious about her answer, following slowly, their boots sinking into the snow beneath them. The whiskey made her a little more gregarious than usual, and Holly took his arm to speed him up, her excitement getting the better of her. Whatever it was on his mind about his father left just then and he smiled that smile of his as he looked down at Holly, only adding to her eagerness. She couldn't wait to show him.

They rounded the corner, and there it was, one of her favorite places: two rows of trees lined up, their trunks hundreds of years old, their branches interwoven above in a vast snow-covered archway that stretched the length of a football field. Holly took a second to admire it before she pulled Joe into it and they started walking toward the large stone fire pit in the center. She'd always wondered what it would look like if someone could weave Christmas lights on the branches way up there. But right now, the moonlight off the snow was causing just enough sparkle to do the job. When they arrived at the fire pit, she pulled the cover off the top of it and set it on one of the benches nearby.

"It won't catch the trees on fire?" Joe asked, tilting his head back to view the enormous branches above them.

Holly flipped the little wheel on the lighter until it sparked. "No, the branches are too high." She held the flame down near one of the logs. When it finally caught hold and began to spread to the other logs, she pulled the bench close enough to feel its heat, brushed the snow off it, and sat down.

"This is incredible," Joe said, his eyes on the lines of trees on either side of them as he lowered himself beside her.

"It's been here for generations. Otis's great-great-grandfather planted them. In the summer, the branches are covered in bright green leaves, the sunlight shining through them. It's so beautiful."

When she turned, Joe was looking at her intently, nodding, and she felt the flutter again. No one else had ever seemed so attentive to the things in her life before. It made her feel interesting, and she knew that she didn't want him to leave after this and never see her again. Even after the wedding, she wanted to know Joe for a long time. She ignored the if-only that niggled the back of her mind and realized that, no matter what, he was someone with whom she had a deep connection, like they'd been meant to be in each other's lives. Maybe this was the start of a great friendship.

"My papa first showed this to me. Otis is one of his really good friends." She hadn't expected it, but being there under the trees, the memory of Otis and Papa sharing stories, her sitting on Papa's lap, her arms stretched behind her to grab the back of his neck, the scruff on his face abrasive against her arms—it made her emotional and the prick of tears caught her off guard. She turned to the fire as if she were warming her hands and tried to get the lump out of her throat.

Joe leaned on his knees. "I'd like to meet Otis," he said softly. She found it charming whenever he did that: his voice seemed to change tone naturally to her moods. It made her wish he'd share more about who he was because he was so fascinating to her that she wanted to know everything about him. It all brought her emotions right to the surface.

Holly cleared her throat.

She hadn't seen Otis yet tonight, and she'd love nothing more than to spend some time with him. She ran her hand along the icy bench where Papa and Otis had talked about so many things: the weather report, the growth of the area, or even Papa's thoughts on Holly's latest boyfriends— Otis was always in her corner on that one. Sometimes, on warm summer nights, they'd just exist beside each other in silence and watch the lightning bugs. She hadn't realized how much she loved sitting there until now.

"You miss your grandfather." He hadn't asked. It had been a statement, an observation.

She nodded.

There was that smile again. "I'm not really close with anyone in my family."

Holly couldn't take her eyes off him.

"You asked about my father...His name is Harvey

Barnes. My mother gave me his last name, but I wish she hadn't."

Holly offered a sympathetic frown, encouraging him silently to tell her more.

Joe looked into the fire. "He created quite a scandal." His attention returned to Holly and she barely even noticed the icy cold around her as he spoke. "My parents dated for a few months. My mother was quite respectable—a lawyer like Katharine. But when she found out she was expecting his child, she told him, and he ran. No one has heard from him since."

"No one?"

"No. He sent my mother a large sum of money and she created an account for me that paid for all my education and gave me a nice nest egg. His money put my mother up in a penthouse in the city, paid all her bills, got her a live-in nanny to help out with me, and sent me to the best schools, but I've never even met him."

Holly was unable to hide the astonishment she felt at that. She couldn't imagine not knowing her family. "My parents have their issues; they're different in a lot of ways from me, but I can't imagine not knowing them. Do you wonder if you look like him?"

"I try not to."

"Have you ever attempted to find him?"

"Yes. I've hired people in the past, but no one can locate him. I've come to terms with it now, but I'd like to hear his side, or at the very least, confront him about it."

"Surely with social media these days, you could find him."

"Maybe," he said, visibly unconvinced. "I like your optimism."

She kept thinking about it, wishing she could do more.

"I'll tell you what. We'll try to look him up together."

"Really?" Holly was excited, already invested.

Joe leaned toward the fire, his hands clasped, his face set in a look of contemplation. Holly's head was whirring with this new information. She wanted to help him, but she had no idea how. Joe was being very brave in front of her, but she could tell that his father's absence had affected him more than he wanted to admit.

"I've never told anyone about him," he said, breaking the silence.

"Anyone?"

"Nope."

"Not even Katharine?"

He shook his head.

"Where does she think your father is?"

"I told her he was dead. To me, he is." His eyes were full of unchecked anger and hurt.

"What made you tell *me*?" she suddenly wondered out loud.

He leaned his head back as if he were looking at the branches that reached out like giant hands above them, but she knew he was inside his own head. "I don't know," he said finally.

He had to know. Subconsciously, he *had* to. But the trouble was, she couldn't figure it out. And now she felt guilty for knowing something that even Katharine didn't know. She could sense herself slipping into the realm of closeness that happened when someone was a match for her, but this time it was stronger than she'd ever felt before. She needed to put the brakes on, come to a skidding stop before she got her heart broken.

"It's great here," he said unexpectedly, sitting up and holding his hands out to the fire to warm them.

"Yes," she agreed.

"I'd definitely like to come back one day. I'm not often surprised, but every now and again a place will grab hold of me..." He looked at her meaningfully but then he let the moment go. He rubbed his hands along his thighs and she wondered if he was warming them up. Then, all of a sudden, he asked, "If you could travel anywhere, where would you go?"

Holly considered the question. "There's nowhere I'd like to be besides here or Nashville," she said, her dreams of eventually going away to New York to design school having melded into the distant memories of all the other things she wanted in her youth. Back when she first enrolled in school, she'd made all kinds of plans for her future, but the realities of life had set in and her ideas seemed to have faded away for now.

"Come on. There has to be somewhere," he pressed her. He'd leaned back, propping his elbow on the back of the bench as he looked at her, the gesture so casual and calming that she felt the stillness in the air. Joe just had that way about him: he could quiet her racing mind in a second.

"I think I'd like to go to New York," she said, without really thinking through what he might interpret from it. Even though she never went to design school there, she always dreamed about visiting New York, wishing she could see the city. And she hadn't meant she'd wanted to go to where he lived. Why hadn't she said somewhere else? As the worry inched in, he twisted toward her.

"That would be great," he said, his smile now genuine. "There's a little café just around the corner from Times Square. It's called Rona's. It's got a gorgeous view of the city and warm coffee in every flavor. I go a lot, even though I'm not much of a coffee drinker. I like to watch all the people pass by the window—it's so quiet inside. I'll bet you'd enjoy it there."

Holly liked the idea. She imagined sitting by the window, drinking her latte, as the snow fell outside. Joe could show her around, she could immerse herself in the holiday clatter of the chaotic city streets, see the Rockefeller Center Christmas tree, and then retreat to the tiny café where the city atmosphere could seep into her soul. She promised herself just now that one day she'd get there. Being with Joe made her feel like her life was just standing still. There was so much more going on outside of her little world, and she deserved to see it. It was up to Holly to make herself happy. What were her dreams? She needed to seriously think about them and then figure out how to start achieving them. But to move forward, she had to face the past.

"Let's go back in." She scooped some snow from beside the bench and threw it on the fire before Joe could question her decision. Then Holly pulled the cover back over the pit and started toward the barn without looking back. She could hear his footsteps as he tried to catch up behind her. She had to face Rhett again sometime. No more standing still.

Chapter Fifteen

When they entered the barn, Rhett had stopped playing to take a break, and was busy in the corner, laughing with a few people, signing a poster for them. Holly rolled her eyes and walked over to the food table. Tammy was there, gathering utensils and putting them in jars for people to take as they filled their plates.

"Hey, y'all!" she said, a sectioned paper plate and wad of plastic cutlery in one hand and a scoop for the fried potatoes in the other. "I was just grabbing a bite for your nana, Holly." Tammy gave her a suggestive look. "Where y'all been?"

"Just walking around," Holly said, purposely being vague to avoid any sort of gossip. "I'm starving." She went to pick up a plate, but Joe had already gotten one and held it out to her. "Thank you," she said to him, not meeting his eyes. Her head was a muddle right now and she just needed to fill her empty stomach and get rid of the whiskey in her system so she could have a clear and rational head.

"Hey, Holly."

She didn't have to look to know who it was. Rhett had

already made his way over to the table as if he had a homing device on.

Just the sound of his voice made her head throb. Joe handed her a napkin as she stood between the two of them, holding the serving spoon for the potatoes. She'd always known how to keep her composure when things were going wrong and she was rattled—it happened all the time at work. The trick was never to let the customer know that their dining experience was being interrupted. She'd had fires on the grill in the kitchen, broken glasses that she'd maneuvered around, incorrect drink orders, a shortage of ingredients for their dishes. None of it had flustered her like she was flustered right now, and she could not, no matter how hard she tried, get herself together.

"Holly," Joe said her name gently, bringing her to. She set her plate onto the table, registering its weight, and realized she'd filled the entire surface of it with potatoes, the scoop still in her grip.

"Can we talk?" Rhett said, placing his hand on her shoulder, making her wince.

"I have to sit down." Holly abandoned Joe, Rhett, and her mountain of potatoes and walked as if on autopilot over to Nana. She needed a friendly face.

"Good Lord, child, what's wrong with you?" Nana said, noticing her state right away.

Was it that obvious? Holly sat in one of the chairs and hung her head down to steady her breathing. Was she having some sort of panic attack? She shook her head, needing a minute before she could answer Nana.

"Trouble in paradise?" Tammy said, setting Nana's plate down. Holly forced herself to meet Tammy's concerned gaze.

"I drank too much of Otis's iced tea, I think," she managed before dropping back down to keep from getting lightheaded.

"You just had the one, right?" Tammy asked. "Was it that strong?"

"I've got her," Rhett said, coming up behind Tammy. "Can you walk?" he asked. His face was pleading as he squatted down next to Holly.

"Yeah." She hadn't thought about her ankle much tonight with everything going on. Despite it not giving her trouble, she didn't want to walk with Rhett. Or talk to him in this state, but she knew he wouldn't stop until she heard whatever it was he had to say.

He helped her up and walked her to the corner, away from everyone. With his finger, Rhett lifted her chin, forcing her to stare straight into the eyes of the person who used to be her best friend in all the world. When she did, the pain of losing him and not having him in her darkest hours came rushing in. Her lips began to wobble and only then did she know that the whole evening she'd been fighting to keep herself from doing this very thing. She didn't want to have to look at his face. It was the face of late-night movies, of laughing outside on the grass until her sides hurt, of baking cookies at Christmastime, of climbing trees together, sitting at the very top, and that night right before he'd left when he'd almost kissed her on Papa's porch... The view of him clouded with her tears and she blinked them away.

"You didn't come to see Papa," she said in a whisper, the tears sliding down her cheeks, the pain finally surfacing through her voice. She took in a jagged breath.

Rhett looked down at his boots, his face revealing his shame.

"Why?" she asked, her anger gone in this moment and replaced with incomprehension.

"Is everything all right?" Joe said, coming up to her, those kind eyes causing the pain in her chest to subside briefly.

Rhett took a step back, assessing Joe. There was something clearly there every time Rhett encountered him, but she couldn't put her finger on it. "Everything's fine," he said, and the intensity she'd seen in his eyes had gone, Rhett becoming distant. "Holly, I just wanted to tell you that I was sorry. That's all I can say."

"Thank you for the apology. It doesn't change anything, because when we needed you, you weren't there."

"I know," he said. He ran his hands through his hair,

and exhaled as if the years of absence had finally escaped on his breath. He shook his head, bewildered. "I should play some more music," he said, changing the subject abruptly. "Mama's coming, by the way. She'd like to see you, I'm sure." His eyes went over to Joe again. "Have a good night."

When Rhett left, Holly rubbed her neck and stared at the barn stage, collecting herself, her stomach churning more than it had been. "What an awful start to the party," she said to Joe with a sniffle. "I'm so sorry to have had all this drama."

"It's fine." Joe looked as though he felt for her and it only made the guilt over causing such a scene worse. She should've been better at keeping her emotions in check.

"I'm still hungry. I never got my...potatoes," she said. "Let's get some food and then go meet Otis."

That made Joe chuckle, which helped.

Joe took her over to the table to grab a bite and then they went in search of Otis. When they approached him, Otis Rigby stretched out those gangly arms that could easily embrace four grown adults. "How's my girl?" he said, pulling Holly close, his unique scent of wood fires and whiskey taking her back to the days she spent with him and Papa. He pulled back and looked fondly at her. His hair had evolved from the silver she remembered to a bright white, and there were a few new sunspots on his hands, but his friendly smile was exactly the same. "How ya been?"

"Good!" she said, not wanting to elaborate in that moment. She'd had a plate of food, which had settled her stomach, but that was the only problem she'd solved. If she started to tell Otis the real answer about Nana and Rhett, or her insecurities about pulling off the planning of Joe's wedding, he'd only try to fix things, and there was no fixing any of her issues.

"I'm sorry your family couldn't come this Christmas," Holly told Otis as Rhett began to play another familiar song. She recognized it. He'd written this one at a bar in Nashville, he'd told her once. Rhett had always been enamored with Music City, and he spent a lot of his time bouncing around to hidden gems, as he called them—bars and restaurants, tucked away from the tourists.

The lyrics sailed into her ears, wrapping around her like a familiar blanket after a long walk in the cold. She tried to block it out.

"Just gives me an excuse to have two parties." Otis winked at her. "Now I'll have to have another one for my family when the snow melts."

Holly had missed Otis. His easygoing personality and contagious happiness always made her very comfortable. He would get Papa laughing so hard he had tears in his eyes. How Holly missed that laughter. She inwardly scolded herself for not visiting more often and decided that, no matter what, she'd make an effort to come say hi every couple of months at least.

"And you must be the infamous Mr. Barnes," Otis said, holding out a hand to Joe.

"Oh!" Holly said. "I'm so sorry. Where are my manners?" Her past was getting the better of her tonight. "Otis, this is Joe." But after she said that, it registered that he'd already known Joe's name.

"Tammy's been all over the floor tonight, telling people about you."

Joe shook Otis's hand. "She has?"

"Yep." He dragged two chairs over and patted the seats before finding one for himself. Otis sat down, his long legs stretching out across the open space in front of him. "She said Holly found herself a keeper."

Both Holly and Joe fell into a fit of denial, shaking their heads and laughing awkwardly, before Otis quieted them with a loud guffaw, slapping his leg. "Don't worry, I asked your nana. She told me what's going on." There was something in that statement that made Holly want to ask Nana what she'd actually said. Otis sat back and folded his arms across his narrow chest, but his enjoyment of the moment was still clear as he looked back and forth between Holly and Joe. "Well, even though the two of you are only *working* partners, you seem to be on good terms, so you should have no problem joining Jean on the dance floor in a few minutes and saving her from Buddy." He nodded toward the front of the barn where Nana and Buddy were doing the two-step under the Christmas lights.

Holly clapped her hand over her mouth. She hadn't witnessed this much life in Nana in ages, and the excitement filled her like a runaway helium balloon. Seeing her now, Holly knew the choice to come to Leiper's Fork had been the right one. Maybe, just maybe, Nana would have a wonderful Christmas after all.

"Why don't *you* get out there and dance, Otis?" Holly asked. "I'll bet those boots have dust on them from all the sitting still. I haven't seen them move tonight the way they did as I remember." Holly thought about how he'd chase her and Rhett around the yard with a water hose when they were little, singing and dancing as if the sprayer were a microphone, soaking them, Holly erupting into giggles and squeals.

"Is that a dare, Miss McAdams?" He stood up and held out his hand. "Because if I remember correctly, your papa taught you some fancy footwork. Why don't we show Joe what to do?"

When she looked over at Joe, he seemed enthralled and charmed at the same time, those eyes sparkling in the candlelight surrounding them. He shifted in his chair with one arm resting on the back of it like he did, his interest clear. She only had that split second to notice him before Otis had pulled her onto the dance floor, spinning her around, those little southern shuffling steps coming to her effortlessly, the way Papa had shown her, the pain in her ankle barely there in all the excitement.

"How'd we get so lucky, Otis?" Buddy called out as they moved closer to him and Nana. "We got the most gorgeous girls in the whole place!"

Nana threw her gaze to the ceiling in mock annoyance just before Buddy spun her around. Watching Nana dance with Buddy was different than the way she moved with Papa. There was a defined space between them, like Holly had with Otis. Whenever she danced with Papa, Nana's features had been relaxed, her smile carefree, her laughter rising into the air like bubbles in champagne. Papa's hands would travel along Nana's with ease, and they moved together as if they were one person.

"So, you planning a wedding for Mr. Fancy over there?" Otis said as he leaned toward her to keep his voice from carrying over the music. His six-foot frame meant he had to tilt way down to reach Holly's ear.

"Yes," she said, taking in Joe. He waved, and she had to fight the urge to want him on the dance floor with them.

He was so different from anyone there. With his perfect-fitting jeans, his expensive hiking boots, and a sweater that would probably cost her a couple of nights in wages, he seemed a little bit formal, like he'd never learned how to really kick back and relax. But there was an element to him that made her feel completely at home. The way he said her name softly, his face as he looked down at her, that laughter of his—it was as if she'd known him forever. She could only imagine what it would be like if she knew him better. They could be great…friends.

"This one's called 'The Two of Us,'" Rhett said into the microphone, his voice booming from the speakers in each corner of the barn. "Remember this one, Holly?"

She looked at him and then away. Of course she did. She remembered them all. Every single song had a story. This song was about best friends; they'd written it together. Well, he'd written it and she'd told him all the lines that he should change. Holly acknowledged him with a quick look, but she wasn't in the mood for his public attempts to smooth things over.

Rhett was always making a mess of things. He was impulsive and fickle, letting his emotions drive him. Even that final night together when he'd tried to kiss her. It had come out of the blue. He hadn't done anything to let Holly know it was coming, and she pulled away, needing time to figure out how she felt about it, but then he left. And she hadn't heard from him since. It was typical of Rhett. She'd seen him do the same thing to other girls, but she thought their friendship had meant more to him than that.

After a couple more songs, Otis beckoned Joe onto the floor. Holly wanted to tell Otis that it was fine if he didn't feel like dancing anymore. She'd be okay sitting down for a while, although it was nice to be out there with Nana. When Nana closed her eyes tonight, Holly wanted to be in her memory.

Joe complied, stepping onto the makeshift dance floor. Rhett had started playing *their* song. She hadn't heard him play it live in quite a while. He'd changed it from the upbeat tempo, the way they'd originally written it, to a ballad that hung in the top ten last month and peaked at number one a few weeks ago. Holly heard about the celebrations among their friends, and the recording studio on Music Row had put a giant banner with Rhett's face on it outside their doors. Holly had driven the long way to work to avoid having to look at it.

"Could you take my place, young man? My back's starting to ache and I wouldn't want to leave Miss Holly to dance all alone. What kind of gentleman would do that?"

"Of course," Joe said, cautiously placing his hand in Holly's.

Joe's grasp was still and steady, and she tried not to think about how secure it made her feel. She liked his touch, but she knew his hand wasn't hers to hold. She was just borrowing him for a dance or two so she could stay out there with Nana and enjoy herself.

"I won't have to line dance, will I?" he said into her ear so she could hear over the sound, giving her goose bumps down her arm.

Holly laughed. "No. I think you're safe."

Joe's other hand found her lower back and he gently pulled her toward his body. She put her hand on his shoulder, trying to keep her distance and fighting that ever-present movie reel of the first night on the sofa. Why did it keep replaying in her mind? She was starting to feel the twinge of panic, and she needed something to break the cycle of thought. Wedding. Focus on the wedding. She was working. Getting to know the customer.

"I was thinking," she said, trying to keep things professional, given the circumstances. She'd let her guard down tonight and it was time to return to reality. No more of Otis's iced tea, no more long talks out under the trees. "I should probably call Katharine and go over the wedding choices I've made so far."

Joe blinked as if her sudden line of discussion surprised him, but then it *was* an odd conversation to have on the dance floor. Their entire situation was odd, though. "Absolutely. I'm sure Katharine would love a check-in."

She felt his shoulder rise under her hand. It was subtle,

but it was there—that slight stress or...something. What was it?

"I'd also like to get your input on the floor runner for the ceremony."

His chest moved against her with his breath as he nodded.

"And do you have a list of RSVPs? I'll need to check that against the invite list so we can possibly send a gentle reminder to the late responders. We need a final head count to update the order for the appropriate cake size and plan for reception tables by the twenty-third. That's in two days."

He'd stopped responding, his eyes on her, and she didn't know how to read it. Their bodies were still moving to the music, but his expression was disconnected. Afraid he could feel her heart beating against his chest, she continued rattling off her list.

"We'll need to check with the caterers to see if there's any final tasting that needs to happen prior—have you done that?"

"Holly," he finally said in that quiet way of his, when he wanted her attention. But then he fell silent. They'd stopped dancing and she waited, her pulse in her ears, to hear what he was about to say. Finally, he spoke. "We don't have to do it all tonight, do we? We have time. Let's just enjoy ourselves. Then tomorrow, you and I can make a list of what needs to be done."

Holly chewed on her lip as Rhett's music played around them. Life certainly could get difficult.

Chapter Sixteen

"Rhett!" Tammy called out through her cupped hands while Rhett adjusted something on his guitar. "Take a break! Come here!" She poured everyone at the old wooden table another glass of wine that she'd brought over from the back room at Puckett's. Several empty bottles were scattered along the table. The stone fireplace outside the barn, where Otis always cooked his steaks and ribs, was roaring, the wood smell filling the air. Mingled with snow and the alcohol of the wine, it felt uniquely like Leiper's Fork at Christmastime.

Nana's cheeks were rosy and the corners of her mouth were set in an upward position, making Holly happy. Buddy was beside Nana, his weathered hands wrapped around a mason jar of Otis's iced tea. The rest of them had had more than a few glasses of wine, and Holly was feeling pretty relaxed, her businesslike façade having faded away with the hours.

"What *is* this wine?" Joe asked, those shoulders now loose and relaxed, his fingers grazing the label as he squinted toward the lettering.

"Muscadine," Holly told him.

"It doesn't taste like any wine I've ever had. It's...overwhelming my palate." He looked into his glass and swirled it around, the skin between his eyes wrinkling endearingly.

Holly turned back toward the bottle to avoid the rise of amusement she got from his evaluation of the wine. When she'd collected herself, she explained. "It doesn't have the greatest reputation, but I think it gets a bad rap," she said, laughter escaping. "It's a southern wine."

He lifted the glass to his lips and took another sip, clearly trying to process the distinctive flavors that only muscadine grapes offered, noticing her once he set it back down. She liked the way he smiled when he had a little alcohol in him—it was slow but deliberate, his eyes looking sleepier, his breathing steady and unhurried. She'd had enough wine herself to feel a little buzz, but, if she were honest, Joe could do the same thing to her without the alcohol. How cruel this world was to put someone so wonderful in her path that was so far out of reach that they shouldn't even be sitting at the same table, given her thoughts. Her instinct was to get up and flee from the situation, but she couldn't bring herself to move a muscle. She allowed the memory of his arms around her to filter into her mind, knowing she'd scold herself once the wine had worn off.

"Y'all just gonna stare at each other all night, or are you going to answer my question?" Rhett said, pulling Holly's attention away from Joe. His comment had been harsh, making her feel a flush of guilt, but when she met Rhett's eyes, he was grinning.

"What was your question?" she asked.

The entire table was looking at her and she'd only just now noticed. Nana's smile had contorted to a look of warning, and Holly's cheeks burned with remorse about her thoughts. Holly knew better, and she deserved better than to fantasize about someone else's man.

"I was wondering if we should do game night, like we used to."

"Uh," she fumbled for coherency. "Sure."

"How about two truths and a lie?" Rhett said.

"Okay, I'll start," Holly said, taking another sip of her wine while attempting to sharpen her concentration. She was actually glad Rhett had chosen to do this game because it was a great way for her to take her mind off the things that had been occupying it tonight. "I love cats. I'm shorter than my sister. My favorite food is a cheeseburger." Her poker face was second to none.

"May I guess?" Joe said, sitting forward to participate. The others at the table urged him on. "So I pick which one I think is a lie?"

"Yes," she said.

Joe squinted at her, studying her face as if it could give

away the answer, but she was amazing at this game. "I see you as a dog-lover."

He leaned back in his chair clearly happy with himself. He had every right to be, because he was correct. She'd never said a thing to him about pets, but he guessed quite easily that she loved dogs.

"How did you do that?"

He offered a crooked smile, the wine obviously affecting him.

"You got lucky," she said, teasing him. "Your turn. I'll bet I can guess your lie."

He chuckled. "Okay…" He grabbed the bottle of wine and refilled his glass. "I'm an only child. My favorite food is…pizza. I collect art."

"You made it easy," she said, laughing at him. "I could tell by your hesitation. You're terrible at this game!" Seeing the enjoyment on his face warmed her, and she liked it when he let her joke around with him. "You don't love pizza? Who doesn't love pizza?"

"I like pizza," he countered. "But it's not my favorite food."

"What is your favorite food?" Holly noticed she was leaning on her hand heavily, fighting the sleep that wanted to come. She sat up, her head fuzzier than it had been with Otis's drink.

"I'll go," Rhett nearly snapped, his voice booming between them, leaving Holly's question for Joe hanging without an answer.

Holly turned slowly toward Rhett. She knew by his gritted teeth what he thought about her and Joe, but he'd misunderstood. Tammy probably told him complete gossip; Holly had never set her straight that she and Joe weren't a couple. Even still, the idea crept in that the thoughts she'd had about Joe tonight would haunt her in the daylight hours, once the night was over.

"Here are my three. Ready? I'm not sure you are." Rhett went straight into it anyway. "All my songs are about Holly—all of them. I'm in love with her. That's why I couldn't come home."

Where was the lie? Was it the second one? Holly prayed it was the second one. She burned through the buzz of the alcohol, her heart wanting to jump right out of her chest, a shooting pain bouncing around in her head like a speeding bullet that couldn't find its way out. If the second was a truth, then he was crossing into territory that she didn't even want to think about. She was already furious with him. But the reality was that, while she was terribly angry with him, she still missed him. Deep down, that had been what had bothered her so much. She *really* missed him. And only now had that realization hit her.

Suddenly aware of tears under her eyes, she wiped them away, her lip wobbling.

"Whoops," Rhett said, his voice monotone, his blue eyes boring into her. "I forgot to tell a lie."

Tammy gasped while the others stared on in complete shock. Holly felt like she'd been kicked in the stomach. She struggled to get a breath, the tears assaulting her, falling down her face faster than she could wipe them. Once again, he'd only thought about himself, derailing the entire night, ruining a light, happy Christmas moment with their friends to dramatically announce this news as if Holly were going to run into his arms.

Not to mention, if Tammy *had* told Rhett, Holly and Joe were an item, what if her gossip had been correct? How audacious he was to think that he could walk in after all this time without a word, bark that he loved her in front of everyone, and have her step away from the person she'd come with to be with him. Did Rhett have any consideration for Holly's or Joe's feelings in the matter?

The table was silent. Holly could hear a pin drop.

Nana stood up. "Rhett, my darling boy, I'm going home. I'm tired." Her voice cut through the tension like a warm knife through apple-butter. Rhett turned to her, clearly shaken by his own admission. Nana continued. "I think you might want to slow down on the iced tea," she said, the word "iced tea" through gritted teeth, and then it occurred to Holly that Rhett had been handling his nerves all night with alcohol. "I'm sure Holly would be happy to come over and see you tomorrow. I'm sorry we missed your mama coming, and I'm sure she'll want to catch up with Holly sometime."

"I'll get the tractor running," Buddy said, standing up and scrambling for his keys, not a word coming from the rest of the table.

Holly still hadn't spoken. She was shell-shocked, confused. She just kept thinking how she shouldn't have come. The minute she heard that Rhett was back, she should've run in the other direction. She'd only wanted to show Nana a good time, and now Rhett had ruined that too. She wanted to talk to him, to have time when they were both calm to go over everything that had happened, but she knew that tonight wasn't the night. He should've said all this before he left. Not now.

They both needed to sleep this off and have some clarity before they could discuss it properly.

"I'll come by tomorrow," she finally said to Rhett, the exhaustion of the night winding its way through every inch of her body, making her feel like she hadn't slept in three days.

Rhett had relaxed now, noticeably more composed after having gotten that off his chest. He nodded, his eyes never leaving hers.

Holly turned to Joe, who'd already stood up and was helping Nana with her coat. She felt just awful for putting him in this situation, and she planned to apologize once they got back to the quiet of the cabin. He turned around and gave her a small, consoling smile, allowing her to relax just a little.

"Ready?" he asked, that soft voice calming her.

"Yes." Holly waved to the people at the table while they all goggled at her, and then left them to their rising, buzzing chatter as she, Nana, and Joe walked out of the barn.

Chapter Seventeen

"As crazy as it was," Nana said as she pulled back her bed covers, "I had fun tonight."

"Fun?" Holly asked, still mortified by Rhett's display.

"Rhett's drama aside, those are our people, and it felt good to be with them. It made me happy."

"I'm glad." Holly kissed Nana on the cheek.

Holly got Nana settled in bed, and when she peeked out of her room, Joe had already shut his door for the night, so Holly turned in as well. But she was restless. The clock ticked as if marking every minute that Holly lay awake next to Nana, wishing she could talk to Joe about everything or at least apologize. She also replayed all the times she'd spent with Rhett through the new lens he'd created tonight.

Holly remembered the day he left. The night before was the night he'd almost kissed her. They were sitting on the steps of Papa's porch like they always did but this time, he leaned in a little too close and, as he made a move, she actually considered it. They both stopped, and she pulled back, neither of them going any further but both of them knowing they'd thought about it. The next day, he was doing a small tour of venues across the South, and he asked if she'd go with him. He teased her and said that he couldn't do it without her. Holly had just picked up a new job at a restaurant and she didn't want to lose it. She explained that to him and told him that he didn't need her, and she encouraged him to go.

"What if we ran away—just you and me?" Rhett said that night. "You could work anywhere."

She laughed and now that she understood his real feelings, she remembered the sadness in his face. She thought at the time that it was just his self-centered yearning to have a friend on the road, but now she wondered if he'd meant that he wanted her to run away with him forever, not to go on the road, but to be his partner in life.

"You never take any risks," he complained. "How can you find what you love if you never make that next step into the unknown?"

Now she wondered if his almost-kiss had been an invitation, a *step into that unknown* he spoke of.

She originally supposed he'd been talking about himself, trying to validate his tour. But after tonight, she thought he might have meant: how can you find *who* you love if you never make that next step?

So many conversations like this one raced through her

head all night, giving her further evidence that the friendship she had with Rhett was one-sided. He thought more of her than that, and she never believed it until he spelled it out for her. Acid burned in the pit of her stomach. She just didn't think of him that way. She loved him, absolutely, but she wasn't *in* love with him—not like that. They were so different...Now what would they do? She wanted her best friend back; she wanted him to make right what he'd ruined. But something told her that he might be gone for good, his pride keeping him from returning.

Holly rolled over and looked at the clock: 2:00 a.m. She was restless, irritable, her head was throbbing, and she probably needed some ibuprofen and water if she ever wanted to get some sleep. Quietly, she slipped out from under the covers, trying not to bother Nana, and padded across the room. The hinges creaked just slightly, so she slowed her pull on the door to reduce the noise. Holly must have left the kitchen light on, a long, thin yellow beam illuminating the hallway floor.

When she got there, Joe looked up from the table.

"Hi," he said, his eyes following her across the room.

"I...couldn't sleep."

"Me neither."

The first thing she noticed was the sunglasses—the Joseph and Katharine ones—resting in the middle of the table. And a pair of nice blue-and-green flannel bottoms and a navy T-shirt that complemented his dark eyes had replaced those silver pajamas. He was leaning on his forearms, his hands resting on either side of a glass.

"Is that...buttermilk?" Holly said with a smile.

"Guilty." He picked up the glass and swirled the thick liquid around. "It's a last resort. I thought maybe Buddy's idea would work, and it would help me fall asleep." He grabbed the bottle of buttermilk that was beside the glass. "Want some?"

"Why not?"

Holly pulled another glass down from the cabinet and retrieved two ibuprofen that she had brought for the headaches Nana had been having lately. Joe filled her glass, sliding it toward her. She popped the two ibuprofen into her mouth and chased them with the thick sweet buttermilk.

"Sooo," he said, the word coming out on an exhale. "Rhett has a big personality."

"Yes." She took another drink of her milk, this sip much smaller than her last.

"How do you know him?"

"I spent every summer and holiday with Nana and Papa here at the cabin, and Rhett and I grew up together. We were inseparable."

Holly had gone from spending long days near the water,

wearing sundresses and ponytails as a little girl to baseball caps and cut-off shorts as a teenager. Their little feet that hung above the water when she and Rhett sat on the pier had grown along with their limbs, their adolescent legs in the cool stream as she watched her bobber sink with the bite of something on the end of it. The thing she'd loved most about Rhett was how he listened with a sort of excitement, and for a teenage girl who had a lot to say, he was great. Looking back now, she knew that he'd listened because he cared about her and he'd used every single feeling she'd had in his music. So, in a way, their talks had been like research for him.

"It seemed..." Joe began, his eyes flickering over to the sunglasses on the table, "that Rhett's admission tonight surprised you."

"Yes." Holly took another sip of her buttermilk.

"You didn't respond to what he said," he pointed out. "It took a lot of guts to do what he did."

Holly shrugged. "Not for Rhett. He finds it easy to lay his feelings on the line. That's what makes him such a great artist. It comes through in his lyrics and when he sings." Holly acted like it hadn't been a big deal, because she was still angry with him—for leaving, for showing up and ruining the night, for changing everything—but she knew it *was* a big deal. She'd never seen Rhett so intense.

"You're going to talk to him tomorrow?" Joe asked, pulling her back into the conversation.

"Yeah."

Perhaps Rhett's announcement tonight had been some kind of divine intervention, a way to keep her from daydreaming about the unattainable. As Holly looked at Joe, all she could think about was a lost opportunity. What if they'd met before he'd dated Katharine? What if they'd crossed paths sooner? Would anything have happened between them? She couldn't drive herself crazy thinking about it. Because, in the end, they hadn't met before he was engaged, and there was a wedding to finish planning.

Why had Joe come into her life? Was it just to give her an opportunity to be a wedding planner? Maybe that was it. Perhaps it was that simple.

"No wonder you're not sleeping," Joe said.

Holly realized she'd been staring at her buttermilk, everything coming down on her again like it had while she'd been trying to relax in bed.

"You need to turn that brain off. It's going a hundred miles an hour, I can tell..." When she looked up at him, his gaze dropped to the table, his eyes unstill, and she wondered if he was trying to work out what she'd been thinking about.

"You two and your late-night shenanigans. Neither of

you seem to know how to rest." Nana's voice took them both off guard. She eyed their glasses, and her disapproval was clear.

In that instant, Holly felt as though there was an imaginary line with her and Joe on one side of it and Nana on the other. It was very clear that Nana didn't like the idea of Holly and Joe spending any time together. Would that line still be there if Rhett were sitting at the table in Joe's place?

But at the end of the day, it was Nana Holly cared most about. That was why they'd come here in the first place, why they'd brought all their Christmas decorations and presents. Joe distracted them from their holiday together. Why had Holly let it happen? If she looked at things objectively, she could see that she and Joe had two very different paths ahead of them in the upcoming weeks. Holly needed to step over that line Nana had drawn, making it her and Nana on one side and Joe on the other. She was his wedding planner, nothing more. Maybe if she could make a clear distinction about that, he'd step back and give her some space, which would help Holly get over her feelings.

"We were just talking about Rhett," Holly said, knowing that name would change Nana's demeanor.

Nana, who was now headfirst in the fridge, turned around, clearly interested, just as Holly had guessed.

"I couldn't sleep thinking about what he said," she lied a little. She'd been thinking as much about Joe as she had about the ridiculousness of Rhett's confession. But she didn't mention Joe on purpose just now. It was important that Holly focused on Rhett because if she seemed interested in him, then she wouldn't look at all interested in Joe. That was how it had to be. "I need to talk to him."

"Yes, you should," Nana encouraged her. "I missed that boy. I hope we get to see him again before he leaves."

Holly resisted the urge to offer a dismissive look. She kept her face contemplative. She needed Joe to think that she was considering Rhett's advances as well. It would be the only way she could show Nana their relationship was strictly platonic. "I'm sure we'll see him," she said. But how would Holly feel when she saw him again?

Chapter Eighteen

Holly had almost forgotten the sun could be that bright; she hadn't seen it in so long. She stretched into the empty side of the bed where Nana usually slept and realized she was alone. Her body ached, as her feet hit the cold floor. She peered out the window. The sun shimmered off the fallen snow like diamonds, the sky now an electric blue. The clock read 9:18. Holly thought that waking after nine, she should feel rested, but she had only gotten about six hours of sleep.

She still hadn't made her way through the mental haze of last night. But she knew that if she could organize her day, she could keep herself focused on a list of tasks, one at a time. First, she was going to see Rhett. She'd ask him to come get her in the tractor—Buddy would let him borrow his, certainly. After that, she was going to get some things done for Joe and Katharine's wedding. Maybe he'd let her do a Facebook post about his dad...

Then, that evening, she wanted to spend some time with Nana. After all, it was Christmastime! Maybe Holly could break out the newest one-thousand-piece puzzle she'd bought. It was a picture of Santa Claus coming down a chimney, his big black leather-clad feet hanging above the logs, his red-and-white hat dangling from one boot.

There was a knock on the door, startling her. The hinges creaked as Joe peeked his head in. "You're up," he said, widening the opening. "I made us scrambled eggs and toast. Your nana's already had three pieces and a cup of tea." He smiled, giving her a rush. Had Nana finally taken to Joe?

Holly ran her fingers through her knotted hair. "Okay," she said, her eyes still groggy enough that she could barely notice that Joe was cleaned up for the day, his hair combed and face shaved, and he had fresh clothes on.

"I also made coffee." He winked at her.

Why was he so spunky today? He'd cooked? For Nana? And he made Holly coffee when he wasn't even a big coffee drinker. She wasn't complaining, certainly, but she did find it a bit odd.

Holly brushed her teeth, washed her face, and slid on her fuzzy slippers—the striped ones that looked like candy canes—then opened the door. Christmas music sailed through the air. Bing Crosby? Before she could start singing along, a mug found its way into her view.

Nana was at the table, knitting and humming to the music, and, for an instant, Holly wondered if she was in the middle of some sort of Christmas dream. But then concern floated up through Nana's tiny grin when Joe got a little closer to Holly to hand her the cup of coffee. That was when Holly knew she was awake.

"I put a spoonful of sugar in it and topped it with cream," Joe said. "Isn't that what you usually do?"

"Yes," she said guardedly. Had Nana told him, or had he remembered how she made her coffee?

Nana's hands were now still, her attention on Joe.

"Can we plan the wedding in a few hours? After I go see Rhett?" Holly asked Joe, Rhett's name coming out gently pronounced, a subconscious message to Nana to stop worrying. She also wondered if mentioning Rhett might clear any lingering apprehension Nana had toward Joe. She sat down at the table.

"Yep," Joe said, returning to the pan on the stove before dropping a pile of scrambled eggs onto a plate with his spatula.

Holly eyed him as he slid it in front of her.

He set two pieces of toast down beside the eggs and handed Holly the butter.

"Those six hours of sleep must have done you well," Holly said, still guarded by the general good cheer in the air. Nana was happily sipping her coffee again.

"Yes." He smiled, but there it was; she knew that smile already. In that one gesture he'd allowed a crack in his façade. It was the counterfeit smile that he used when he wasn't really comfortable.

Ha! She caught him. But then more questions followed. Why was he attempting to be so chipper? Had Rhett's little outburst made him uncomfortable? Or was he trying to keep the atmosphere light for Nana? It wasn't like Nana didn't know what was going on with Rhett—she'd been there last night too. There was no reason to pretend.

"You two been up long?" Holly asked, directing the question toward Nana.

"Long enough to have a nice chat about Joe's wedding. I told him I'd be more than happy to have Katharine visit us here at the cabin once the snow melts."

"At some point, we probably should get you two together anyway to finalize things once we've got it all in motion," Joe added. "Your eggs are getting cold," he said.

She tried to decipher his look, but she couldn't get a thing from it.

"Sorry," she said, scooping up a forkful. "Nana, I'm heading to Rhett's in a minute. Want me to take over some of those Christmas cookies you made?" Holly took a bite of her eggs, her other hand on her phone, texting madly. She didn't like this new atmosphere and she needed the distance from Joe to begin right now.

She texted: *Rhett, you up? I'm coming over.*

The message felt so natural, like old times. Except that she had no idea what she was going to say to Rhett when they saw each other, face to face. But she'd better figure it out because she'd just hit send. Holly grabbed her coffee, Nana's obvious happiness showing after she'd made contact, causing Holly to swallow the fiery liquid too quickly.

Her phone pinged.

Can't wait. I'll send Buddy with the tractor if I can get him. Keep you posted.

Joe caught sight of it before meeting her eyes. When he did, he flashed that artificial smile. Why did Holly get the feeling that today was going to get complicated?

※

"Oh my stars!" Kay said at the door, grabbing Holly and burying her in a warm hug. "Aren't you a sight for sore eyes? I missed ya last night at Otis's. Rhett says you were there but you went home early. Not feeling well?" Her youthful-looking face was crumpled in concern, the soft brown curls that had always brushed her cheeks pulled back today.

"You could say that," Holly said to Rhett's mother, the woman who'd been her riding coach every summer. Kay Burton had three horses: Strap, Bo, and Imogene. Imogene was the gentlest of the three, and Holly had learned to ride her unbridled through the fields. Imogene could stop on a dime and make turns by voice commands and tiny taps of Holly's feet. Every summer day, after practice, she and Rhett would take a bag full of carrots from their garden and feed the horses while they cooled off in the barn.

"Well, Otis's tea has that effect on people." She winked at Holly.

"Brought you some of Nana's cookies." Holly held out the tin. Nana had been eager to make one tin for Buddy, who'd graciously picked up Holly and taken her to Rhett's, grinning the whole way, and another tin for Kay.

"You know how I love your nana's baking!" Kay linked arms with Holly, pulling her inside. "Get yourself out of the cold before you catch one!" Then, she called up the stairs, "Rhett! Rhett! Holly's here!" just like she always had through the years. Miss Kay, as Holly called her when they were young, had a rule: no girls upstairs. So every time Holly came over, Miss Kay yelled up the stairs to Rhett and he came bouncing down them, already smiling like he knew something special that Holly hadn't been told yet.

"Come on into the kitchen and wait for Rhett. I'll get us a cup of coffee." Kay pulled two mugs from the cabinet and started the machine, filling it with grounds and water.

Holly walked over to the corner of the room where Rhett's Gibson guitar was sitting, the one he'd saved up for by cutting lawns all over Nashville and fixing cars for five years. It was his baby. She ran her fingers along the neck of it, the strings humming with her touch, and suppressed the pain of losing her best friend for Kay's benefit.

Kay patted Holly's shoulders before returning to the counter and checking the carafe still filling with coffee. "What have you been up to these last few years? I heard you fixed up your papa's cabin. Anything else exciting?" The coffeemaker gurgled as Kay stretched across the counter to retrieve the little dish of sugar.

"Yes, ma'am, I did fix it up. The rest of the time I've been taking care of Nana and working in town."

"Wish you and Rhett could've caught up once or twice."

A tiny shot of anger pinged through Holly as she thought about how close she worked to Music Row, yet Rhett hadn't even tried to reach out to her. They could've had lunch between recording times when he'd come home from touring. But then again, she knew his schedule was tight because only a day after news from her friends of him being home to record a new album, she'd seen him live on some television program up in New York.

"Hey." Rhett appeared on the other side of the room.

"Speak of the devil," Kay said. "You drinking coffee after nine in the morning these days or is it out of style?" She smirked at her son, but his eyes were already on Holly.

"I'm good," he said. "I don't need a cup, but thank you, Mama."

There was a different air to him this morning. He was more settled, his expression almost humbled. Holly guessed he'd probably had to answer a whole lot of questions after she left. He looked a little tired too, and she imagined he'd been up tossing and turning with the rest of them last night. His hair was back to normal—no style in it this morning—and he had a slight scruff on his face.

"I promise to let you two catch up, Mama," he said, "but can I talk to Holly alone for a little while? It's been a long time…"

"Yes you can," Kay said with a doting smile. "Get the half-and-half out of the fridge for her in case she wants some in her coffee. Holly, do you take half-and-half or milk?"

Holly smiled. She hadn't had a chance to see Kay since Rhett left, and it was nice to have her fluttering around them again. That was how Kay always was: wanting to please people. She liked it when her guests had their feet up, something to drink in their hands, and smiles on their faces. She'd buzz around all day, catering to everybody because that was what made her the happiest.

"I'll take the half-and-half," Holly said.

"I got it." Rhett shooed Kay away kindly and opened the refrigerator door, grabbing the little carton of cream and milk mixture and setting it down, and Kay left them, heading upstairs.

Holly, being used to rooting around their kitchen like she was one of Kay's kids herself, washed her hands at the sink and then grabbed a spoon from the drawer where Kay always kept them. She poured herself a coffee before settling across from Rhett at the kitchen table.

"I suppose you want to talk about last night," he said quietly with no introductions. "Before you say anything, I just wanted to say I'm sorry. I didn't mean to dump all that on you, but I hadn't expected to see you there and then I could tell you were upset with me. And you'd brought someone... The whole thing just caught me off guard, and you know how I get when things make me uptight."

She knew exactly how he got. Whenever something was bothering him, Rhett got irritable. She'd almost forgotten it, though, because it took a whole lot to trouble him. Heat coursed through her face as she made the connection that his feelings for her had really gotten to him, but regardless of how calm he was now, and how lovely it had been to see Kay again, she was still angry with him. Holly stirred in her cream and sugar and then wrapped both hands around her mug.

"Thank you for your apology but it's not enough, Rhett. Last night was worse because of how you left things. We need to talk about that first. I still think you should've at least come back when Papa died. Nana and I needed you and you didn't stop for a second to be there for us. After all Papa had done for you, coming back then was the least you could do."

He nodded, contemplative. "I just couldn't, Holly. I'd have to see you and all I wanted to do was be with you. I was afraid to comfort you for fear I couldn't handle my emotions about us. You didn't need that when you were trying to grieve Papa." He rolled his head on his shoulders. "And losing Papa took me back to those days after my dad…"

He was struggling to get the words out, which wasn't like Rhett at all. He always had words for everything. But she understood because Rhett had been only five when his father passed away in the car crash, just old enough to know something terrible had happened and be able to process it. Kay took Rhett to counseling for years, but he never really got over it because Rhett and his daddy did everything together. The only thing that made it better for Rhett was when Papa stopped by, so every day that he was in Leiper's Fork, Papa asked Kay if he could pick up Rhett and take him to the cabin to fish in the pond down the hill or help Papa wash his car—anything to support little Rhett as he came through the loss.

Rhett stared at her, his eyes filling with tears, so vulnerable.

"I missed Papa like I missed my own dad, and I knew it was my place to comfort you, but I also knew I wouldn't be strong when you needed me."

Holly's anger slid right out of her in that moment, and there he was: her best friend.

"I thought you'd just forgotten about us all," she said, her voice breaking.

"How could you ever think that?" He leaned in, his face right in front of hers, his tears still present.

"You didn't give me any reason to think otherwise."

"I didn't handle it well at all." He shook his head. "Any of it. My emotions got the better of me and all I can do is try to make it up to you." He took her hand and she resisted the urge to pull it away, her outrage over his absence still right on the surface despite their moment together. She'd been angry with him for so long now, it was difficult to feel anything else.

"I know you were hurting too, but you handled it selfishly. We could've gotten through it together. And whatever you felt for me, we could've figured that out too. *Together*."

"Whatever I *feel* for you," he corrected her. "I should've kissed you before I left. I wanted to but something stopped me."

Holly restrained herself from dragging her hands down her face in frustration. He hadn't even given her enough time to stop being furious with him before he came at her with something else. She longed for the simpler times.

"You're in your head so much," he pointed out. "Just be, Holly." He intertwined his fingers in hers. "I know what we should do. I know what we're best at."

She met his gaze.

"Let's write a song."

He couldn't have said anything better. Songwriting was Rhett's way of channeling his emotions and her way of shutting everything else off. It took all the problems and set them aside, the music pushing its way to the forefront and giving them both a much-needed break from reality. And even though all their issues were still there, she wanted to forget them for just a little while and be with her best friend.

Rhett dropped her hand and stood up to get his guitar. "Come on." He nodded toward the living room. "Bring your coffee."

Rhett sat down on the sofa, the guitar poised on his lap. Those recognizable fingers of his ran along the strings the way they did whenever he was thinking about writing. "Would you get my notebook from the drawer over there?" He pointed to the antique secretary desk where he always kept it.

The familiarity of the process was a welcoming change

from everything that had been going on. She retrieved a pencil and the battered notebook and brought them over, opening to a clean page before setting the pad on the table. Rhett was plucking the strings, trying to find that chord that would pull all his thoughts into a single first line. That was his method. Hearing the process was like music itself, the tune of their younger years.

He turned toward her and smiled before singing, *"I've got this girl…"* He moved along the strings, the chords fast and bluesy. *"I thought I'd found."* He leaned over his guitar and scratched the words onto his notebook, humming the tune as he wrote them. Then he went back to his guitar. *"Don't know what's left of me when she's not around."* He hit a big chord, his frustration coming out in song. *"And she's gone,"* he held that last word, his eyes moving over to her, bringing her back to the present. There was a screech on the strings from his fingers, the music stopping. He didn't write the last line down and she knew his head had gotten the best of him, making even writing difficult today.

"If this song is about me, then I hope you know that I haven't gone anywhere. You have."

He shook his head. "That's not true. I saw you at Otis's. The way you look at that guy you're with, you're gone."

Her breath caught. "You've misinterpreted things," she said.

He raised his eyebrows in doubt, his arm slung over the neck of the guitar. "Have I, Holly?"

"Yes." The word came out demanding that he believe it.

"I don't think so. He's not exactly subtle with his feelings for you either. Watching you two is what made me want to explode."

Holly struggled for a response, panic slicing through every thought. Did she and Joe have some sort of obvious chemistry? Had everyone seen it last night...?

But then it hit her: Rhett was bluffing. That had to be it. He was feeling her out to see if he should make a move. Because, while he was self-centered at times, he was a good person and, now sober in the light of morning, he wouldn't interfere if he thought he might ruin her happiness. He just had an odd way of approaching the situation.

"I only just met him—"

Rhett set his guitar down with a giant exhale, stopping her in midsentence. "Great. You just met the guy and you're head over heels."

Maybe he wasn't bluffing. He had it completely wrong, but at the same time, she didn't like how he was handling it at all. What if she *had* been head over heels? She'd have liked a little support from the person she'd known for so long. Jealous or not, he should man up and be happy for her.

"You know, you don't consider anyone else's feelings but

your own, Rhett. How do you think it feels for me to hear that you aren't supportive of what I might want? You make assumptions and get all pouty and it makes me so angry I can't stand it. Grow up."

He stared at her, fury growing behind his eyes. "Grow up? How about the fact that I know you so well that I feel like I can tell you anything? That's not being pouty. That's called passion. Have you ever experienced real desire for something, Holly—the kind of feeling that would make you do anything? Because that's what I feel for you."

Holly slumped back onto the sofa, her head so full of confusion that she couldn't speak. Why was life so hard? Here was Rhett, telling her that he was totally in love with her, and yet she kept going back to the little moments she'd spent with Joe, who was unattainable in the most permanent way. On paper, Rhett was perfect for her: they had the same interests, they'd grown up together, she knew everything about him, her family loved him, and he had undeniable feelings for her. She sat up and faced him, unsure of what to say.

"One thing I've learned is that in life, I don't move forward without risk and determination. That's what got me where I am, and I have to trust it." He put his hands on her face and before she could process whether or not she wanted him to, he pressed his lips to hers and kissed her.

Chapter Nineteen

"You're a block of ice!" Nana said when Holly came through the door.

"I walked home." Holly hadn't waited for Buddy. She'd told Rhett to let Kay know she'd catch up with her, she needed some time, and she'd left, the fresh crisp air doing her good. Her teeth were chattering and she just knew her ankle was swelling again—she shouldn't have pushed herself—but she had to get out of there.

"Yes, I know. Kay called in a tizzy. She said you'd run off without even telling her goodbye. That's not like you." Nana helped Holly unwind her scarf. "I'll get you some hot cocoa and a blanket to warm you up, and then I'd be delighted if you would explain yourself."

Holly scanned the room for Joe, and she was glad to see his closed door. She slid off her boots and coat, and shuffled over to the fire, sitting down in front of it. Nana wrapped a throw around her shoulders and went into the kitchen.

The feeling had just started to come back into her fingers when Nana came back, handing her a warm mug full of hot chocolate with whipped cream. Nana sat down in the corner chair, her own mug resting in her lap, her feet crossed at the ankle. Slightly thawed enough to move, Holly got up and limped over to the sofa that sat in the center of the room, the fire sending its heat her way.

"I don't know what to do, Nana," she confessed. "I'm so confused."

"About what, child?" Nana's concern was clear until her mug hid it when she took a slow sip.

"Can I ask you something?" She really didn't even know where to begin, so she figured this was as good a place as any to start to get answers. "Why aren't you angry with Rhett for not coming home when Papa died?"

Nana stared at her for a second, clearly surprised by the direction of the conversation, but then she took in a breath and seemed to regroup. "He sent me a lovely card with a letter, telling me he was sorry, and that he wasn't in the country. While I'd have liked to see him, I was happy because he was out there doing something with his life, and I was okay with that."

"He sent you a letter?"

"Yes. He said he loved me, and it was too hard, but if I needed him, to call."

"Why didn't you tell me this?"

"You never asked. I got hundreds of cards from all kinds of loved ones."

"Well that makes me feel a little better about it. But I wonder why he didn't reach out to me? I would've liked to have his support too."

Nana nodded knowingly. "I'd imagine it would be difficult for him, given his feelings for you. People handle grief in very different ways."

"I suppose. But he still should've come."

"He's home now. And you were barely there any time at all. Want to tell me why you chose hypothermia over waiting for Buddy to bring you home?"

Holly filled her lungs with the warm cabin air and let it out slowly, the events replaying in her head still just as muddled as they had been when they'd first happened. "Rhett was my best friend. And I was so mad at him..." She looked down at her hot cocoa, the whipped cream now a thin sheet of bubbly white on the top as the steam pushed its way through it. "He kissed me."

Nana's eyes grew round, her lips parting as if she wanted to say something, but couldn't find the words. Then, her gaze moved above Holly's head, her lips pressing together and turning downward again, making Holly twist around in response. Joe had come out of his room and was standing behind the sofa.

"I'm sorry," he said awkwardly. "I didn't mean to interrupt. I thought you'd come in, but I hadn't heard the tractor…" He looked startled, and she wasn't sure if it was that he'd heard her admission to Nana or the fact that she'd appeared without Buddy's help. He paused, appearing to gather himself. "If you'd like, I thought we could finalize some of those plans you'd mentioned last night."

"Of course."

"Great. I'll be in my room whenever you're ready."

"Okay." Just the sight of Joe sent a wave of uncertainty washing over her.

"It's nice to see Rhett going after what he wants, as usual," Nana said once Joe was back in his room, dismissing his presence entirely. Rhett was clearly a much more interesting topic of conversation for her.

"Is it? Because it's pretty confusing to me."

"What's confusing about it?" Nana leaned forward with a frown.

"It was a lot easier to be around him when we were both on the same page, but now he's gone and changed everything and made it difficult."

"It's only difficult because you're making it that way. If you were in love with him, it would be the easiest thing you've ever done. Love is effortless if you allow it to be, Holly. The feelings are just with you, like air, and you don't have to work at it."

She knew exactly what Nana meant.

The frustration over the situation was giving her a headache and she didn't want to talk about it anymore. "I guess I should work on the wedding planning," she said. "But after that, you and I are going to do something Christmassy. I promise."

"Don't worry yourself over me. I've got my book, my knitting, and my hot cocoa. I'll be just fine. Focus on planning the wedding. You need to get that boy married."

Holly knew Nana would be fine, but she wanted her to be more than fine. She wanted this Christmas to be spectacular. But as life often did, it crept in and now Holly had to figure out how to quickly navigate it so she and Nana could enjoy the holiday. That was her number one goal.

She knocked on the door, and Joe opened it. He grabbed his laptop. "Want to work on this at the kitchen table?" he suggested.

Holly was glad for that, because then she wouldn't have to be bombarded with his personal items and she could concentrate on the task at hand. "Sure. I just want to get a handle on where things are in the process. Why don't we begin with the guest list?" They made their way to the table where Joe set up his computer and pulled two chairs side by side.

"Yep. I have a spreadsheet with those who RSVPed. Brea suggested sending reminder cards."

"With the mail not running, we can't do cards, but we

could send a quick email to close friends and family." She sat down next to him, the topic of work an easy distraction.

"If you'd like. Let's see…Katharine's family names are in blue." He started scrolling. "Looks like they've all responded."

"What about yours?"

His fingers stilled on the keyboard. "I don't have any family to invite. I'm an only child, remember? My mother's no longer living and I'm not terribly close with my extended family on her side."

"I'm sorry about your mom," she said.

He regarded her fondly. "Cancer. Three years ago."

"Mm. So your father may be your only living immediate relative?"

"Yes."

"The fact that you've looked for him makes me feel like he should be there. You need family to witness this major event in your life, Joe. It's big. You're getting married— that's a very important life change. You will never again be just you. You'll be forever Joe and Katharine. Joseph and Katharine," she corrected herself, his whole first name feeling odd now on her lips.

Joe stared off into the distance, perhaps contemplating.

"If we found him, all he could say is no."

"We're a matter of days from the wedding. And we're snowed in and can't even send reminder cards. I doubt we

could start a search. But I do wish he could be there..."
Joe fell silent and the atmosphere between them was full of their thoughts. "Would you help me take a look on social media now? Maybe he has a Facebook page."

"Of course. We could do a public post as well to see if anyone recognizes him."

He shook his head. "What would we say? Anyone know Harvey Barnes? I have no idea what he looks like, where he lives, or anything about his life, but he's an older gentleman..."

"I'll think on it." Holly pulled out her phone and searched Facebook for Harvey Barnes. Joe leaned over to view the screen. Scrolling through, she said, "There are so many. It could be this guy." She clicked on his profile.

Joe squinted at the screen. "He's a rare dog breeder."

"That has its perks." She clicked back to the list of people.

The corner of Joe's mouth twitched in amusement. "What about that one?"

Holly tapped the profile. "He's a high school principal."

"Never say never."

"The rest are all too young..." She went over to Twitter and typed in his name. "Oh! Here's a...gospel singer."

"I could send them all a quick message just to see..." she said, already typing on her phone.

"I feel like we don't have much to go on. We might have to think of something else."

Holly took a few minutes to send the three people a message, telling them that if they happen to know Joseph Barnes, she would greatly appreciate a message in return. Then she put her phone onto the table.

Joe's face became somber to clearly let her know he wasn't joking anymore before he said, "Thank you for trying." It changed the tone of their conversation considerably.

Holly knew by the emotion in his words how much finding his father would mean to him.

❊

"The pile of logs on the front porch is nearly gone," Holly said, poking the fire to keep it going before adding another log.

Nana looked on from her chair in the corner, a book open on her lap and her reading glasses resting on the end of her nose so she could view Holly.

After about an hour, Holly and Joe had decided to take a break from planning. She wanted to get the room nice and toasty, turn on the Christmas lights, and create some great family memories. Perhaps they could do a board game or something. "We've got some more wood in the barn out back."

"I'll help you get it," Joe said, his boots already on from bringing the last pieces of wood from the porch in for them.

Holly guessed he'd be happy to help because it seemed as though he'd do anything not to have to plan his wedding.

He'd been agreeable on every point and hadn't offered a whole lot in the way of opinions. Holly had done most of the talking. On each item, he'd said, "Sounds great. Whatever you think," his demeanor making her feel hurried, as if he didn't want to ponder any of it, which is what made her suggest they take a break.

She'd never seen two people more disengaged in their own wedding planning before. It was the strangest thing, and it didn't match Joe's usual behavior at all. He was so thoughtful about everything, careful... But to each, his own.

With cold fingers, Holly pried the latch on the barn door, and the double doors swung open. Glad to have Joe there to calm her mind, the musty smell of the barn hit her harder than she'd expected this time, stopping her. It was the scent of old summer days when Papa had worked in there while she sat outside on the grass with her lemonade. She took in the dresser, half of it sanded down to clean wood, the original drawer pulls still sitting on his bench where she'd put them last time she was in the barn. The sander was on top of one of the tables, dust from sanding covering nearby pieces of furniture. The project had sidetracked her, and now she wished she'd spent more time cleaning up instead of refinishing the dresser. They would barely have a path to the woodpile.

Papa had chopped and lined the wood against one wall

to keep it out of the elements. Holly remembered giggling at him, telling him there was no reason to carry it back to the barn, that he had too much, and they'd never need it all. But he said, "Holly, you never know. We could have the coldest winter on record and I'll be the only one ready. Gotta keep my family warm."

Papa always knew.

Holly surveyed the room through Joe's eyes. Papa's gasoline can for his mower sat in the corner where he always put it, his old radio dial still set to his favorite country station.

"Your hands are shaking," Joe said. He reached out as if he were going to put his arm around her to comfort her but seemed to think better of it, taking a step back, his face a bit stunned for a second.

"I've been in the barn before, but today, for some reason, I see so much of Papa in here."

Holly walked to the back and ran her hand along his safety goggles that sat next to his saw. She picked them up and smiled before setting them back down carefully. As she looked around, Joe stood patiently in the doorway, his eyes on her, his face gentle and kind, that curiosity lurking behind his gaze.

"I haven't really looked through any of his stuff since Papa died," she explained. "I've just used the front space for the furniture."

Joe took a step inside, and walked her way, standing near her as if to give her quiet support. Her emotions had come on suddenly, but they always seemed to do that, showing up without warning, against her will. She was happy he was there with her to share this moment. His presence made it a little easier to bear.

He took a few steps and looked around with unobtrusive respect. She realized that this was the first time she'd gone into the barn to get something that Papa had put in there, and it made her unusually emotional, missing him and knowing that when they took the wood out, this time, he wasn't there to refill the pile. The task of making sure there was enough to heat the cabin through the winters now fell on Holly. As he moved into the back of the place, she focused on Joe, on his compassionate face, to get her through without breaking down.

"What's that?" Joe asked, pointing to a box under Papa's workbench. Until now, she hadn't dared to allow her eyes to travel from him into Papa's most frequented area. She just knew that when she did, Papa's presence would overwhelm her. In permanent marker, scribbled on the top of a small box, it said, "For Holly" and a cold shock of fear and anticipation shot down her spine.

Stunned to see her name in Papa's handwriting, she peered down at it. "I have no idea." Holly gave it a dusty slide, moving the box into the center of the floor. She pulled open the flaps to see what was inside. It was full of balled up newspapers with an envelope on the top, also bearing her name. She picked it up and ran her fingers inside to retrieve the letter, her heart pattering, knowing she was actually about to hear from Papa. Before she read a thing, she sat down on the dirty floor and Joe did the same, having moved a little closer to her, providing that support she'd felt when they'd entered.

With a deep breath, she read the letter:

My sweet Holly,

The doctors are telling me I'm not doing well, so I wanted to put this together in the hopes that it will ease your nana's first Christmas without me...

She felt the tears come, knowing she hadn't discovered this until now. If only she'd found it last year. Nana hadn't let them come to the cabin, and Holly had concentrated on the interior of the place, so there was no way she could've found it until this moment, but at the same time, it was as if they needed him now more than ever. Holly kept reading.

She's going to be cranky. But please know that it's because she hides her worry with anger. And she'll be worried, for sure. She worries for you and knowing how close you and I are, she'll be anxious about filling that space when I'm gone. Talk to her. Tell her all your feelings. Confide in her like you did in me. And if you do, she'll start to smile again. I just know it.

Now, on to the fun stuff. She's going to feel alone, even if you're there with her. But I'm right here. Your nana won't believe it, so let's help her. You know I always hide her Christmas presents. I've filled this little box with enough to get you through this year. Will you wrap them and hide them for me? You remember how I did it, right? Put the first one on the mantel on Christmas morning with a note.

I love you, Holly. I know you well too, and you're probably giving up a lot to be with your nana. But what will make her the happiest is if you get out there and live. She'll be okay. She's a strong woman. Enjoy life! Don't try to preserve the past. When you're in my shoes, what will you have to look back on?

I'll see you later. Promise. And when I do, I want to hear your stories!

Love,

Papa

"This is too much," Holly said, allowing the tears to spill over her eyes. She gasped, trying to catch her breath, her whole body shaking, the paper bending in her grip, distorting that handwriting that she knew so well. She started to cry and, right then, she wasn't sure if she'd be able to stop, the last years' anger and fear and sadness overflowing and finally spilling out.

Joe finally put his arms around her and drew her in, his embrace so strong it felt like he was holding her together, stilling her trembling. "It's amazing," he whispered into her ear. She dropped the letter in her lap, and buried her head in his chest, finally allowing herself to let out all the emotions she'd been holding in for Nana's sake. Joe's scent, his touch, the gentle rising and falling of his chest—it made her feel whole, and she was so thankful to have him there to help her through this moment.

When her crying had subsided, she was aware of Joe's hand caressing the back of her head, his face by her ear. She inhaled his clean, spicy fragrance again, noting how easily he'd calmed her. Holly looked up at him to thank him, and they both held each other's stare, neither of them speaking, a mere thank-you not enough for how he'd made her feel. They had an unspoken language—it was an indescribable feeling that made her believe that, no matter how long they were apart, he'd always be able to make her feel this way. Then, as if it had registered simultaneously for both of them, they sprang apart.

"I can get the wood," he said, leaving the moment entirely.

"And I'll distract your grandmother—I'll ask her to show me where she'd like to start a new pile on the porch. Then you bring the box in through the back door and hide it in my room."

Still trying to climb out of the moment, Holly folded the letter and placed it on top of the newspaper and dragged her fingers under her eyes. Then she grabbed the box, sliding her fingers under the bottom of it and lifting it easily, not looking into Joe's eyes for fear she'd reveal how much his embrace had meant to her.

"What if Nana sees?" Holly fretted aloud, shifting the box into her arms and hurrying toward the door, anxiety filling her.

"Holly," he said gently, like he'd done when she could tell he had things on his mind, stopping her. He waited until she looked him in the eye. "We're just getting wood. That's all. Don't worry."

Holly wondered if Joe was talking about more than just keeping Papa's gifts from Nana when he said not to worry. And against all that she felt was right in the universe, she simply said, "Okay."

Joe gathered the wood, and, together, they walked back to the house in silence. With every step in the snow, Holly felt the need to run as fast as she could and get out of there before she said something that could change everything.

Chapter Twenty

Holly hadn't seen Joe since their moment yesterday. She stayed away, spending most of the evening finishing the dresser out in the barn, thinking about her future. Nana came out a few times to check on her, but Holly hadn't been ready to talk until now.

She shut the bedroom door for privacy. Nana had been in there since early this morning, dusting and tidying the en suite bathroom when Holly finally decided, with encouragement from Papa's letter, to get something off her chest.

After she and Joe got the box past Nana, Holly hadn't gone back in to Joe's room for the rest of the evening, and he hadn't come out of his room either. Using the distance they'd created, she took some time to digest what Papa had told her about confiding in Nana. She prayed that it was the right thing to do, and she had to trust Papa like she always had.

All evening and now this morning, all she could think about was that she was starting to feel trapped there with Joe, fully aware of how people felt when they met that perfect person and they just knew it was right. When her friends had said things like that, Holly never believed them. But now she understood—there was a clear and obvious energy around her and Joe. It was inexplicable and irrational, and she wouldn't be able to put it into words if she tried, but she had to attempt to explain herself to Nana. After pondering scenarios for the last few hours, she'd made some pretty big decisions that Holly felt compelled to share with her.

"I need to tell you something," she said quietly, sitting down on the bed, so nervous she could hardly get out what she wanted to say. Before now, she hadn't done anything for herself, but in light of her current situation and Papa's words, she'd come to a firm conclusion.

Nana's dusting rag came to a stop and she turned around, facing Holly.

"What is it?" Nana asked. "Does it have anything to do with your new determination to stay outside in that barn?"

She nodded. "I feel a…" She looked over at the door to make sure it was secure and then, in a whisper, finished. "…connection with Joe. I really like him," she finally admitted. Just saying it out loud made her heart ache, and guilt washed over her.

She expected a frown, a stomp across the room, but instead, Nana had sympathy in her eyes. Papa was right; Nana was listening.

"He hasn't done anything, Nana. It's just how I feel." She swallowed, shame filling her with every word. "I'm worried that he's going to break my heart. In fact, I know he is." Her chest felt like it could explode from the stress of her predicament. "It's early enough that I can take a step away, but I'm falling fast for him." She closed her eyes and sent up a silent prayer that Nana would be okay before she finished. Then, with a deep breath, she said, "I'm going to do the right thing. I'll plan this wedding and then I need to leave for a little while so I can clear my head."

She heard Papa's voice in the words of that letter: *Get out there and live!*

She'd already thought through a few options about getting different people to check in on Nana if she refused to go with Holly and, hopefully, stayed on at the cabin—especially as at the moment they had no rentals for the foreseeable future. Otis certainly would, and Buddy. Holly could ask Tammy to bring by some meals. Kay would unquestionably drive Nana anywhere she needed to go. They'd made plenty of money on the rentals and could easily afford to have Nana stay at the cabin indefinitely.

But Holly knew she didn't need to explain any further. With Rhett back in town and now her feelings for Joe, it was clear that Nana understood that leaving would be the best thing to do, and Holly had thought it through. This was the best thing for everyone.

"I called work. I told them I'm quitting."

Nana was clearly waiting to show any emotion until she'd heard the rest of what Holly had to say.

"I'm planning a pretty big trip…"

Holly had enough inheritance to handle a sizeable excursion, and she'd make sure Nana would be taken care of.

Nana nodded. "I already knew how you felt about Joe, but I didn't want to put any thoughts in your head." It seemed as if she had more to say, but instead, she asked, "How long will you be gone?"

"I don't know. Maybe a year? No idea. I need to be somewhere else, change my perspective. Take my mind off everything. Then, when I have a clear head, I'll come back home." A long vacation like this was a lot to put on Nana without any warning, but it was the best way Holly knew to handle it. "You could come with me," she offered, knowing how Nana felt about traveling.

To Holly's complete surprise, Nana smiled. "I think this is something you need to do, not me. I'm so glad you figured it out without me having to shout at you," she teased. "That's what I've wanted for you for ages. There's so much out there, and I fear you're missing it on my account." She took Holly's hand. "I think you're doing the right thing," she said. "You deserve someone who will sweep you off your feet. And you won't feel confident about anyone else until you find yourself. So go."

"Thank you, Nana." Her emotion on the surface, Holly wrapped her arms around Nana and held her tightly. "The minute you need me back home, I'm coming. Just say the word."

"I'll be fine. But promise me you'll come home for the holidays."

"I promise," she said, the thrill of doing something new rising up inside her.

❄

"Holly," that soft voice meandered over her shoulder.

Joe's door was shut the whole morning. Holly had felt the urge to knock on it to let him know he could sit in the living room with her, but she figured he might be working. Since Nana was taking a nap, Holly was reading on the sofa, unbothered. Now that she'd decided to leave, Holly felt a new sense of restraint around Joe, and she'd convinced herself that she could easily make it through the holiday.

Joe sat down beside her, his face concerned. "I've been thinking a lot since we...got the wood out of the shed."

She'd made a mistake crying in the barn and allowing him to comfort her, and she wouldn't do it again. Holly squared her shoulders and braced herself for what he was about to say.

"Seeing your connection with your papa made me want to find my dad more than ever. I think the what-ifs are getting to me."

Holly let out an exhale in relief.

"Did anyone respond to your messages?" he asked.

"No, I'm sorry."

He nodded and then extended his hand, offering her an aged photo of a young boy, his hair combed to the side, a few runaway strands poking out at the back. He had a narrow jaw and happy eyes.

Holly took the photo and peered down at it more closely, attempting to wipe a small water spot from the surface that had put a speck on the child's face.

"Maybe we could use this."

"What is this?" she asked.

"When she told him she was pregnant, my mother asked my father for pictures of him as a child. She'd wanted to see if I looked like him as I grew up. He left without a trace, but one day, she came home to find this photo wedged into the doorframe of our house. She knew it was him immediately. I wasn't told any of this until she was sick with cancer. That was when she shared the photo with me."

"Did the investigators have this?"

He shook his head. "She gave it to me a few years after I'd hired them and their search hadn't yielded anything.

But, to be honest, it wouldn't come down to some old grade-school photo, would it?"

"I don't know," she said honestly. "They didn't find *anything*?" She looked back down at the boy in the picture.

"His parents are both deceased. He has no family that we know of. My mother said he's an only child like me."

"So he has no one."

"If he's still alive himself."

"And you have no one."

"Yes."

She looked up at Joe. "Wouldn't it be great to find him?"

He shrugged. "I'm not sure. But I'd like to try."

"You should probably start by telling Katharine you may have a father."

Joe took in a chest full of air. "Yes, you're right. I'll tell her soon." He placed the photo on the side table next to Holly.

"In the meantime," she said. "We could post the photo on Facebook and see if anyone recognizes it."

"Okay."

Holly snapped a picture with her phone and handed the photo back to Joe.

"Maybe, by some miracle, we'll have a mutual friend," he said.

"You're talking miracles. Does this mean you *do* believe in Christmas magic?"

He grinned, shaking his head. "I'll only believe in Christmas magic if you actually manage to locate him."

"Hey," she said as he turned to go back to his room. There was no need for him to spend the whole day in that tiny space. "When Nana wakes up, I'd like to put on Bing Crosby and cook a big supper. You're welcome to join us. And it would be nice to have a few extra hands in the kitchen."

"I'd be happy to," he said, and it was as if he understood their unspoken arrangement to keep it friendly, nothing too personal.

Perhaps that had been what he was trying to do when he'd cooked Nana breakfast. Could he sense the need to step back from her as well? If so, he'd faltered in the barn. But now Holly had made the decision not to get close to him again and she'd be strong enough for the both of them.

He walked back over to her. "While your grandmother is sleeping, would you like to go through the box?" he asked quietly. "It might be a good time to wrap the gifts."

"Yes," she said. "Let me grab the gift-wrapping supplies."

She grabbed the roll of wrapping paper, a pair of scissors, and the tape from the hall closet where she'd stored them when they'd arrived and then went to Joe's room and knocked. Joe let her in. He pulled the box into the middle of the floor and opened it. Holly set down the supplies and retrieved the first item, noticing now that they were all numbered. She unwound the wadded newspaper on gift number one until she got a glimpse of it. It was an antique tin, shined to a bright silver, with little hand-painted flowers on the top. Holly popped the latch and opened it up. To her surprise, it was musical, the tinkling tune of "You Are My Sunshine" playing as Papa's handwriting on a slip of paper inside gave her pause. She calmed herself and read his message: *For your knitting needles*, it said. *Go to the linen closet.*

"She's always talking about needing somewhere to put them," Holly said as she cut a square of paper and gently set the box in the center, pulling each side up and securing it with a piece of tape. She unrolled a stretch of ribbon and snipped it from the spool, tying a simple bow on top, then added the message to the bottom with another piece of tape.

Joe reached in this time, handing her the second present. Holly removed the newspaper to reveal a CD. She turned it over in her hand. "Oh! It has an early version of 'Santa Claus Is Comin' to Town'!" She flipped it around to show Joe, her excitement making her forget about everything but the holiday. "It's a vintage Christmas music compilation from the thirties. I grew up listening to this." The memory of it made her nostalgic. "Nana couldn't find the record some Christmases ago, and she was huffing and puffing, turning every closet inside out to find it." She grinned down at the shiny cover.

Resisting the urge to play it, she wrapped it instead. Papa's next note was nestled in the wad of newspaper. It read: *I'll bet you never did find that record, did you?* Holly could hear him laughing. *Check under the sofa for my next gift. If your back hurts, make Holly do it.* Biting back her amusement, Holly lovingly set it aside with the musical tin.

"I can't wait to see what else is in here," she said, the atmosphere of Christmas now settling around her, making her feel like Papa was with them.

Joe had a glimmer in his eye, and it was clear that he enjoyed finding these gifts too. "We should wrap quickly before your nana wakes up," he warned.

"Yes, you're right."

She took the third gift from the box. It was heavier than the other two.

"*War and Peace*?" Joe looked up from the gift, obviously confused.

A loud laugh escaped from Holly's lips and she slapped her hand over her mouth to quiet it, still giggling at the sight of Papa's old, battered novel. She read the note: *At the very least, it makes a good paperweight. I swear, though, you should read it. Head over to the kitchen window.*

"Papa used to read this book over and over," she explained,

"and Nana said it was just to annoy her, because the premise bored her to tears. He'd chase after her, reading lines from it, and Nana would ignore him, as he followed her around, until she couldn't stand it anymore. Then she'd put her hands on his face and kiss him to shut him up. Papa said that that was the real reason he always did it."

Joe held her gaze, introspective, but whatever he was thinking wasn't showing. Then he handed her present number four. It was small and fit in the palm of her hand. She unwrapped the newspaper and a thrill shot through her when she saw a jewelry box. Carefully, she lifted the lid and gasped. "Wowzers," she said in a whisper, disbelief that this had sat in the barn for all this time. Cushioned down in a bubble of white satin was an enormous sapphire-and-silver ring, with little diamonds around the center stone. Holly took it out and slipped it on her finger to examine it. "It's Nana's birthstone," she said. It shimmered in the light.

She returned it to the box and read the final note:

On our wedding day, you had something old, something new, something borrowed and something blue. I wanted to repeat that one more time to remind you of our vows and the life we created because of them. Our time together was nothing short of amazing. How wonderful to think, that when we see each other next, we'll get to start it all over again. Until then, Merry Christmas.

All my love,

Art

"I've only just learned his name," Joe said, taking the note from her to reread it.

"He went by Art most of the time; it was short for Arthur. When Nana was being stern with him, she called him Arthur, but otherwise, he was Art."

"I can tell he loved her," Joe said, handing Holly the paper, a frown of consideration on his lips.

"He always told me, 'Love will get you through anything.'"

Chapter Twenty-One

Holly helped Joe make a public Facebook post about his dad, which included the photograph. They stated that Joe would like to find an old friend named Harvey and any information about him would be greatly appreciated. Holly asked Joe if Katharine might share it for him, but he said she didn't use social media—she was way too busy, he'd told her. So Holly shared it onto her own wall with her email address just to show him how much she wanted to help.

After, Joe went off to finish some work, and Holly made her way out to the barn to tidy up and to make sure there weren't any other surprises left by Papa. With nothing else out of the ordinary there, she made an organized grouping of furniture and a path to the extra wood in case they needed any more. Then she came in to help with dinner.

"We have three notifications on Harvey's post," Joe said to her with no introductions, the phone in his grip. "Want to take a look?" He left a bowl full of potato peels and a kitchen towel on the counter and met her in the middle of the room. From the looks of it, he was helping Nana prepare supper. It looked like her famous winter squash and chicken casserole.

Holly leaned over his phone, the scent of him all around her. It was becoming recognizable. Just like the smell of Nana's casserole: when she was around it, cooking, she hardly noticed, but when she'd come in from outside she smelled it immediately and she breathed in the familiar aroma with purpose.

Joe opened the notifications.

Only three post likes.

He closed the app and shrugged it off. "Oh well," he said.

"Don't get discouraged. It's early still. It only takes one person to see it and everything can change."

He smiled at her and put his phone back into his pocket, their eyes locked in solidarity. Holly was the first to look away.

"Is that a plow I see out the window?" she asked. A salt truck grumbled as it moved down the main road behind the plow.

Nana peered around her, visibly relieved, and Holly had to wonder if she would be glad to get Joe on the road the minute the flights were running again.

"The streets will still be a sheet of ice until the sun beats down on them tomorrow," Nana said, holding a dish with two oven mitts on. "But that's fine, because tomorrow's Christmas Eve, and everything will be shut down anyway."

Nana slid the casserole into the oven. "I've invited Kay and Rhett over tonight for supper," she said casually, as if it were no big deal.

Holly was aghast. She knew that this was Nana's way of putting more space between Holly and Joe while simultaneously giving Holly something else to think about, but did she realize the drama she'd cause by having Rhett over? Holly hadn't spoken to him since their kiss, and she still didn't really know what to say about it. She was scrambling for a response, but Joe interjected.

"That will be nice," he said, but she noticed those shoulders going up again. He spent an extra few seconds folding the towel, as if he needed something to occupy his hands while he gathered his thoughts.

"It's good to have people around," Nana said. "Holly and I have been by ourselves too much lately." Nana didn't look at Holly as she spoke, probably because she didn't want to see Holly's reaction to her inviting Rhett. "We need to have Katharine visit as soon as possible, Joseph," she said. "I'm sure she'll want to meet Holly and see the location for the wedding firsthand." Nana's suggestion was strongly given and direct as if to say, "You'd better get your fiancée out here so you two can act like an actual couple."

"Yes, you're right," he agreed, and the atmosphere was reminiscent of the two of them acting kind and overly friendly when Joe had cooked breakfast for Nana, but it was clear they were having to work to put it on. "I'll call her soon."

"Perfect," Nana said. "Perhaps we'll make her dinner. But right now, we'd better get going on tonight's. We've got company coming."

Holly was certainly surprised by Nana's invite, but she wouldn't let it rattle her. She could handle this, no problem. Right?

※

The air was saturated with the smells of a winter supper and the Christmas tree glimmered in the corner of the living room. Holly had redone her makeup, brushed her hair, and chosen a red sweater to wear with her jeans. She was jittery, sitting on the sofa but unable to stay still, so she rearranged the knickknacks on the coffee table a few times.

Tomorrow was Christmas Eve. They'd be spending Christmas with Joe. As Holly looked at the presents under the tree, she thought about how Joe didn't have any. She wished she could put something down there for him, but the streets were barely clear enough yet to get back into Nashville. Even if she could get out, she didn't know what she'd find for him.

There was a knock at the front door, and Holly jumped out of her skin. She knew it was Rhett and Kay, and she couldn't bear the anxiety it caused her. Holly got up to answer it and met Joe head on. He was wearing a blue-and-red button down and jeans, his face clean-shaven, his hair combed in that way he always did it, and the spicy scent of him cut through the air, making her more nervous. All she could do was offer him an uncomfortable look as she opened the door.

"Hey there, Miss Princess!" Kay said, barreling through the door and plastering Holly with a hug, her hair tickling Holly's nose.

Holly wanted to hold on to her, not letting go, so she wouldn't have to face Rhett. She knew he'd press her for answers about her feelings for him, and she just wasn't ready to have that conversation. She didn't know where they were supposed to go from this point.

When Kay finally moved away from her to introduce herself to Joe, Holly was face to face with Rhett. He was all cleaned up. He'd styled his hair again, his eyes already full of questions, as he held out a basket. "Food," he said with a crooked grin. "Mama made biscuits and her famous dill dip and veggies." Then he shot her a knowing look before clamping his eyes on Joe, his voice still addressing Holly. "And we made you sweet potato pie. I know it's your *favorite*." He said that last word as if he were the most knowledgeable of anyone about Holly's favorite things.

Joe smiled politely, unruffled.

Kay took the basket from Rhett and headed toward the kitchen while Rhett stepped inside, shutting the door behind him. "Where's your nana?" Kay asked, not waiting for an answer as she unpacked the basket on the kitchen counter.

"I'll see if Kay needs help," Joe said, noticeably giving Rhett and Holly a moment. He left them without another word.

"Please don't spend the whole night spouting passive-aggressive jealous comments," she barked right off the bat, her voice at a clipped whisper. Rhett had hardly gotten through the door before the jab about knowing her favorite pie. Joe had done nothing to deserve that.

Rhett stepped back, looking offended. But then he bucked up again, his emotions on some kind of roller coaster. "That guy's not your type," he said with an annoyed grimace. It was apparent that he couldn't stand the idea of Holly with anyone.

"How would you know? You've been gone so long you can't claim to be an expert on my type. Unless you just *assume* that my type is someone like you."

He wavered again and she was aware of how quickly she could hurt him. "We could be pretty good together, Holly. Being with you is so easy," he said, his voice calmer now, the past slithering between them. "He brings out the worst in me."

Holly followed Rhett's line of sight to where Joe was

standing in the kitchen, and she saw that Joe was looking back at her. Nana stepped up beside him and he quickly cleared his throat and asked her if she needed anything.

Rhett took a step toward her, his tall frame filling up the space between them, his soft stare looming over her as he put his hands on her arms tenderly and kissed the top of her head. "I'll try to keep my opinions in check," he said. "I'll do it for you." Then he bent his knees just a little to face her, eye to eye. "But I still want to talk about us later."

"Us?" she said, pointing out yet another assumption.

Rhett slid his hands down her arms and intertwined his fingers with hers. "Yeah, us." He gave her that grin that she imagined would melt the hearts of every twenty-something that pressed herself against the stage at his concerts. "We may be in different places—I don't know yet—but when I think about all the memories I have with you, it's definitely an 'us' for me."

Her resolve crumbled just a little at his admission because she knew exactly what Rhett meant. She missed him terribly. "Can we just be the 'us' that we *were* for a little while and not push things?" she asked.

Before he could answer, Nana was behind them. "I'm setting the table," she announced. "And I've opened a bottle of wine. I think it would be wise for all of us to drink some."

When Holly got to the kitchen, she saw that Nana had

put her favorite wine glass with the purple stem at one end of the table, and Joe and Rhett were on either side by her. Kay's plate was beside Rhett's and Nana was next to Joe.

"That looks delicious, Nana," Rhett said. He kissed her cheek as he rounded the corner of the table to sit down next to his mother, his chair making a scraping sound against the new kitchen tile.

"I remember a little boy who wouldn't touch casserole," Nana said, a rare smile emerging.

"Do you remember when we were kids and Nana made us eat that green bean casserole that day, Holly?" Rhett looked over at her, laughing. "We told her we'd eaten it, but we'd stuffed it inside napkins in our laps. Nana, you told us how good we were for using our manners."

Holly hadn't thought about that in years. "After lunch, we were so hungry, we took our chore money down to Puckett's and bought Moon Pies and RC Cola."

"I've wondered what's wrong with you two over the years," Nana teased. "That's why the both of you are such a mess—eating chocolate cookies and soda as brain nourishment when you could've had my green bean and chicken casserole. You'd better make up for lost time now." She reached over and heaped an enormous lump onto Rhett's plate, sliding it to the other side of the table. He blew her a kiss, charming her as he always did.

"What's a Moon Pie?" Joe asked, the entire table turning his way.

The others looked a bit puzzled by Joe's question, but Holly found it endearing. She wanted to get up from the table right now, take him by the hand, and walk down to Puckett's to get him one. Rhett gave her a look that said, "I told you he's not your type."

"It's a graham cracker and marshmallow sandwich dipped in chocolate," she said to him, trying not to allow her gaze to linger. She wanted to drink in that curiosity of his and let it fill her up, but she knew, just like Otis's iced tea, that it wasn't good for her.

"They come in different flavors, though," Kay added. "I like the vanilla ones, myself. How about you, Jean?"

Nana rubbed her face in contemplation, the decision clearly a tough one. "I have a hard time choosing," she said.

Rhett was quiet, which wasn't like him at all. When Holly turned toward him, she noticed his eyes darting between her and Joe, and she realized that, despite her internal warning, she'd kept her attention on him after the others had started talking. Rhett's silence was at least a step in the right direction. He hadn't made any sarcastic comments. But she did feel embarrassed that he'd caught her looking at Joe.

There was a palpable silence after the Moon Pie discussion—Nana had clearly noticed—their conversation dwindling into quiet bites of casserole. They ate together, soundlessly, with only a little conversation between Nana and Kay until it was nearly unbearable, but with Rhett and Joe at the same table, Holly didn't really know what to say. She tried to think of all the things she did at work to get the conversation going, but her mind was totally blank, so she just ate.

Due to the lack of conversation, everyone ate relatively quickly. "Rhett," Nana finally said, undoubtedly to break the silence. They were finishing dinner and Holly prayed they could all get up and turn on the TV or Christmas music before they had to endure dessert under the same awkward hush. "What do you have on the agenda for after Christmas? Any new music coming our way?"

Rhett held a forkful of his last bite of casserole above his plate as he addressed Holly with his answer. "I'm going on a tour of the West Coast for a few months, and then I'll be back in the studio."

"How lovely!" Nana eyed Holly, trying to urge her to mention something, but Holly wasn't sure what she wanted her to say. With a small frustrated breath meant just for her, Nana smiled and said to Rhett, "You know, Holly's planning to travel extensively soon. Perhaps you two could meet up somewhere."

"Really?" Rhett said, shocked.

A new interest sheeted over Joe's face like a downpour on a summer night.

"I haven't known Holly to be the traveling type." Rhett set his fork down and leaned on his elbows, grinning.

"That would be nice, Rhett," Kay said. "Maybe y'all could spend New Year's together."

"Holly, we'll still be planning the wedding then," Joe said, clearly concerned.

Rhett dropped his fork and it fell with a clatter onto his plate, his eyes the size of saucers. He almost said something before he clamped his mouth shut, his jaw tightening. Clearly trying to keep control of himself, he got up and gathered his dishes. "Thank you for the delicious dinner," he said, and Holly wondered if she was the only one who could hear the strain in his voice. "My guitar's outside in the truck. I need to go get it. Holly, come with me?"

Not wanting Rhett to make some kind of scene with whatever his stress was now, she complied, following him to the front door. "Be right back," she said to Joe as she left, hoping that Nana and Kay would include him in conversation.

They'd barely shut the door behind them on the front porch when Rhett whirled around, his face full of fury, causing Holly to stumble backward and catch herself by grabbing the doorframe.

"You're *marrying* that guy?" he spit the words at her.

That's when it all made sense, and she let out a laugh, only serving to infuriate him further. "No!" she said quickly to keep Rhett from completely losing his temper. But she couldn't get the explanation out for the laughing. She got herself together so she could set him straight. "Rhett, he's getting married to another woman. I'm planning the wedding for them."

To her surprise, this clarification seemed to confuse him more than when he thought she was the one walking down the aisle. He stared at her, his lips parted just slightly, the skin between his eyes puckered in bewilderment. He took a step away from her, some sort of clarity dawning.

"What?" she asked, his reaction bothering her.

"You have the hots for a married guy?"

"He isn't married. He's *getting* married." She knew right away that she'd focused on the wrong point there... Even to her, the answer was flimsy and transparent. "But no, I don't," she added quickly.

Rhett searched her face, skeptical. He was looking at her the way he did when they played board games and he was formulating his strategy. "You don't have the hots for him?"

"Stop saying that," she said, getting frustrated. "And no, I don't have the hots for Joe Barnes." She hoped that over time she could convince herself of this.

He still didn't look convinced, but challenge filled his eyes. "Then come to California with me."

"What?"

"I can work my plans around that wedding. When is it?" He didn't let her answer. "There's nothing keeping you here. You want to travel all of a sudden. Knowing you, you haven't even researched where you're going. I can show you the country. I've been all over it."

An unexpected memory floated into Holly's mind: when they were teenagers, they used to hike through the woods outside Leiper's Fork. Holly would get turned around, lost, unable to find her way back, but Rhett always took her hand and led the way, and no matter how far they went, when she followed him, he got her back home.

"I don't think so." The point of this trip was to clear her head, and she doubted very seriously that being with Rhett would allow her to do that.

"You know you don't want to travel by yourself. Really, Holly. Think it through."

She was *trying* to think it through and all that came to mind was the real reason for the trip. It couldn't work...

"I'll be on my best behavior, I promise. I know how you don't like crowds. I won't make you come to the concerts. It'll be just you and me and the wide-open road. Come on, Hol. I promise it'll be like old times." He made an air cross over his heart, those eyes of his so much like they had been before he'd left, making her ache for the days she'd spent with her best friend. His honesty was evident.

Their years of experiences together, if stacked up, towered over the measly pile of excuses for going alone, and Holly wondered if she'd shot the idea down too quickly. It might actually be nice having Rhett with her to see the country. She'd never considered it before, but the way he was acting toward her now, it seemed like a viable possibility. She could have her best friend back...

"You know that we're only going as friends," she warned.

Excitement ballooned in his eyes and Rhett picked her up right there on the porch and spun her around. "Is that a yes?"

She pushed against him until he set her back down. "If you promise to keep yourself under control. The minute you pressure me to be anything more than what we already are, I'll be on the next flight out."

Rhett let out a hoot of joy and then ran to the truck, nearly slipping on the ice in his elation. "We're gonna have the time of our lives," he called over to her. That self-assured smile spread across his face.

"I hope so," she said. And she meant it.

After Rhett had been to the truck, they went back up

to the house. He swung his guitar case through the open doorway by the handle, his other arm around Holly. Everyone had moved to the living room, their heads all turned in Holly's direction.

"Guess who I talked into going to California with me," Rhett said, giving Holly a kiss on the cheek before hopping over the back of the sofa and bouncing down, guitar and all, beside Nana, giving her a start.

Nana laughed, her eyes dancing delightedly over to Holly.

Joe got up suddenly to poke the dwindling fire, his back to them before Holly had a chance to catch his expression. What was she hoping to see anyway? Why would he have any opinion whatsoever about what she did with her free time? It would be after the wedding, so she was certain he'd be fine with it. The fire popped and flickered angrily as Joe moved a log. When he turned around, he smiled respectfully again, his face completely unreadable.

His phone buzzed in his pocket and he pulled it out to check it.

"Please, excuse me a moment," he said, leaving the room without even a glance in Holly's direction.

Rhett opened his case and pulled out his guitar. Even in the flashy videos Holly had tried not to watch when they'd come on, she'd noticed that he still had the same guitar.

Knowing Rhett, he could end up a multimillionaire and he still wouldn't get a new one. It was like a family member, a brother, that loyal companion that never left his side.

He strummed a few notes of "White Christmas," as Kay and Nana looked on, and Holly immediately fell into the trance of it. It took her back to all the holidays he'd played for her, the Christmas Days when Rhett would show up with his guitar slung across his back, and whatever new gadget he'd unwrapped that morning in his hand. He'd always been too impatient to wait to show her, and he'd run all the way down the road first thing Christmas morning.

Now, with Kay and Nana there, the lights of the tree, stockings on the mantel, and Rhett back in town, it finally felt like home. And she wondered: the last time Rhett had asked her to travel with him, if perhaps she was supposed to have gone. Maybe that was her destiny. Was she fighting against what was meant for her? Holly studied him, those familiar breaths of his between quiet lyrics and the way his fingers moved on the strings in a way that only his did. It certainly would make things much easier if she were in love with Rhett—her problems would be solved.

"I apologize," Joe said, coming back into the room, interrupting Holly's spell of nostalgia and contemplation. He finally looked Holly in the eyes and Rhett stopped strumming. "That was Katharine. My fiancée," he added for the benefit of Rhett and Kay. "She said the Nashville Airport is up and running again and she booked a ticket for December twenty-sixth. Think the roads will be good enough to bring her out here?"

"I'll go get her myself," Rhett said. His words to Joe came off kind finally, but Holly was willing to bet that if Rhett had his way, he'd marry them the minute Katharine set foot on solid ground.

"Or we could go into Nashville to meet her," Nana suggested. If Rhett would marry them, Nana would roll out the runner leading to the altar.

Kay leaned forward in her chair to join the conversation. "I think the high temperature tomorrow and Christmas Day is well above freezing, so a lot of this mess will melt. You should be fine, but regardless, we'll get her here. I'm sure you miss her."

Holly waited for a mannerly response like he was so good at, but it never came. Instead, he nodded, a faraway look in his eyes.

Chapter Twenty-Two

After Rhett and Kay left, Nana shooed Holly and Joe away when they tried to help clean up after dinner, and when she finished, Nana went on to her room to read and settle down before bed. Holly asked Joe to stay in the living room a little while longer to go over the specifics of the wedding so she could have some real answers for Katharine when she arrived.

"Are you or Katharine planning to send a little gift to your wedding party?" Holly asked, chewing on the end of a pencil as Joe poured them each a glass of wine. She'd brought in a bottle that was left from dinner and two glasses. The fire was still going, and they'd settled on the sofa, both of their laptops open on the coffee table in front of them.

Joe set the bottle down and picked up his glass. "What for?" he asked, taking a drink.

"Well, either you can give them a small gift at rehearsal or you can have something sent to their homes to say you're honored to have them there. It's sort of a thank-you."

Joe leaned forward and opened a browser on his computer. "Let's search for a good bottle of wine to have delivered to them," he said, then grabbed his own glass and held it up as if he were toasting someone, that genuine smile surfacing and making her wish she could have known him under different circumstances.

She took a large glug of her own wine, not wanting to think about it. Instead, she allowed an image to filter into her mind of Rhett taking her to a bar where they'd stay up too late and laugh all the way back to the hotel. He could always make her laugh. Sometimes, they'd get going so much that her sides would ache, only making them both laugh harder. Rhett was part of the fabric of her youth; he made her who she was. Sure, he had his faults, but nobody was perfect.

"This one looks good." Joe scrolled down the rest of the wines before making a selection. "Where are their addresses?" he asked, typing away.

Holly unclipped her papers and located the invitation list, handing it to him.

Joe reached into his pocket and retrieved his wallet, sliding out a credit card for the purchase and placing it on the table. Then he finished typing in the information for delivery. After a bout of typing, he hit the final button. "Done." He turned to her as if he were going to say something, but instead, he just stayed silent, in the moment, every muscle in his body content. His shoulders were low, an easy smile played around the edges of his mouth, his elbow rested on the arm of the sofa.

Her spine straightened in response, and she kicked into gear. "Does your wedding party already have their attire and accessories?"

"Yes. Brea did that. All the fittings are finished." He was studying her, clearly aware of the change in her body.

Holly took a sip of wine, keeping herself in complete control. "What about hair/facials/nails for the bridesmaids before the wedding? Who's doing that, or are they doing it themselves?"

"Uh, you'll have to ask Katharine that one."

"Okay." Holly scribbled down a quick note next to the bullet to remind her to add it to the new to-do list she'd make for Katharine.

"What about accommodations? Have you blocked off rooms in area hotels for guests?"

He took in a quiet breath. "Yes. We have rooms at the Renaissance Nashville and The Hermitage."

Holly paused, the luxury of those hotels making her wonder again what the wedding venue in Brentwood would be like. It was bound to be nothing short of extravagant. Putting the clip back on the pile of papers, the handwritten to-do list she'd made on top, she checked off the box for "wedding party" and moved on to the next one. "Have you or will you insure the rings?"

"Yes. Done."

He took a swig of his wine, and he was starting to get that faraway look in his eyes, but she pressed on.

"Does your best man have Katharine's ring for the ceremony?"

"No. I've been holding on to them for safekeeping. They're in my suitcase in the bedroom," he said, tossing his thumb behind him toward the hallway. "We're tying them to the ring bearer's pillow."

Holly swallowed. The idea that the bands were in the house made the wedding feel more real than it ever had. "Where's the ring bearer's pillow?"

"Katharine has it." Another drink.

"Okay." She made a note.

"Would you like me to touch base with the photographer, caterer, florist, minister, and musicians to make sure they're all on top of things, or has Brea already done that?"

"I'm not sure what she's finalized, so yes. Thank you."

She noticed that his wine was nearly gone already, and he was filling his glass again. Holly had barely had any of hers. She made herself take a sip to be polite, since he poured her some, but she really just wanted to keep going because rattling off questions was easier than allowing herself to speak casually to Joe. He was sitting next to her, his knee almost touching her leg and just the sight of it made her feel like she was doing something wrong, so she focused on the list again.

"Gift registries all done?"

He nodded.

"Arrangements confirmed for your honeymoon?"

He took another drink of wine. "Yeah."

"Got your passports, tickets...?"

"Yep." He drew in a large breath and let it out quietly.

"Marriage license?"

"Yes."

"Are you writing your own vows?"

"No. We're doing traditional vows." He set his wine down slowly, that distant look in his eyes that she'd seen before, now in full force.

"Great." She ignored it and checked off another box. "Did Brea complete the reception menu?"

His relaxed demeanor had completely gone, his face pale.

"Not sure. We'll need to contact the estate office to see. If she didn't, just pick whatever food you think would be great. I trust you." He rubbed his neck and stood up abruptly, his face looking as though he were suffocating. "I'm sorry. I have a terrible headache. Perhaps it's the wine..." He dragged his hands down his face as if he could actually pull the headache off of himself, letting out a little groan. "Do we have any ibuprofen?"

"Don't take it while you're drinking. Maybe just lie down."

He pinched the bridge of his nose, his breathing quite fast.

"You look like you're having a panic attack," she said, standing up and facing him, worry consuming her. He was clearly overwhelmed. "Your wedding is a big thing, I know," she said softly.

She couldn't even imagine the permanence that would wash over someone about to make a leap like this.

"In the end," she said, using all her strength to give him the support he needed, "all this will be over and it'll be just you and Katharine spending your lives together."

He opened his eyes wide, penetrating her with his stare, something trying to come through, but it just wouldn't. Did he want to tell her something? He opened his mouth slightly to speak, but he only allowed his breath to come out before he gently pressed his lips together, his gaze dropping to the floor as if in defeat.

"Yes, you're right," he said, his inner thoughts clearly not matching up with the conclusion he'd made out loud.

While Holly couldn't believe *she* ever would, she'd heard about people getting cold feet before their wedding. Joe was a quiet person who didn't seem to thrive on attention, and perhaps this was quite challenging for him. She'd been launching questions at him like a rapid-fire New Year's fireworks display, and she might have overwhelmed him. Gently, using restraint to keep her actions separate from her emotions, she put her hand on his arm.

Joe's gaze flew to her hand and then searched her face, and she knew she needed to get him to relax.

"Sit for a second?" she asked, lowering herself back down onto the sofa. He sat beside her immediately, staring deeply into her eyes as if she could save him from something. But he didn't need saving—he was marrying the love of his life, right? Joe didn't strike her as a person who would propose to someone unless he was truly committed. When they started talking details again, Holly would pull back on her questions, give him more time to think between each one. She decided to take his mind off the wedding for a little while.

"Let's shift focus for a minute, get our minds off the wedding." She folded the papers and slid them underneath her laptop.

"Yes," he exhaled and cleared his throat, collecting himself.

"I have something that's been nagging me," she admitted, hoping the complete change in topic would ease his headache.

Those dark eyes nearly swallowed her, while he waited for her to finish.

"Tomorrow is Christmas Eve. And you don't have anything under the tree."

He blinked a few times, and she wondered if she'd surprised him with her admission. Then he regarded her warmly, whatever had been eating at him sliding away. "It's fine," he said, his voice still a little gruff.

"I know it's fine," she said with a lighthearted grin. "You're a big boy and you can handle it, I'm sure. But it isn't much fun. It's Christmas! I want to include you when Nana and I unwrap our gifts."

"Well, unless you start wrapping things in the cabin, there's not much you can do, and it really is okay." She could see his stress diminishing in just that small amount of time. "But if you *are* wrapping things, that candle over there would smell really good in my apartment," he teased, and it was a relief to see.

"Now you won't get it because it won't be a surprise!" she said.

"How about I make a list of things then." He looked around the room. "I like that picture you have on the wall..." Finally, he allowed a small smile, flooding Holly with happiness. It was amazing how changing the conversation had eased his nerves so quickly.

"You know what we could do?" The thought just hit Holly, the Christmas spirit filling her. She sat on the edge of the sofa and faced him, making him smile at her excitement to this idea.

"What?" he asked, that curiosity washing over him.

"We could both go down to Puckett's tomorrow! What if we have to choose three things to wrap for the other person, but you can only pick from what's on the shelf?" She sat back, proud of herself for such a revelation.

Joe allowed a little chuckle. "You want me to wrap up a bottle of mustard?"

"You can never have too much mustard."

That made him laugh, and she had to remind herself to put that mental distance between them. It could dissipate in an instant whenever they were together. "You might surprise yourself with what you can find there."

"You're on," he said, and Holly could tell that she'd done her job. Joe was back to his wonderful self again.

Chapter Twenty-Three

"Don't look!" Holly said when Joe peeked around the corner of the grocery aisle in Puckett's. They went right after breakfast.

"I'm just checking to see how many items you have," he said. "I've found two."

"I have two! One more for each of us. Now go back to your aisle before you spoil the surprise," she said good-naturedly.

He peeked around the aisle again and Holly hunched over her basket before he could see. He laughed from the other side.

Five elderly gentlemen at their table looked over at Holly and Joe nosily, their chatter withering for a second. It was this table that everyone always saved for the same local men who drank coffee there every morning. Holly waved to them and they went back to their conversations.

"What in Heaven's name are y'all doin' over there?" Tammy called from the register.

"Shopping," Joe said pointedly as if he came to Puckett's every day. His back to Holly, he carried his items over to the checkout counter. "Would you, please, double bag mine quickly, Tammy? I'd like to keep my selections from Holly."

Tammy examined the things in his basket and raised an eyebrow. "Okaaay," she said, hitting buttons on the register as she placed each item into the bag. "That'll be eleven eighty-three, Joey." He handed her a twenty-dollar bill.

"I'll just wait outside," Joe called to Holly before tying his bag and carrying it to the door.

"Okay," she called back.

When Holly came out of Puckett's, Joe was nowhere to be found. She warmed her hands at the nearby fire pit, her own bag dangling from the crook of her arm, when she caught him leaving the art gallery. And then she remembered during two truths and a lie at Otis's that he'd said he collected art.

"Sorry." He seemed startled to see her. "I didn't mean to leave you. I just saw this art gallery and thought I'd take a look inside."

With only his Puckett's bag in his hand, she assumed he hadn't found any major works of art to buy, but she asked anyway, "See anything good?"

"A lot, actually." He beamed. "But I'm not really prepared to buy art right at the moment. Maybe one day I'll be back."

"Yes, you're more than welcome to visit anytime," she said, and the hope that rose in her chest wasn't healthy at all.

Then something occurred to her. "Have you gotten any presents for Katharine? Do you have some back in New York?"

He shook his head. "With the case research she has going on, the trial she's finishing up, and me here, we decided not to have Christmas this year."

How awful. "Well, anyone within a two-mile radius of me gets Christmas *every* year. I wouldn't be able to cope without it. Christmas is when everyone forgets all the troubles around them and just celebrates being with one another. And I know you might not think so, but, in my opinion, it's that one time of year when magic really is possible."

He smiled and she noticed, happily, that this time, he didn't try to refute her mention of magic.

❄

Nana had been invited to Buddy's for the day, and, with the streets now salted, he came to pick her up in his old Ford truck. She returned late in the evening, looking more relaxed than she had before, and Holly was glad that her friends were around her to give her something other than her loss to think about.

While Nana had been at Buddy's, Joe worked on the sofa and Holly divided her time between baking blueberry muffins and contacting all the event staff to be sure everything was on track for the wedding. The only things she had to run by Katharine regarding the venue were the final say on the photography package and the archway of roses that was being built over the entrance of the venue. Apparently, for the number of roses Katharine had selected, they'd need to pull in two more florists, which was going to change the cost. She felt accomplished and her fears about finishing this wedding were subsiding a little.

Now, with both Holly and Joe at a good stopping point for the night, they decided, because it had been a good amount of time since Nana had gone to bed, they should set up the gifts from Papa and they could also put their presents from Puckett's under the tree.

"Watcha got there?" Holly said, once Joe retrieved her presents from his room. She reached out to touch one of the packages he was holding. They were gift-wrapped haphazardly, with lots of tape on the ends.

Joe pulled back. "Careful," he warned as he kept them steady. "This one needs to go into the fridge." He nodded toward a flat gift that was the size of one of Nana's old forty-five records.

A grin spread across Holly's face. "One of my presents requires refrigeration?"

"Yes." He stepped aside to avoid her, and walked to the kitchen, sliding the present into the refrigerator and closing the door. "No peeking." He winked at her. He'd let go of whatever it was that had caused him so much stress, clearly giving in to the festive spirit of Christmas.

The other two presents were smaller. She followed him into the living room where he set them carefully under the tree next to the ones she'd placed there for him. She squatted down to inspect them.

"Nope," he said, taking her hands and pulling her up. His touch was like electricity, so she let go quickly and stood next to him. "You need a distraction. I can't have you guessing my presents before you unwrap them."

Holly laughed. "Let's have some hot cocoa so that I'm not tempted to shake them to see what's inside," she teased, walking over to the kitchen and filling the kettle with water and two mugs with Nana's secret homemade hot cocoa mix.

While the kettle finished boiling, Holly lit the candles in the kitchen and living room. The smell of hot cocoa filled the air the minute she poured her and Joe a mug full—her Christmas Eve tradition. Nana had passed on it this year, and Holly knew that it was probably because she was having a difficult time being at the cabin without Papa. Not to mention being with Buddy had probably tired her right out.

For a little Christmas flare, Holly lumped a dollop of whipped cream on the top and then ran a chocolate bar over the cheese grater, little flakes falling like snow on top of the steaming liquid. After she cleaned up the counter, she plunged a candy cane into each one.

"I can't believe we found that box in the barn just before Christmas," Joe said quietly, nodding toward Nana's room. "What are the odds? Had we not run low on wood…"

"I know." She handed him a mug. "And if you hadn't been here, I may not have noticed it. I'm nearly certain Papa put it in the barn because he knew that Nana never went out there. If he'd hidden it in here, he chanced her discovering it, since she wouldn't let anything leave the closets without first approving. Sometimes things just work out like that. When I was a little girl, Papa used to say that luck is magic going incognito. That's where we got the Christmas magic idea—Papa was always filling our heads with it."

Joe smiled. "I love that you have those family stories."

"You'll make some," she said encouragingly. It was too bad that Joe hadn't had the family experience that Holly had. She wondered again about his father. "I wish someone had come forward with information about your dad," she said. "Have you had any comments on the post or anything?"

He shook his head. "Holly, we aren't skilled enough detectives to locate him. It was wishful thinking. You almost convinced me that it was possible with all your magic talk," he said with a grin, filling her with happiness. "But if an investigator couldn't do it, we certainly wouldn't have a lot of luck—picture or no picture. We need a whole lot more of that magic you keep talking about."

"Well, if we get any magic, it'll be at Christmas. That's when it's all around."

He shook his head, amused, that curiosity back with a vengeance. Holly could feel the affection for him welling up regardless of her need to keep it pushed away.

Her phone pinged across the room, dragging her attention away from Joe. She walked over to it and checked the text that was waiting. It was Rhett: *Watcha doing tomorrow afternoon after you open presents?*

She peered down at it, her decision to travel with Rhett to California whirring around in her head. She prayed that she hadn't given Rhett false hope by agreeing to go with him. She knew him well: he was optimistic and confident, always believing he could change the world. Did he think he could change her mind about their relationship?

"Everything okay?" Joe asked from his barstool as he swirled his hot cocoa with the candy cane.

Holly swam out of her thoughts. "Oh! Yes. It's just Rhett." She waved her phone. "He's asking what I'm doing tomorrow afternoon."

"Oh." Joe sipped from his mug, not saying anything else, and the loss of his attention stung. She craved the moment they'd just had, knowing that it was wrong to want it.

Holly looked down at the screen and typed, *Why?*

Rhett came back: *I want to take you somewhere.*

On Christmas? she typed back.

Yes. On Christmas! Like a date…

"He wants to take me on a date," she heard herself say, but she'd really just meant to ponder the idea rather than say it out loud.

She was still thinking about it when she noticed that Joe hadn't responded. She looked over at him and the attentiveness she'd seen earlier had faded completely now.

The only thing she could think of was that it must be because Joe believed she might have feelings for Rhett and he was being considerate by pulling away. While she hated the absence of his interest, she knew it would be better for everyone involved if she could keep them on neutral ground. She'd tried before, but with Rhett asking for a date, this might be a foolproof way of maintaining her distance.

She texted back: *Where do you want to take me?*

It's a surprise, Rhett returned.

"Rhett wants to take me on a surprise Christmas date," she said, playing it up. After all, why wouldn't someone be interested in Rhett Burton? He was fun to be around, and there were hundreds, maybe thousands, of squealing, bleach-blond-perfect-legged girls in every one of his shows who would absolutely want to be with him.

Call me tomorrow with specifics, she told Rhett. Then Holly put her phone down and went back over to Joe.

"He usually comes over on Christmas Day anyway," she said brightly, her new role as Rhett's love interest coming easily for her. The illusion was easy to hide behind. "I can't say he ever plans dates on Christmas though. That's new." She shook her head and smiled, inwardly wondering what Rhett had arranged.

Joe looked pensive all of a sudden, that preoccupied stare returning. Then he stood up, and she noticed how edgy he looked. Had Holly's and Rhett's exchange brought back the stress of the wedding somehow—perhaps the "date" making him think of the big day? He seemed just like he'd been when Holly had overwhelmed him with her questions. "Shall we place your grandmother's presents now? I think I'm going to turn in for the night. All that work today made me tired."

"Sure," she said, his reaction confusing her. She hadn't meant to upset him. She'd only wanted to make sure she wasn't overstepping her bounds.

She wanted to tell him that everything was okay, that he had to trust his heart, but she stayed silent. Joe turned around and went into his room to get Papa's gifts, leaving Holly with her hot cocoa and the quiet lights of the Christmas tree.

Chapter Twenty-Four

Holly leaned over Nana as her grandmother opened her eyes, the sun streaming in through the window, bouncing off the lingering ice on the sill outside. Nana sat up slowly, clearly wondering why Holly was so excited. By the look she gave, Nana didn't seem to feel any differently about today than she did any day. But, knowing that Nana was about to hear from Papa again, Holly was nearly certain that was about to change.

Holly took her hands.

"Nana, it's Christmas!" she said, the thrill of what was ahead of them making her want to burst, but she kept calm. "You've had a hard time coming back here," she acknowledged gently.

Nana pursed her lips, nodding, the pain showing in the creases on her face.

"Remember how Papa always used to tell us that Christmas was a magical time? It was when the impossible became possible."

Nana allowed a small but loving smile at the idea of it.

"If you could have anything for Christmas," Holly whispered dramatically, "what is your one wish?"

Nana focused on her face, seriousness taking over. "I'd like to have your papa back, you know that. So, while I adore your enthusiasm for the day, it'll be difficult for me. That's just how things are. But please don't let me put a damper on the holiday for you."

Holly had to use all her strength not to allow the tears to come and to keep her voice as neutral as possible because, in true form, Papa had managed Nana's only Christmas wish. "I'll let you get ready for the day," she said. "And then I'll meet you in the living room." Then Holly closed the door behind her and went to get the muffins and coffee ready.

❄

"Why do you have that silly grin on your face?" Nana said to Holly, once she finally emerged from the bedroom. She consulted Joe for an answer, but he shrugged as if it were a mystery to him.

Holly set a blueberry muffin and a cup of coffee on the table for Nana, another of their Christmas traditions. They always had a tiny bite to eat just to get them through opening presents, and then they put on the Christmas music and cooked a big breakfast together to celebrate the day.

"Thank you, dear, but I'm not hungry," Nana said, leaving

the muffin sitting. "If you two have eaten already, we can dive right into presents."

She knew that Nana didn't like to eat when she was worried or upset, and she was visibly missing Papa. Christmas was difficult for her, and Holly prayed that Papa's gesture would ease the emptiness Nana felt without him. "You sure?" Holly asked.

"Yes, dear. I'm sure."

"Okay then." Holly walked over to her and took her by the hand. "I need you to close your eyes."

Nana watched her, openly trying to figure out what she was up to.

"Trust me," Holly said. "Give in to the magic."

Nana had a look of slight disapproval but then she closed her eyes and allowed Holly to lead her to the living room until she was centered in front of the mantel.

"Okay, look."

Nana opened her eyes and noticed the gift right away, emotion surfacing immediately. She let go of Holly and clasped her hands as if she were about to say a prayer, every inch of her body directly lined up with the little wrapped package on the mantel. "Your papa always used to put my first gift here," she said, her voice wobbly. "Then he'd hide the rest—did you remember that he did that?"

"Of course I remember. And he's done it again," she

whispered in her ear. "One last time. Just for you." Holly held on to her, this time to give herself some support.

Obviously perplexed by Holly's comment, Nana's fingers trembling, she reached out and gently took the gift. Holly was barely able to swallow, given the lump in her throat. Joe changed position in her peripheral vision, and she was surprised to see emotion on his face as well.

With slow movements, Nana peeled back the tape that had secured the paper and pulled the tin out of the wrapping. "It's lovely," she said as she opened it, and then she stopped in her tracks. The only sound in the room as she found Papa's note, and peered down at his writing, was the tinkling of the music from inside the box.

Nana was still, the tin open in her withered hands, and her whole body started to quiver. She turned to Holly for answers, her eyes wide and full of wonder.

"He left a box for me in the barn. I didn't know it was there until Joe found it."

Nana turned and observed Joe with a look as if he'd just saved her life. In a way, Holly believed he had. Nana walked over and gave him the biggest hug, squeezing him tightly the way she did when she embraced family.

Then she looked back down at the note. Tenderly, Nana held it to her face, breathing in, probably hoping she could still smell him there. Her eyes closed, a tear made its way down her grooved cheeks, all those years of laughter left along the edges of her face. When she opened her eyes, Joe handed her a tissue as he looked on warmly. Holly was so glad he was there.

"Thank you," Nana told him. She gave a dainty sniffle and dabbed her eyes. "Is there really another gift in the linen closet?" she asked, her eyes wide with excitement. It was the same look she had when Papa used to grab her and spin her around in the middle of her housework.

Holly nodded, feeling like she was witnessing a miracle.

With agile steps, Nana shuffled over to the linen closet in the hallway where the second gift was located. Holly had set it on top of the guest towels she'd bought for the renters. Nana swung the door open and reached in for the gift, unwrapping it quickly, the way Holly used to devour her own presents as a child.

"It's our favorite Christmas song, 'Santa Claus Is Comin' to Town'!" she said excitedly, half giggling and half crying. "Papa used to whisper the lyrics about how he sees me sleeping into my ear on Christmas morning." She peered down at the note. "He's right! I never did find that record. I think Papa took it to the secondhand shop by accident," she said dramatically as if she were divulging a secret. "He was always cleaning out old junk." She turned the CD over in her hand. "I want to play this right now."

Joe leaned in and gestured for her to hand it to him so he could remove the cellophane that encased it. With eager hands, Nana held it out, and this time, she smiled kindly at him.

"This note says that if my back hurts to make you get the next gift under the sofa," Nana said, waving Papa's slip of paper in the air as she followed Holly back into the living room.

Joe put the CD in the player and turned it on. The whole room felt festive with the music playing and Nana happy—just like old times.

"I wish the rest of the family could see this," Holly said.

Nana gave her a thoughtful look.

Holly reached under the sofa to retrieve the third gift and gave it to Nana.

Nana unwrapped *War and Peace* and rolled her eyes, throwing her head back and laughing. "He wants to bore me even now!" She flipped through the pages, spending a little extra time on the opening, and Holly wondered if she'd finally give the book a chance, just for Papa. "My last gift is at the window," she said, reading Papa's message, and Holly noted a twinge of fear in her hesitation. "I'm going to leave it for a bit." By the look on her face, Nana was savoring the moment.

"Okay, Nana." Holly understood completely. As she

viewed that last gift—the little ring box—on the sill, it felt like Papa was still with them, watching over them.

"How about you two open some gifts? I've been monopolizing the morning." She clutched the old book in her hands as if she were holding on for dear life.

"I'd say you're allowed to," Holly said with a laugh. "But I do have some presents for Joe."

"Yes," Nana said slowly, the skin between her eyes wrinkling more deeply. "I've been dying to know what's in my refrigerator."

"Holly has to open that one last," Joe said, only piquing Holly's interest more.

With the music still playing, Nana carried her book over to the sofa and took a seat. "Holly, why don't you go first?"

Eager to see Joe unwrap her gifts, Holly didn't protest, jumping right in and grabbing the first one. She sat down next to Joe, passing it to him.

With a quick grin at her, he took the present she'd gotten at Puckett's and unwrapped it.

"Ah, a Moon Pie."

Nana laughed.

Joe pinched either side of the wrapper. "Shall I try your childhood delicacy?"

"Yes! And if you don't like it, I won't be offended. I'll be happy to take care of it for you."

Joe opened it and took a bite, chewing slowly as if he wanted to let it sit on his palate for a while to achieve the entire taste.

"It's not that sophisticated," Holly said. "Just chew it up and swallow."

When his bite was finished, he said, "I enjoyed that, thank you." He folded the wrapper over and set it on the table. "I'll save the rest for later. Don't want to ruin my breakfast."

Nana laughed again. "The vanilla ones are my favorites, I think; I trust Kay on that one."

Holly was overjoyed to see Joe and Nana chatting as if they'd been friends all along.

"I'm just delighted that Holly thought enough of me to want me to try it." He winked at Holly, and her heart gave a little patter.

Christmas magic certainly was all around this year.

"Let me give you your first gift," he said to Holly, getting up and reaching under the tree. Joe set a slightly heavy box in her lap.

It was small enough that she could wrap her hands around it. Holly began to remove the paper, feeling another swell of fondness for Joe at the sight of all the tape at the ends. When she got the paper off, she was holding a white coffee mug. In black writing, it said, "Someone's thinking of you in Leiper's Fork." The "O" in "Fork" was a red heart.

"I couldn't be choosy with the options," he said. "It was all they had. But your grandmother asked me to get her a mug from your family stash the other morning." He acknowledged Nana with a happy glance. "She told me a story about each mug. But she didn't mention that there was one under the cabinet that was just yours. Now you have one too."

"I love it," Holly said, charmed by his thoughtfulness.

"You two have to do all your presents first," Nana interjected. "This is so much fun to watch."

Holly took another of her gifts for Joe from under the tree and gave it to him. Joe unwrapped it.

"Ha!" He held up a camouflaged baseball cap with an old patch of an American flag on the front.

"That's perfect, Joe," Nana said, and Holly noticed her use of his nickname. "It's so very suitable for you," she tittered. "Although Holly didn't need to buy you one. I'm sure Buddy and Otis have enough to share."

"I was struggling to find you something," Holly sniggered. "I thought you could wear it to the next barn party."

"The next one?" he asked, enthusiasm in his question that Holly couldn't deny. He liked it here.

"You're welcome anytime," Nana said. Then she clapped her hands together. "Okay, enough chitchat. What do you have for Holly? This is better than one of those Christmas marathons on TV."

Joe got up and gave Holly her second present.

With less tape on this one, she opened it easily. Slipping her finger under the fold of the wrapping, she noticed Joe smiling as he looked on. What had he found that would make him so happy? Holly looked down and gasped when she saw what was nestled in the paper. It was a tiny canvas, the size of a shoebox lid and painted in gorgeous watercolor was Times Square.

"Oh wow," she said, taking in all the detail.

"I thought you'd caught me," Joe said. "I popped into the art gallery to find something for you after leaving you in Puckett's. I couldn't believe it when I saw this. A local artist had done these paintings with locations all over the world. It's an original, one-of-a-kind." He leaned toward her to look at it with her, his presence now as much a part of her Christmas in the new cabin as the flickering vanilla candles and the spruce tree, and she knew that next year, she'd definitely miss it. "You said you'd like to go to New York one day." Then he tapped a little spot on the left of the painting. "Right there. That's the location of Rona's, the café that I mentioned. I know you're going to California with Rhett, but I hope you get to New York, since it's where you've always wanted to go."

Joe had been so thoughtful that she was having trouble managing her feelings. But she'd be strong. "I have one more for you." She grabbed the tiniest gift.

Joe opened it, slipping it onto his finger so it dangled in front of his face. It was a keychain with bubble letters that said, "Joey." His chest heaved with laughter.

Holly was glad for the opportunity to laugh because emotion was taking over. "You'll never forget that," she said, hoping he wouldn't.

"No. I will never forget."

He seemed so truthful in the moment, but would he remember? Or would his time here fade away into just an old memory? Would he go back to his life in some big penthouse in the city, Katharine swishing around in her silk bathrobe every morning, gathering up his newspapers and talking about the rise in stock prices? That was how Holly imagined the two of them anyway.

She'd find out if her impressions were correct soon enough when Katharine arrived tomorrow. But for now, she pushed it out of her mind so she could enjoy Christmas.

"Okay." He stood up. "Your final gift."

He got up and went to the refrigerator. "Ms. McAdams," he said to Nana from across the room. "I owe you a tube of icing."

"Call me Nana. That's what all the kids call me around here."

He gave her a warmhearted nod. "I apologize," he said, returning. "I used the tube of icing that I found in the pantry. I'm assuming it was yours, as it appeared after you all came. I'll get you more."

"It's fine, dear."

"You made me a cake?" Holly said, unable to keep the grin off her face.

He shook his head, sliding it onto the coffee table. "Don't tip it."

Nana leaned in to see what it was.

Carefully, Holly unwrapped it and lifted the lid on the box. "Sweet potato pie." White unsteady lettering read, "Merry Christmas."

He remembered.

"Thank you," she said, wanting to hug him but holding herself back. His gifts had been some of the best gifts she'd ever received, and she couldn't imagine a better Christmas Day.

When she looked over at Nana, her grandmother had a funny expression, studying Joe. It was as if she was trying to figure out some sort of puzzle, but she blinked it away. Then Nana's gaze moved from Joe and his pie to the window in the kitchen where the final gift from Papa sat. "May I open my last one from Papa?" she asked, getting up.

"Absolutely." Holly followed Nana over to the gift, Joe following.

Nana took the present from the windowsill and cupped

it in her hands, cherishing the delight of it, and at the same time, Holly knew that Nana was thinking this would be her final contact with the man she loved. She pulled back the paper slowly and opened the little box. Then her whole body stilled when she saw the ring. Without a reaction yet, she read that lovely message from Papa.

Nana folded the final note from him and held it against her chest, clearly trying to keep herself together. She looked up as if she could see him. Then she slipped the ring onto her finger and, even with her arthritis, it fit perfectly.

"I think what Papa wants you to know is that you're allowed to be happy," Holly said, placing her hand on Nana's arm and rubbing up and down affectionately. She grabbed Nana's hand. "None of his messages talked about how he was gone; they were all about the happiness he shared with you."

After a long time of contemplation, her focus on the ring, and tears in her eyes, Nana finally spoke. "Do you know why Papa used to hide presents?" she asked.

Holly shook her head.

"Because he always said that life is like Christmas. Anyone looking under our tree might just see a bare space, and sometimes we think the same about our day-to-day lives— we overlook the riches that are all around us—but, in life, if we hunt for them, we find treasures hidden everywhere, in places we'd least expect them." Her eyes fluttered over to Joe and she offered him another kindhearted look, clearly delighted in the fact that he'd brought Papa back for just a little bit. "You know, I've been thinking a lot about your mom and dad, your sister, little Emma... Until now, I'd been too grief-stricken to come back to the cabin, and I feel like I've driven them away."

"No, Nana. You can't think like that."

"It's okay. Besides, we were renting out the cabin. While nothing here resembles what your papa and I had anymore, I feel him in this place now. I see his friends here, I still pull his coffee mugs out of the cabinets, I have his things in the barn. But I also have the gift that he gave us of a new space to gather, a wonderful, gorgeous home where we can have Christmas. The family couldn't all fit in my house in Nashville, and they didn't have anywhere to go... but I'm wondering if I should stay at the cabin and we could have the Christmas holidays here every year. I'd like to invite them back."

"I think that's a great idea."

"Why don't you ask them when you make your Christmas call to them today?" And then, out of nowhere, Nana gave her the biggest smile Holly had seen in years. Holly knew right then she'd never forget this Christmas.

Chapter Twenty-Five

The presents were all unwrapped, paper and ribbon still strewn about in the other room, and the Christmas breakfast dishes piled up and sitting empty in the sink. Nana, Joe and Holly settled in at the kitchen table with a slice of pie.

While they were cooking, Holly had washed the mug that Joe got her, and she was sipping from it. The satisfaction over Nana's seemingly permanent smile and the fact that, for the first time, the three of them were chatting so easily wrapped around her like a giant hug.

"I'm so thankful for the snowstorm," Nana said. "Without it, none of this would've been possible."

Before Holly could respond, a soft pounding at the door stopped them. "I'll get it," she said, standing up.

She opened the door to find Rhett, or what she thought might be Rhett from the view of his limbs behind an enormous present. "I couldn't wait till later," he said, plopping it down just inside and stepping through the door.

"Some things never change," Nana said to Joe in the kitchen. "Merry Christmas, Rhett."

"Hey, Nana!" he called, scooting the gift toward Holly as he turned his attention to her. "The streets were clear enough that I could get into Nashville today and I got you something."

"Aren't the stores closed?"

"I texted the owner of this little shop in town and asked if she'd open the store for me. She said she would if I'd take a photo in front of the storefront so she could share it on social media. Whatever it takes, right?" He laughed. "Y'all come on in and join us," he said, beckoning Nana and Joe into the room like he was in his own home. Holly couldn't help but grin—she'd missed this.

"Would you like some pie?" she asked.

"Naw! I don't want pie!" he said, beaming. He was jumpy with excitement like he always was on Christmas morning. "I want you to open my present!"

She laughed, his enthusiasm contagious.

"Nana," he said to Nana as she made her way over, while Holly dragged the enormous gift to the center of the room, "I didn't forget about you! Your gift's in the truck. Once Holly opens hers, I'll give you yours."

Joe lowered himself down onto the sofa, regarding Rhett's gift. What Holly wished she could tell him was no matter what this monstrosity that Rhett had gotten her was, and no matter how much money he'd probably spent on it, she'd much rather have her mug, a slice of sweet potato pie, and that beautiful little painting of a place from her dreams.

"You just gonna stare at it, or are you gonna open it?" Rhett teased.

Holly ripped the paper, tearing a long strip down the front, and revealing a designer suitcase. It was scratch-resistant, polycarbonate, according to the tag that showed under the rest of the wrapping, and cobalt blue with white piping along the edges.

"For when you travel with me!" he said, throwing his arms around her waist and picking her up.

She wriggled free.

"I have the other pieces in the truck—I only wanted to wrap one."

"The other pieces?"

"Yeah, I got you the whole set. I wasn't sure what you needed. I'll bring it in later." He pounced across the room like a distracted toddler. "Nana! You know you can hardly wait to see what I got you, right?" He kissed her cheek, and she rolled her eyes playfully, a chuckle escaping. "Be right back!"

Rhett headed off to get the gifts, and it was as if he'd sucked the sound in the room right out with him. His big, charismatic personality left them all quietly contemplative, and Holly wondered what was on Joe's mind. He was in the corner chair, gazing into the fire.

Before she could ponder it, Rhett was back, holding a bouquet of flowers. Holly wondered with whom he'd had to pose for a picture to get those. He handed the bundle of red and white roses, baby's breath, and petite ivy to Nana. "For you, my lovely lady," he said as he held out the flowers.

"These are beautiful, Rhett." Nana carried them back into the kitchen and set them on the counter where she used to put the bouquets of wildflowers Holly picked her as a girl.

"They aren't as pretty as you," he said when she returned, making her laugh at his syrupy sweetness. Rhett always turned it on strong for Nana just to embarrass her, but she ate it up every time. "I'd like to take Holly for a few hours if that's okay."

"Is this our *date*?" she asked.

"Yep." He raised his eyebrows at Nana, his eagerness clear. "Get your coat. The truck's running."

"You shower us with gifts and then run off," Nana teased.

Rhett shrugged, playful, as if he had no other choice.

Joe stood up. "Excuse me," he said politely. "I have…" He gestured toward his room, but didn't finish his sentence. Holly wondered what he could have on Christmas Day. Certainly, he couldn't have work. Perhaps he was off to call Katharine. "Merry Christmas," he said to Rhett.

Then, he walked down the hallway to his room and shut the door behind him.

"Nana, are you okay if I go?" Holly asked, pulling her eyes from Joe's room down the hallway.

"Of course, dear. Have fun. I'll just bother Joe if I get bored."

Her joke surprised Holly, and she was delighted to see Nana warming to him.

"Okay, then," Holly said. "Back soon!" She grabbed her coat and followed Rhett outside. His regular truck had been replaced by an imposing and clearly brand-spanking-new Chevy Silverado that was purring in the drive.

"New truck?" she asked, opening the massive black shiny door and hoisting herself up inside.

"Yeah, still got the old one, though. It's in my garage. And I also still have the old jeep that you like," he said while she buckled her seatbelt. "But I wanted nothing but the best for my girl today." He closed the door and headed around to his side. Rhett hopped in, belted himself, and hit the gas.

My girl. She hoped it was a term of endearment and not the possessive use of the phrase. She was not *his* in any way, and she thought she'd made that pretty clear. The thing was, anyone who looked at them together would wonder why Holly didn't want to be Rhett's significant other.

Holly and Rhett had a history together, she could trust him with her life, he was an honorable person who would never intentionally hurt her, he made her laugh, and Nana adored him.

But Rhett was busy. He was absent most of the time. Him being here day in and day out for Christmas caused a misconception: he'd be gone again right after the holiday, leaving everyone. And after they went to California, he'd be off touring somewhere else. Holly wouldn't want that life forever. She wanted stability; she wanted long hours on the porch, mornings cocooned in blankets with the person she loved under the early light of day, and home-cooked dinners together when the stars came out.

When she finally focused on the road, Holly apprehended that they weren't on a road at all, but a hidden gravel path meandering through the hills. She held on to the door handle as the large truck tires bumped along the uneven surface, much of the snow still covering the ground under the canopy of trees. Finally, when she was so turned around that she'd never find her way back, Rhett pulled up to a small, snow-covered clearing in the woods.

"What is this?" she asked, glad that she knew Rhett so well or she'd worry about his choice of date location.

"It belongs to me now—eighty acres," he said, turning off the engine.

So Rhett had used his money well and purchased a nice piece of property in Leiper's Fork. Holly couldn't imagine anything better for him. "Are you going to build something here?"

"I already have." Rhett got out and walked around to her side of the truck, but Holly had already hopped out when he got to her. Rhett shut her door and faced the clearing.

She looked left to right—nothing. Were they going to have to hike to wherever it was he was taking them? Surely, he didn't plan to keep her in this freezing cold. She hadn't brought her gloves or scarf.

Rhett stood behind her and put his hands on her shoulders. "Look," he said into her ear. Then he pointed to the top of the trees and Holly sucked in an icy breath of surprise.

It was a tree house. But not like any tree house she had as a kid. This was an actual house in the trees. Hidden by all the branches and evergreens— she'd never have noticed it, but now she could see the golden light in the windows and the rocking chairs on a deck that overlooked a stream past the clearing down below.

"How do we get up there?" she asked, breathless.

Rhett took her hand. "Follow me."

He led her to a close group of trees and, completely concealed from the drive, there were stairs that wrapped their way around the trunk of one of the oaks. Holly climbed up beside Rhett and followed him to the top, every stride allowing a more magnificent view, until they were on the porch that enveloped the entire house. The sight of the hills and valleys, the streams snaking through them, the remnants of snow sprinkled onto every surface like some sort of life-sized oil painting absolutely dazzled her.

A soft mewing came from behind them and she felt something press against her leg. "Oh, look," she said, reaching down and scooping up a tiny kitten, all fluffy white with orange spots. It purred in her arms, nuzzling her face and licking her chin with its scratchy tongue.

"Wow, what the heck?" Rhett laughed. "I could hardly get that cat to come near me. I found it in the back of an alley in the city. It just didn't look like a city cat to me, so I brought it out here, started leaving food and milk for it, until it trusted me. But I guess it trusts everyone now."

"Does it have a name?" She held the kitten out at arm's length and looked into its blue eyes as it wriggled to get close to her again.

"I call her Hattie." He reached over and ran his strong hand over the delicate little head of the kitten. "Found her behind Hattie B's restaurant. I took her straight home without getting any food, and you know how I like their hot chicken."

Holly grinned. "I don't want to ask you why you were in an alley behind Hattie B's..."

"It's the only way I could get in and get some without being mobbed."

Holly sobered. She couldn't imagine that.

The kitten pushed against her to get down, so she let it roam on the decking and looked around. Holly dragged her fingers along one of the two rocking chairs that over-looked the landscape. They were rugged, made of unfinished tree limbs, but sanded enough to feel comfortable under her touch. "This is amazing," she said.

Rhett spread his hands out along the railing, looking at the view, his breath billowing into the air. "It doesn't suck, that's for sure." He turned around, eager. "Let me show you the inside!"

Rhett moved past Holly and opened the glass-paned door. Beside it, she noticed a tiny flap door for Hattie, and it made her smile. "After you," he said, dramatically waving his arm, allowing her to enter.

A fire was roaring in a stone fireplace that towered over them, enveloping one wall all the way up to the beams at the vaulted ceiling. He'd lit candles, and their flames, along with the glow of lamplight, filled the room. An over-sized plaid blanket was draped on a leather sofa that faced the view through a wall of windows and in front of it was an old trunk that he was using as a coffee table, a few local magazines fanned out on the top of it.

While she looked around, Rhett went into the kitchen that faced the den area, the open floor plan allowing them to talk. "What do you think?" he asked, popping the cork off a bottle of champagne, the hollow sound of it filling the space. He poured two glasses and the fizz danced above each glass.

"I'm speechless," she said. "It's ... incredible."

"No one can find me here," he said as he walked around the bar and handed her a glass. He set his own on the trunk and plopped onto the sofa, kicking his feet up. Hattie let herself in and found a comfortable spot in his lap the second he sat down. "I can just be myself." He patted the cushion next to him while he stroked the kitten.

"Is it crazy being Rhett Burton, the star?" She sat next to him and curled her legs underneath her. She hadn't thought about it until now, but to many, he wasn't that boy she knew. He was some larger-than-life caricature of the real Rhett Burton. Holly had gotten glimpses of him on TV, his fans crammed up against makeshift fences, waving paper and pen at him, their phones in his face while he signed autographs before running up on stage to perform above their squeals and screams.

"Yeah," he said. "But it's a good crazy. I like it. I just can't do it twenty-four-seven, you know? Sometimes I need to get back here and be around people who know who I am."

She definitely knew who the real Rhett Burton was. She knew everything about him. And an old memory popped into her head just then. "Yes," she said, "it's good to come home to people who know you. Like people who know you're deathly afraid of bees…" She hid her grin with her glass.

He gave her a challenging but playful look. "It bit me on the ass!"

Holly nearly spit out her champagne in laughter, the bubbles invading her sinuses. She clapped her hand over her mouth to keep it all in, her chest heaving at the memory of it. It took her a minute, but she finally recovered enough to try to look serious. "There was no welt there." She giggled again.

"No. There wasn't. But there was a stinger! And how mortifying that I had to pull it out behind a tree at the age of thirteen when you were looking!"

"Remember Buddy said to put tobacco on it?" She laughed again, nearly snorting. "He swore it would take the sting away."

"As if I wasn't humiliated enough," Rhett said, "I had Buddy coming at me with a can of chewing tobacco, telling me to rub some on my backside in front of a girl!"

Holly started to laugh so hard she couldn't stop, bringing

her to hysterics, the memory of Buddy chasing Rhett, while he held one cheek and ran around the yard yelling, "It hurts!" as clear as if it had happened yesterday. Once the giggles subsided, she wiped her eyes. "Those were fun days, weren't they?"

He gave her that crooked grin. "Yeah, they sure were." Rhett took his feet off the trunk and leaned toward her, his smile wide. Hattie jumped to the floor and walked off toward the kitchen. "And now I know to never allow an interviewer near you! Who knows what kinds of stories he'll dig up on me with you around!"

Then his smile faded.

"I miss those days."

Holly nodded.

"Sometimes they seem so far away." He got up and walked over to the window, his hands in the pockets of his jeans. "I like the me that I am when I'm with you," he said without turning around.

"Who you are with me is who you really are, Rhett. Don't let anyone tell you differently. It doesn't have anything to do with me."

He finally faced her, studying her for a long time. "Maybe I should keep some of Buddy's dip in my back pocket to remind me of that."

"And if you always have some, Buddy won't need to

worry if he forgets his as long as you're around." She made light of it, although she felt the weight of his statement.

He shook his head and chuckled. "I'm glad you're going with me to California."

That was when she wondered if perhaps she would be that token of home that he wanted to keep in his back pocket, that constant reminder of who he was because it was so easy to forget when he was out there on the road. Was that why he really needed her with him? But she wouldn't think about it right now. She needed to just enjoy the moment.

Chapter Twenty-Six

Holly scratched her head through her uncombed hair, yawning as she strained to focus while rooting around behind Nana for her new coffee mug. Yesterday, Holly and Rhett had two bottles of champagne and then they moved on to wine. They talked so long that they both lost track of time, and he offered to cook her dinner. She hadn't eaten all day, so she jumped at the chance for his cooking, remembering how great he was with an outdoor grill. So, unfazed by the winter air, he fired it up and cooked them a feast of steak, grilled vegetables, and potatoes, and they ate at his new farm table under an antique chandelier, all the windows allowing a mesmerizing view of the night sky. When she insisted on getting home for Nana in case she needed her, Rhett had been a perfect gentleman. He bundled Holly up and walked her home, but she had no idea of the hour that she arrived at the cabin.

"Where's Joe?" Holly asked, feeling bad for not seeing him hardly at all yesterday. Although, it was good, because being away made it appear that she and Rhett were an item, and that was exactly how she wanted it to look.

Nana clicked on the coffeepot and Holly realized just then that she was already dressed, her hair in those little pin curls she did, her pearl earrings on.

"He's gone to get Katharine from the airport. He called a taxi a few hours ago."

Adrenaline surged through Holly's veins. "Do you know how long it will be till he gets here?"

Nana twisted the little gold watch on her wrist. "We exchanged numbers before he left. I can call him . . ."

"You exchanged numbers? With Joe?" How things had changed between them.

"He texted that he'd secured a rental car for the next few days, and they were on their way about ten minutes ago, so probably forty more minutes."

"Nana!" Swinging her empty mug, Holly lunged toward the coffeepot, but it hadn't generated enough liquid to fill an entire cup yet. She turned to Nana, but then thought better about spending precious time debating whether she should have given Holly more notice, and started down the hall. "Why didn't you wake me up?" she called from the bedroom while she went through her suitcase like a bulldozer on overdrive. She couldn't find her best pair of jeans, the designer ones, the ones that flattered her figure the most and made her look sophisticated like Katharine probably would be. She scanned the room.

"I saw you and Rhett coming up the stairs last night," Nana said, setting a full mug of coffee on the dresser, unaffected by Holly's panic, "and it was clear that I should let you sleep all that off."

"Yeah, but I have to make a good impression!" Holly dove headfirst back into the suitcase. "Where are my jeans?"

Nana grabbed them off the chair and offered them to her. Holly swiped at them just as Nana pulled them out of reach. "Slow down, dear. Take a breath." In those words, Nana meant so much more, she could tell. It was clear that Nana knew Holly's worries encompassed more than not being ready on time. "You'll be just fine." Nana handed the jeans to her. "Have some coffee, take a shower, and relax. I'll keep Joe and Katharine busy until you're ready."

❄

Holly's heartbeat was in her throat, her fingers unsteady as she put her ear against her bedroom door. She heard a feminine laugh—polite, quiet—and she knew it was Katharine. Holly looked down at her attire. Maybe she should have dressed up a little, be more professional? But this was her house, so that might be weird. She heard Nana's voice and then Katharine's again, but they were muffled, so she couldn't make out what they were saying.

Holly was frozen in place, unable to make her limbs work,

the reality of Joe's fiancée sitting in her living room turning her to stone. This was the woman with whom she would be working side by side, the woman who would walk down the aisle toward Joe and promise to love him until death do her part. Holly was about to get a very small glimpse into his world and how he lived. She was already curious about their mannerisms toward each other. Was Joe sitting next to her, his knee invading Katharine's personal space like it had when he'd sat next to Holly? Would he have the same interest in his eyes?

Steeling herself, Holly forced her hand onto the doorknob, the click loud enough to most likely let them know she was coming. She channeled that part of her that was so good at keeping herself under control. Then she squared her shoulders and walked out into the living room to greet Joe's soon-to-be bride.

The woman stood from the sofa. She was strikingly beautiful. Her dark brown hair was swept into an up-do, her eyes large and attentive, and Holly considered how intimidating her gaze would be in a courtroom, but her smile was genuine when she held a commanding hand out to Holly. "Katharine Harrison," she said with a firm handshake. "I hear you're my new wedding planner."

"Yes," Holly said, keeping herself poised. "Brea has done an amazing job so far. I'm happy to finish planning this for you."

"Ugh, Brea…" Katharine said, that intensity flickering in her eyes. "This could've turned into a total disaster without your help. I'm so glad Joseph found you!"

An air of complete confidence circled Katharine like a whirlwind as she regarded Joe with a smile, and it was clear in that moment that Holly wasn't a thing like this woman. Katharine was self-confident, reserved, her wealthy upbringing evident in every movement she made. Holly was willing to bet she'd never climbed a tree all the way to the top or spent her childhood looking for four-leaf clovers and run barefoot at least a mile down a dirt road to show her family when she'd found one. Katharine stepped toward the fire and rubbed her hands together, a diamond the size of a boulder swinging around her finger, the diamond that Joe had obviously given her.

Holly glanced over at him and recognized by his look that he'd noticed her assessment, and his face seemed almost apologetic. But there was nothing to apologize for. The difference between Holly's life and Katharine's stretched wider than the Grand Canyon. No wonder Joe had seemed so curious around Holly; she was probably like some stray puppy to Katharine's champion greyhound. But she had to remember that their differences didn't make either of them less of a woman.

"Thank you for having me in your home," Katharine

said. "I'd love to stay, but I know that Joseph has already imposed on your holiday long enough." Her words regarding Joe were kind and more bantering than accusatory. "So I'll get him out of your hair." She let out a small chuckle at her own line, not knowing that having Joe leave would be the very last thing Holly would want. "I got us a room at a hotel in Brentwood. I figured you and I could quickly go over the final details together before we leave, Holly, and then I'll get all my wedding mess out from under your feet so you and your grandmother can enjoy yourselves."

"I'd hate to know you'd found accommodations on our account," Nana said. She'd been sitting quietly on the sofa. "You're more than welcome to stay."

"Thank you for your hospitality, Ms. McAdams," she said, her high heels out of place for the weather, making her seem more imposing than she probably was, "but I'll be slaving away at research, so I wouldn't be much fun. And it'll be nice to be closer to the venue as well. I'd like to take a break from my work for a quick tour of it and then make Joseph take me out in Nashville." She flashed that smile at Joe. "I've been so busy that I haven't had a moment to relax. I'd like to steal a few free evenings from my calendar before I dive in full force." Turning from Nana, she said, "Joseph, why don't you work on packing, and I'll sit down with Holly to write out a schedule."

Joe got up and left the room. Holly wished she could go after him and spend their last few minutes together talking, but she knew she couldn't. Unexpectedly, her chest felt like it had a cinder block sitting on it at the thought of him walking out of the cabin and not returning. She felt guilty for spending so much time at Rhett's last night, but she hadn't grasped that their unexpected days being snowed in together had now come to an end.

It was probably better this way. It would give her time to get over it and move forward with her life, because she wasn't doing herself any favors feeling the way she did for him. She just couldn't ignore that charged involuntary feeling of knowing without a doubt that he could be someone significant in her life, and they'd never know what that significance could've been. If he was going to break her heart, best he do it right now, as quickly as possible. The more she considered this, the faster she wanted him to leave, as the thoughts of the fun she had with him sped through her mind like a freight train. She wanted more time to get to know him, to find out what he loved, what he hated, what drove him crazy. She wanted to see that look in his eyes again that he got when she surprised him with something she said.

"Is that all right, Holly?" Katharine's face appeared in front of her and when Holly came to, she realized she was still staring at Joe's door down the hallway.

She produced a pleasant expression for Katharine, her eyebrows raised in mock interest, her lips set in the same inviting way that she did when she had an unruly customer and she was employing the old motto that "the customer is always right."

"I'm sorry," Holly said, covering. "I was already listing things in my head! Let me get my laptop and papers and we'll have a quick chat at the kitchen table. Nana, do you need anything before we get started?"

"I don't need a thing, dear." Nana gave her a knowing stare, making Holly look away.

"Great," Holly said. "Back in a sec."

When Holly returned, Nana had made herself comfortable with her book in the living room. Katharine was perched at the kitchen table, her spine straight with empty space between her body and the back of the chair, her legs crossed delicately, her posture so comfortable in that position that it was clear that this was exactly the way she sat most days. She pulled a notebook and pen from the Louis Vuitton bag by her chair. Holly set an untidy pile of papers on the table, straightening the corners that had gotten bent as she'd worked on the planning.

"I checked on the photography package," Holly started in. "They need your final decision on the wall-sized oil painting of your bridal portrait. If you choose this, they will rush it, to get it done by the wedding day, because they think it would be nice to display it on an easel as guests enter." She checked her timings. "I see here you have a final fitting for your dress. But you've had your portrait taken, yes?"

Katharine was scribbling in her notebook. "I have one more dress fitting for a few last tucks in the waist and hem. We need to make sure it fits like a glove on the big day, so I asked for an extra fitting right before the wedding. I moved the appointment to tomorrow, since I'm in town—they overnighted the dress from the boutique in New York to their Nashville location. Would you be there with me to make sure it all goes well, and then you can pick up the dress and take it to the estate?"

"Absolutely. And your portraits?" Holly made another note, while wondering if she could actually stomach this.

"It's all fine—I've already had my portraits done," she said without looking up. "They retouched any imperfections in the dress. I say, tell the photographers it's a go on the oil."

"All right." Holly made a note to call the photographer. "Also the florists don't have enough inventory for the archway that you chose. They'll need to pull in two more florists. I gave them the go-ahead on this, figuring you wouldn't want a sparsely decorated archway."

"Great." Katharine nodded. "Just make any of those

decisions yourself, if they're easy. Only contact me for the things you can't answer without me. I trust you. Joseph told me you're incredible."

"He did?" The word "incredible" dangled in front of her, giving her a thrill but also causing a hollow feeling in her chest as if she were losing something. But when she noticed Katharine studying her, she cleared her throat and continued, redirecting the conversation. "What wedding shoes are you wearing? Will you have heels?"

"Yes. They're Jimmy Choos," Katharine said, lighting up a little when she said it, and Holly was glad to have moved her on so quickly, promising herself she wouldn't let her emotions show again.

"Lovely," Holly continued, her mind returning to the shoes. "Have you started wearing them in the house to break them in? We wouldn't want you to have blisters when you're spinning around the dance floor." She thought of Joe, twirling Katharine while her dress fanned out around her.

"Great idea," Katharine said as though Holly had just saved her life. "Plus, it'll give me more time to wear those shoes."

Holly smiled.

"I got my things packed," Joe said, setting his suitcase down with a thud beside him, his gaze flickering over to Holly. "I'll just start gathering the wedding boxes now."

"Great," Katharine returned as he left the room again.

"Holly and I will only be a few minutes more," she called after him. "We can text the rest, and I'm sure I'll have Holly by my side most of next week."

Would Joe stay clear of Holly next week and let her focus on her work? Would he instinctively know to do that for her? Because seeing him now, that suitcase sitting alone in the center of the kitchen, she missed him already. Missing him was part of the process, but having to spend time with him was another matter. It just made getting over her feelings harder.

"Will you call the office tomorrow to see if we can get into the estate?" Katharine asked. "Joseph tells me how detail-oriented you are, and I'd like to consult you on a few things."

Joe came back in, his arms full of boxes. He continued across the room, exiting through the front door.

"Certainly." She made a note and rubbed the back of her neck.

Joe came back in, the door slamming behind him. "It's all in the car," he said, and just like that, there was no shred of him left in the cabin. Like all the other renters before him, he'd packed up, and was heading out. Katharine closed her notebook and stuffed it into her bag. Nana, who'd been silent this whole time, stood up from her chair to say goodbye.

"Let's have a little fun," Katharine told Joe, walking over to him and slipping her arm in his. "I need it. I found a gorgeous restaurant in The Gulch with a drink menu the size of Long Island. They have frozen rosé."

Joe didn't look Holly in the eye, and she worried he could sense her ache to see him go. She swallowed, feeling like she had cement in her throat.

"I'm so happy Joseph found you, Holly. I can't say that enough," Katharine said from beside Joe. "It's a delight to have you as part of our wedding."

Holly forced a smile, overwhelmed by the irony of Katharine's statement.

"Thank you for . . . everything," Joe said, finally looking into her eyes and then addressing Nana.

"It'll be quiet without you," Nana said. "I've enjoyed having you with us this Christmas."

Joe smiled. "I won't forget it." He threw a quick glance back to Holly. "So, I suppose this is goodbye. For now."

Holly nodded, her words failing her.

Katharine walked over to the door and Joe followed, opening it for her. He put his hand on the small of her back to lead her out onto the porch safely.

"Have a wonderful time in Nashville," Nana said, waving.

Holly chewed on her lip, watching them go.

Chapter Twenty-Seven

The next morning, Holly pulled up in front of the bridal shop in Green Hills, an area known for its amazing shopping, as well as being home to both the infamous Bluebird Café and some of the most desirable real estate in the city. She got up extra early to get ready and make the drive into Nashville, happy the snow had melted considerably enough to allow her time to stop at a gourmet coffee shop on the way.

She picked up a coffee for herself and one for Katharine along with a tray of crackers and cheese. Her years at the restaurant had taught her that the customer might not remember the food or the conversation, but they would remember how they were treated. If she was going to do this wedding planning right, she was going to do it in style.

Keeping the carrier tray of coffees steady in the passenger seat with one hand, she parked her Honda next to a shiny black Range Rover, and, as she got out, Katharine exited that vehicle.

"Good morning," Katharine said over the car, holding her hand up in a wave. Everything she did was controlled.

"Good morning." Holly reached across her seat and grabbed the tray with two coffees and the bag of nibbles before shutting her door. "I got you an extra skinny vanilla almond milk latte and something to take the edge off if the fitting takes longer than expected," she said. "Hope you like it."

"You are a lifesaver!" Katharine clicked down the sidewalk toward her on heels that were so tall and pointed at the toe that Holly wondered how she could manage the pain. She shifted her designer bag on her shoulder and repositioned the shoebox under her arm that held, presumably, her Jimmy Choo wedding shoes.

"This coffee is one of the best in Nashville," Holly said with a grin, handing the cup to her. "I doubt it's better than Rona's though."

"What's Rona's?" Katharine asked.

"The café in New York," Holly clarified. She'd tried to hit a familiar note in conversation. She took a slight risk not knowing Katharine well, but since Joe seemed to like the café so much, Holly was nearly certain Katharine would have been there before. He'd made it sound like such a romantic place that Holly figured he'd have told Katharine. But maybe Holly just interpreted it as romantic when it wasn't. Perhaps Joe had just popped in on his lunch breaks or something.

"Is it good? I've never heard of it," Katharine said, taking a sip of her coffee.

"Uh...I heard it's great, yes," she said, not wanting to make more of it than it was. She'd misread Joe's language when he'd told her about it, which wasn't like her at all. "It's near Times Square."

"Good to know." Katharine took another long drink from her cup. "I worked all night last night on my case after dinner. Then Joseph went for a run this morning before I got up and I was so tired that I almost overslept! I drove straight here. I haven't eaten a thing."

"He runs?" Holly snapped her mouth shut, the question coming out when she hadn't meant it to, but she felt oddly excited to know a new fact about him. With the snow he probably hadn't been able to go for a jog, but he hadn't even mentioned it.

"I think it's something new he's starting. Maybe an early New Year's resolution, I don't know." Katharine waved her manicured hands in the air dismissively and then reached out for the coffee, shifting the box under her arm before Holly took it to give her a hand.

"He was still gone when I left." Katharine took a grateful sip and headed toward the shop.

Holly opened the oversized glass door and followed Katharine inside. The boutique was something out of a bridal magazine: everything was white—the floors, the roses and their curving vases, the billowing chiffon and beaded dresses, hanging one after another like rows of heavenly curtains. The only color in the whole place came from the exposed brick wall at the back and a silver logo in script upon it that read, "Shimmer."

A woman in a very tailored blazer with matching trousers greeted them, shuffling up to the front with tiny, hurried taps. When she reached them, the woman leaned in and kissed Katharine on both cheeks.

"My dear," she said, a very slight southern accent coming through her overworked tone, her face so animated that it looked as if she were getting married herself. "Are you not dying right now? You're only days from your wedding!" Katharine hadn't even answered the question yet, and the woman took in an elongated breath.

"Where's Brea?" she asked, her voice directed at Katharine but her sideways eyes on Holly.

Holly straightened her back, lifted her chin to show her assertiveness, and, before Katharine had to explain, she answered, "Hello, my name is Holly McAdams. I'll be planning the rest of the wedding. It's lovely to meet you, Diane." She inwardly fist-pumped to herself for remembering the note on Joe's spreadsheet that said the Nashville bridal seamstress's name: Diane Long. Don't mess with her high-end waitressing skills. Holly could remember a customer's name for years. She'd tag them with some sort of trait—their bushy eyebrows, their crooked tooth, their freckles—and then she'd never forget them.

Looking a bit stunned, Diane smiled brightly and said, "Well, it's lovely to meet you. Shall we start the fitting?"

Diane led Holly and Katharine to the back of the shop and made a sharp left into a room resembling a miniature dance studio with its glossy floors, impeccable lighting, and mirrored walls.

In the center, under a soft, romantic spotlight, a single silver stand was positioned toward the mirrors, holding the most incredible wedding dress Holly had ever laid eyes on. It was a simple cut, straight across the bust, three-quarter-length sleeves, with a seamless waist and a skirt of white satin that tumbled elegantly to the floor where its lightly beaded train trailed behind it.

Diane moved the veil with its matching ornate beadwork, the airy fabric falling delicately from a diamond tiara, and began to unbutton the dress at the back. There were so many buttons that they resembled an outstretched pearl necklace. It took her a little while, but when she finished the last button, Diane said, "I'll leave you two ladies to chat amongst yourselves and then you can let me know what final preparations will be required. I find it's helpful if I'm not in here so you can talk freely about what you'd like done. I'll check back in just a few minutes." Then she waggled her penciled eyebrows at Katharine. "I. Can. Not. Wait! To see you in this dress," she said dramatically. "You will be stunning." Then, as she left, she pointed to a small dresser-like piece of furniture. "Your undergarments are in the top drawer."

Katharine slipped off her coat and then her heels, placing them to the side of the small stage with the three-way mirror. She padded over to the dress, quietly viewing it in all its glory. For the first time since they'd met, Katharine seemed pensive, as if she wasn't sure what to say, which was very possible, as the dress was simply breathtaking. Holly searched for even one stitch line but every single tuck and fold hid any sight of thread as if it were one giant piece of tailored fabric, magically held together by all those pearl buttons at the back.

Holly stared at it, the knowledge of what it stood for hitting her in full force. She could already picture Katharine in it. Standing next to Joe. Promising to love him forever. It seemed so wrong, like two puzzle pieces that didn't fit just right, but she had to remind herself that the Joe she'd met might not be the same person he was on a daily basis.

"It took one phone call and we had this shipped from the store in New York," Katharine said quietly, her gaze running down the satin and back up. "It seems so real now, having the dress here, in Nashville." As if the garment itself could entrance her, Katharine had gone from the bubbly, shoebox-holding, chatting woman she'd been upon arrival to silent and thoughtful, her aura seeming to shrink down to a more average size. In that instant, Holly felt like she was someone she could actually talk to.

But it seemed as though Katharine needed a minute, and Holly didn't know her well enough to feel like she should assist her dressing anyway, so she said, "I'll be just outside the door. Let me know when you'd like me to step in and help with all those buttons."

Katharine was still staring at the dress when Holly let herself out.

Diane hovered around at the front, fashioning a new display, the sun coming in through the large windows and making the whole room glow as if it were powered by an electric current. Shimmer was the sister company to one in New York, and, according to Brea's notes that Joe had on his computer, Diane and the person in New York had been collaborating on this dress as a special project. It all felt so formal and that wasn't how she viewed Joe at all. It made her wonder if she'd really known him at all.

Holly realized she'd been outside the room for quite some time now. Wondering if Katharine was having trouble with the dress, she peeked her head in, and to her surprise, Katharine had it on, the back gaping open, as she sat on the edge of the stage, her knees pulled up and her arms around them.

"What's the matter?" Holly said, rushing in. Did the dress not fit? Was there something wrong with it?

Katharine looked up, her wide eyes helpless. "I don't know if it's right," she said.

It was a little late now to decide on another dress. "It's a beautiful dress," she said quickly. "But is there something we could change on it to make you more comfortable? I'm sure Diane—"

"Not this," Katharine cut Holly off and fluffed her dress, the satin catching the air under it and ballooning out before deflating onto her legs once more. "My marriage. I don't know if I'm doing the right thing, marrying Joseph. I'm worried that it won't work between us, that we'll fall into that fifty percent of couples who don't make it. That's half—one out of every two marriages ends in divorce."

Holly gaped at her. What was she supposed to say to that? It was clear that Katharine was a confident, smart woman, and if she'd promised herself to Joe, she hadn't made the decision lightly. Holly could never live with herself if she didn't talk Katharine through this. "Do you remember Joe—Joseph's—proposal?"

Katharine nodded, a bit of that strong presence of hers returning as the memory emerged.

"Did you feel like you could be with him for the rest of your life in that moment?"

"Yes." Katharine ran her French manicured fingernails along the edge of the fabric, her mind clearly returning to that day.

"Channel that. And then go with your gut." Holly took the tiara off the stand, the veil spilling over her arm, and carried it over to Katharine. "From what I've heard, planning this has put a strain on you, given your workload."

Katharine looked up at her, listening.

"But it's a day of celebration, a day of enjoying the person beside you and knowing that the two of you will get through anything." Holly set the tiara on Katharine's head. "Why don't you let me get those buttons for you and we'll see how the dress fits."

After a long, thoughtful moment, Katharine stood up and then slowly turned around and faced the mirrors, slipping her hair and veil over her shoulder.

Silently, Holly began to fasten the pearl buttons.

Chapter Twenty-Eight

After the dress fitting, Holly arranged for the estate to be opened so she and Katharine could take a look at the property. Katharine was quiet, but she seemed purposeful in her comments, and Holly wondered if she was mentally preparing for the big day. After all, Katharine's whole working life was about readying herself for anything that was thrown at her—she was a lawyer. That could've been the reason for her earlier wobble during the fitting: Katharine wasn't used to having to rely on others. A marriage required two people to make it work and Katharine wasn't in control of Joe. It had to be difficult for her.

With the final alterations now being finished on the dress, it was time to consider placement of the wedding party, musicians, artwork, and the locations of various tables.

She had a couple of hours to kill, so she grabbed an early bite to eat, telling Katharine she'd meet her there, and Katharine went back to her hotel. While she was nibbling on a sandwich at a local takeout, Holly noticed she had a notification. It was an email message and the subject was "The Boy." Curious, she opened it. An unsigned email followed, the address as cryptic as the message: 786@hb.com. She read the email:

> *I recognize the boy in the photo you shared on Facebook. I can get him a message. What would you like me to tell him?*

Holly stared at the screen, paralyzed. What if it was just a prank? How would she know? Was it just a stranger out there, or was this some of Papa's Christmas magic? Her fingers hovered over the screen as she decided on her response. She typed back:

> *Hello!*
> *Thank you for your email. I'd love you to tell him that Joe Barnes would like to meet him. Can you give me some sort of information to prove you really know him?*
> *Thank you,*
> *Holly McAdams*

She sent the message, nervous energy pulsing through her hands. Should she contact Joe and tell him she'd had a message? No. Maybe not yet. She wouldn't want to get his hopes up. Holly decided she'd wait until something actually came of it. It was probably nothing.

After leaving the restaurant, Holly tried to forget about the email until she got a more informative response. The whole drive, her mind was on the wedding she had to finish. She pulled her car to a stop behind a pair of colossal scrolled iron gates at the estate and hit the button. "Holly McAdams, here for the Barnes wedding preparations."

There was a buzz and the enormous iron doors swung open slowly. Holly proceeded to the circular drive out front and parked the car. When she got out, she put her hands on her hips and took in the view, the estate towering over her like a monument to the rich and famous. A sprawling mass of white, with a portico supported by columns that were bigger than two hundred-year-old oak trees loomed over her. The whole thing sat on an expansive piece of land that managed to have green grass even in the winter, the leftover snow magically lifted from every surface. How had they done it?

Just then, the Range Rover pulled up. Holly turned to greet Katharine through the car window but stopped when she saw Joe was driving. He caught her eye as he parked and got out.

"Hey," he said, that one word seeming to have so much more meaning than just a hello. Was she imagining it?

"Hi." Holly caught herself chewing on the inside of her lip after she said it and made herself stop to eliminate any show of emotion, however small. This wedding was happening no matter how she felt, and she had a job to do.

Katharine exited the passenger side and walked around the car to greet Holly. "Ready?" she asked as she took Joe's hand in hers.

Holly looked away from them toward an empty bench sitting under a large maple tree. In the winter, with its cold seat and empty branches on the tree above it, it seemed cold and barren. She could just imagine it in the springtime with the glow of sunshine all around it, the tree in full bloom... The crunch of light gravel under their feet brought Holly's attention back to the wedding couple. They'd started walking. So Holly followed, stepping up on the other side of Joe, ready to work. Joe deserved a great wedding and she was going to give it everything she had.

They climbed the massive steps, leading to the double doors that, when opened, could be the size of an entire wall in her own home. When they arrived, the one on the left opened, a man in a suit greeting them.

"Hello. You must be the Harrison-Barnes party," he said with a nod. "My name is Jay Woodson, house manager. Please, come in." When all the introductions were made, Mr. Woodson invited them to look around and told them he'd be in his office off the parlor should they have any questions. Then he graciously left the room.

Holly got to work immediately. She started, "This is a good place to have your guests sign in, take their coats..." She walked across the black-and-white tiled floor, under a glass chandelier the size of a small condo, and waved her arms toward the sweeping staircases that flanked the room. "I've been looking at photos of the interior online, and I have some ideas. Against the side of these steps here, I thought we could put your portrait. We want it far enough from the door that it will draw guests inward, leaving space for new arrivals."

Joe followed Holly's steps with his gaze, quiet.

"And along that wall there, I thought we'd have the table with the favors—the snowflake ornaments." She felt a little fizzle of affection when she remembered planning with him, but she pushed it away. "Would that work, Joe?"

"Hm?" he looked between them blankly.

"The favors?" Katharine repeated, inquisitively observing him.

He seemed to come to.

"The ones you'd told me about, remember?" Katharine said, nodding.

"Oh, yes," he said on an inhale of breath. "Perfect."

Was he getting overwhelmed like he had when she'd

run too much by him? This was her job, though, so she kept going. Having studied the floor plan of the building and extensively researching since Joe left the cabin, Holly was on her game and Joe and Katharine needed her to be. "This leads straight into the grand hall through the entrance there." Holly turned around and peered back at the double doors at the front. "Hang on a second. Let me see something." She walked over to them and pulled on their enormous brass handles, swinging both of them open, the winter sunlight pouring in from outside. Then she stepped back, thinking.

"The cold is lost on this big room for a moment, as long as we don't keep these doors open all day…" She went over to the grand hall and walked into the room, turning back around to face them, a smile emerging. "I thought so. Come in here."

Katharine clicked her way across the floor with Joe beside her, entering the grand hall where they would have the ceremony. When Katharine faced the entryway, she gasped.

The doorway to the entrance of the estate was so large that, when the doors were open, it created a perfect frame behind the opening to the grand hall with a backdrop of lush winter green gardens, and the sunlight illuminated the floor all the way to them.

"It's like a natural spotlight," Holly said. "You will literally glow. If we are lucky enough to get sun, it will bounce off of every diamond in your tiara, every bead in your train, and all that perfect white of the dress will be against the gorgeous landscape out there as you are revealed to the guests for the first time. We'll close the doors to the grand hall right after the bridal procession and then, when everyone stands, we'll have ushers open the doors here, as well as the front doors at the same time, and there you'll be, standing like a princess." She waved her arms toward the doorframe. "I'd like to see those roses here instead of on the exterior. I think they could be better used as an addition to the visual framework around that first glimpse of you in the dress."

"Oh my God, Holly. You're amazing. Your attention to detail is astonishing. Joe was right, you are incredible."

Holly felt a thrill at Katharine's comment.

"Thank you," she said with a confident smile. She did enjoy wedding planning. "Once you start walking, we'll close the front doors again immediately so the cold won't seep in," she continued, turning away from them and going toward the front of the estate.

When they got back to the entrance area, she noticed Joe looking on intently—so different than how she'd known him—and it brought back memories of laughing over those ridiculous sunglasses, his arms around her on the dance floor in Otis's barn, the attentive smile he had when he unwrapped the keychain she'd bought that said, "Joey." To her, he was Joey. Joe. Never Joseph. Never this man that had been so quiet the whole time.

Holly closed the heavy doors and turned around. "If we put the roses inside, and go with the dark-red-and-white ensemble, the deep red runner I've chosen will pop against your dress. I'd like to also do small floral stands of roses on the ends of each row along the runner. I already cleared it with the florist, having used pictures of the estate from the web. The white folding chairs will start here." She brushed Joe's arm by accident as she passed, catching a whiff of his familiar scent. It made her feel surprisingly calm, like he'd always been able to make her feel. "And they'll end there about a foot from the back of the room where you'll enter."

Katharine nodded, concentrating on the directions. Holly was delighted that the person who had seemed completely disinterested in her own wedding was so enthralled under her direction.

Holly was more energized than she had been in years, and for the first time, she got an indication of what Rhett must feel when he was performing. It was so natural and effortless, and the more interest she got from Katharine, the more encouraged she felt.

"The musicians could be set up over here on the side. We can put the strings on this platform and the flutes will be just below." She finally looked at Joe, and he was smiling at her—could he tell how much she was enjoying this? "Joe, you'll stand here," she said, stepping into position at the front, her attention on his spot on the floor. "The bridal party could be fanned out on either side."

"Lovely," Katharine said. She wriggled her hand under Joe's arm and linked hers with his.

"Everything sounds fantastic, Holly," Joe finally said when she'd finished, the sound of his voice making her happy.

"I'm just going to visit the ladies' room," Katharine said. "Then Joe and I are going out for the day! I hope you enjoy the rest of yours, Holly. It's chilly but the sunshine is glorious."

Holly nodded.

Katharine dropped Joe's arm. "Be right back." She walked away, leaving Joe and Holly in the entryway.

Silence immediately fell between them.

"I...Uh..." Holly started, trying to fill the void but knowing that anything she said wouldn't work in this instance. "I..."

"Holly," he said gently and every nerve in her body responded to it.

She wished she could somehow let him know that regardless of how their lives ended up, she really cared about him.

She cared about whether he ever found his dad and whether he went to that café he liked near Times Square, or whether he had a chance to kick back and be Joey again one day since it seemed like he'd really enjoyed it.

The two of them stood, totally absorbed in the space between them, as if their surroundings had faded into nothingness and it was just Joe and Holly. Neither of them said anything. What could they say in this situation? Whatever they had experienced while staying together at the cabin wasn't real life, Holly told herself. But it definitely was *real* to her. So real that she felt tears starting to surface, causing her to blink them away. Perhaps she was emotional because it was the first Christmas since Papa died where she'd had fun—at least that was what she was going to tell herself. Planning this wedding had been like one of those hidden gifts Papa talked about, the treasures that she had to look for to see. There would be more for her, she was certain.

"Thank you for waiting," Katharine's voice inched its way into her head.

She was glad that neither of them had said anything, because nothing good would've come of it. And this day wasn't about Holly at all. It was about making great memories that would last generations. In a way, Holly could understand Katharine's lack of interest in the wedding details now. When the roses were gone, the dress boxed up, all that mattered was the promise that Katharine and Joe would make to each other. The promise that would span their entire lives. The promise Joe had made to Katharine way before he'd ever set foot in the cabin this Christmas. That was what mattered most: love. How could she get in the way of that? But she knew one way to show Joe she cared: Holly could manage the details for them—she was great at that.

"I'm glad you liked my ideas," Holly said. She stepped back from Joe and turned toward Katharine. "Is there anything else you'd like me to go over? Any questions you still have after seeing the estate?"

"Not that I can think of. Looks like you have it covered," Katharine said.

Holly was glad for that. "Okay, then. Enjoy your day and text if you need anything at all." Then, she hurried out the door. She couldn't wait to tell Nana all about the plans she made today and how happy she felt making them.

Chapter Twenty-Nine

Holly was in the barn just as the sun slid above the horizon this morning. It was cold even with the furnace heat. Unable to sleep in at all, she'd gotten up and worked on the dresser, giving it a thin whitewash. While it dried, she sanded the old drawer pulls and then rubbed them with apple cider vinegar to distress them. Then she headed inside to get some breakfast.

Nana was in her chair, reading. They had spent last night playing board games, and Holly had told her all about the wedding. Despite the diversion, Holly had tossed and turned the entire night and then been awake before the sun this morning.

Papa's sapphire ring glistened on Nana's finger as she sat silently, turning the pages of her book. She acknowledged Holly with a glance but then went back to the text, her reading glasses on the end of her nose.

Holly grinned when she realized the book Nana had in her lap was *War and Peace*. "How's the reading?" she asked.

"Like living in Papa's head," she said. "Not my cup of tea, but if he says I should read it, I'd better, because when I see him again, he's going to ask. I just know it." She rolled her eyes lovingly. Then she put her finger in the book and closed it for a second. "Rhett texted. He said he tried to get you, but you weren't answering. He wants to come over in a bit."

"Oh, I didn't have my phone. I was in the barn," Holly said. She'd be happy to immerse herself in whatever Rhett wanted to do. This Christmas had brought them close again, and she'd forgotten how much fun he could be.

So an hour later, when there was a knock on the door, Holly jumped up to get it.

"Hey!" Rhett slipped past her, kissing her on the cheek on his way in.

Holly shut the door.

"Nana, you're looking lovely this morning."

Nana grinned, shaking her head.

Rhett spun around to face Holly the way a child responds when his mother calls him sharply, but she hadn't said anything. "You look like hell."

"Thanks."

"You're beautiful," he elaborated. "But you look like something's put you through the wringer. You been partying without me?" He cut his eyes at her jokingly.

"I didn't sleep very well last night."

"You try Buddy's buttermilk idea and everything?"

Buddy had clearly shared that tidbit with Rhett as well. "No. Maybe I should've."

"Or maybe you just need to hang out with me more. Bet you slept like a baby after being at my place the other night."

"She did," Nana piped up. "Didn't move the entire night and slept in the next morning."

"Well, that's an easy problem to solve then." He opened his arms as if he were about to wrap Holly in a bear hug. "I'm at your service!"

Holly laughed and batted him away, ignoring his gesture. "That's the thing about you, Rhett Burton: you think you can do anything."

"Think?" Without warning, he scooped her up, throwing her over his shoulder. "I *know* I can do anything!" Grabbing her coat that was hanging by the door, he called, "I'll have her back by dark, Nana! Love you!"

If that had been any other person, she'd have socked them one for picking her up against her will, but she and Rhett had a different kind of relationship. They could fight like siblings and they had so many experiences together that she could be completely herself with him, and she knew he felt the same way.

He didn't set her down until they were at his vehicle, the old rattling hum like music to her ears.

Holly felt a surge of nostalgia when she saw it. "You brought the jeep."

He opened her door, acknowledging her statement with a grin, and ushered her inside. He'd left it running and the interior was warm and comfortable. Rhett had owned this jeep since he was sixteen. He'd restored it himself and managed to keep it running and in great condition. It was where they'd had so many teenage talks about life, before either of them really knew what they were facing, where they ate ice cream together while watching the old drive-in movies in the lot outside of town, where they'd first heard his single on the radio, the year before Papa died, both of them squealing with delight.

Rhett went around and hopped in.

"Where are we going?" she asked.

"Nashville." He put it in drive and headed down the hill toward the road.

❧

"Broadway?" Holly asked when Rhett pulled the jeep to a stop, parallel parking along the side of one of the busiest nightspots in Nashville. Holly opened her door, bluesy melodies already coming at her from every direction. Located on Lower Broadway, this spot in the road consisted of bar after bar, each one with live music spilling onto the streets every single day—rain or shine.

They stood in front of one of the larger of the bars, its

neon sign glowing brightly in reds and yellows against the crisp blue sky. Many of the big-named country music superstars had played there. It was just opening for the day, its doors unlocked and the doorman out front.

"Oh my God!" A shriek came from behind them and both Holly and Rhett turned around. "Rhett Burton?" A young bleach blonde in her twenties with eyes like a doe and a row of bright white teeth was bouncing on her toes, her cell phone intermittently obscuring her face as she snapped photos with shaky hands. "No one's going to believe this!" she nearly squealed as she snapped away. When she'd gotten enough images to single-handedly flood the Internet, she dropped her phone down by her side and asked, "May I have your autograph?"

As Rhett took a flyer from the doorman and the girl wriggled around in her bag to find a pen, a buzz began to radiate out to passers-by. They were slowing, taking photos, hovering around, scrounging for scraps of paper and pens to get his autograph like the lucky girl who'd stopped him. Holly stood, feeling as if she were invisible to everyone, completely blindsided by the spectacle he was causing. She was aware of his popularity, but until she saw it firsthand, it hadn't seemed real somehow.

Before she knew it, their part of the street was full of people making their way over, and Rhett had to politely tell them that he needed to go in, taking Holly by the hand and pointing to the door. The marquee above them flashed his name before a screen full of digital fireworks that spelled "New Year's Eve." Some of the on-lookers followed them inside, and the doorman had to act as a shield between them and Rhett to allow him some space.

"Sorry about that," he said, taking Holly over to a table and offering her a chair. He waved to one of the managers, who was lining up a row of guitars along the tables. "I thought we were plenty early and I'd parked close enough to avoid any chaos, but they just seem to find me."

People were snapping photos of them while they chatted, making Holly anxious. The manager came over and introduced himself, but she missed his name with all the commotion. He handed Rhett a permanent marker and then said something about merchandise. Another bystander took her photo. She didn't necessarily want pictures of herself floating around. But Rhett didn't seem bothered at all. Had he already gotten used to this madness?

Rhett led her to the guitars where he scribbled his signature across the face of each of them. Then he picked one up and held it in the air as he addressed the manager who seemed thrilled to see what Rhett would do with it. He grabbed Holly's hand and took her up onto the stage with him. "Watcha think of this?" he asked.

Holly turned her attention away from the crowd that had grown in size and peered over at the large expanse of lights and speakers, the microphone stands dwarfed by the width and breadth of the platform. An American flag hung against a white-bricked wall behind it, whiskey barrels set along the edge at various places for drinks and music, she supposed. There were open boxes lined up, full of gray T-shirts with Rhett's name in red lettering.

"It's nice."

"Nice? It's awesome, don't you think?"

"Sorry. Yes, it's awesome." She smiled at him. "Those people are distracting me."

"Oh, don't let them bother you. They're just excited. It used to be a shock when people stopped me like that. To make sense of it, I had to create two worlds for myself: there's their world, the one they see, the photos they're taking of the guy on the radio, and then there's my world, the one right in front of me." He put two fingers to his eyes and then pointed them toward hers. "Stay in my world," he said.

Rhett took her by the hand again, leading her to the center of the stage and sending the cell phones into a frenzy. She tried to ignore them like Rhett had instructed. He offered her a wooden stool next to his and she sat beside him while he got comfortable with the guitar. To the delight of the crowd, he propped it up on his knee. Then he did the finger point from his eyes to hers again.

"*Some say maybe one day…*" he started to sing, and the place began filling up out of nowhere, a couple of hoots rang out from a few as they hurried to the edge of the stage, but Rhett held her gaze. "*But I say right now…*" He hit the chords, the song speeding up and making her heart race. And that was when she felt what Rhett had just explained. The people watching knew these words because they'd heard them on the radio or had seen Rhett play them on TV, but they didn't know that he'd written them the day he'd decided, at the age of fourteen, over one of Papa's grilled cheeseburgers, that he was going to be famous one day and he was going to start the journey right then.

He and Holly were painting the picket fence at his mother's that summer, both of them covered in white speckles, and he started humming this tune, the notes coming to him by some cosmic creative force like they always did. He grabbed her arm with a paint-covered hand and they ran back to the house so he could get a pencil and his notebook and scribble down the words that had found their home in his mind. Papa made them both eat dinner so they wouldn't "waste away," Papa said.

"I'm going to sing this on stage one day," Rhett told her then.

And here they were.

At the end of the song, he thanked the crowd and, with the place now filling up, he set down the guitar and led Holly to a back room where the musicians must get ready before their performances. She took a seat on a cowhide-covered sofa across from a mirror-lined wall and counter.

"I'm headlining here on New Year's," he said, dropping down beside Holly and putting his arm around her.

"Wow! New Year's Eve on Broadway—Rhett, that's what you've always wanted to do. I'm so thrilled for you." Rhett could sell out stadiums all by himself, so she could only imagine the pandemonium he'd cause in such a small venue.

"Wanna come see me play? I'd like you to."

Apart from the moment they'd just had, and at Otis's, she'd never seen Rhett play publicly. She knew how much this performance meant to him. This was his home, and every one of his friends would be among the crowd. He'd played all over the world, but Nashville was different for him. He didn't want to mess it up. It was clear he was asking for her support. "I'd love to," she said.

"I'm having a driver drop me at the back door the evening of the show before the crowds start to gather. I can send him to get you after. It might be too much for Nana, but if she wants to watch, I could find her a pair of headphones and sit her in the back, just off stage."

The idea was amusing. "She won't stay up that late. But she'll be delighted that you thought of her." Holly paused, taking in the intense look he was giving her.

"I love having you with me," he said suddenly. "Holly, I want to kiss you right now."

"Rhett," she said slowly, shaking her head.

"Okay." He looked away, resigned.

"At least you asked this time," she said with a half grin, bringing him back to her.

He broke into an enormous smile.

Chapter Thirty

The next few days, Holly busied herself with final wedding preparations for Joe and Katharine, putting the last coat of sealer and last few touches on the dresser out in the barn, and keeping Nana entertained. Thankfully, Holly had finished everything for the wedding via phone calls and texts and hadn't seen Joe again, and, while she definitely felt his absence in the house, she managed to focus on the wonderful things around her.

Nana was thrilled with the look of the dresser once Holly finished it. Holly could just imagine a mirror above it, a lamp flanking each side, a small vase of flowers…

"You could open a shop with refinished furniture," Nana said when she saw it.

"Possibly," she said. She'd surprised herself. Holly loved the piece and couldn't wait to start thinking about what she wanted to do with it.

Over the last few days, she and Nana had had lunch with Kay, and they visited Otis. Nana was smiling again. She'd made it an incredible two-thirds of the way through

War and Peace, and they'd put an entire puzzle together. Holly had also been to Rhett's house in the trees. They'd even written part of a new song, like old times. She held Hattie, worried about who would care for the kitten when they went to California. He reassured her that Kay would be taking care of the kitten, and Nana had offered to be a backup should they need anyone.

The soft undercurrent of normalcy had just started to settle through the cabin again when Nana dropped the bomb. "I spoke to Joe yesterday," she said over her shoulder.

Holly, who'd been putting away laundry, stopped in the living room on her way to the bedroom, the basket of whites in her arms, and stared at her.

"He and Katharine are going to see Rhett play tonight for New Year's."

"What?" was all she could get out, but it was enough for Nana to respond.

"He called my phone while you were with Rhett. Said he couldn't find one of his lists with the addresses of the wedding party." She got up out of her chair and walked toward Holly, taking the basket from her arms and setting it down on the coffee table. "He eventually found it with his things and we got to talking. He mentioned not having plans for New Year's, so I suggested he and Katharine go."

"But Nana," Holly said, the unique cocktail of elation

over being able to see Joe again in a festive and laid-back atmosphere and panic about Katharine being there with him pumped through her veins. "I was hoping not to have to see him again until the wedding."

"I'm not sure that's wise, dear." Nana began folding the clothes in the laundry basket, making little piles on the coffee table.

"Why not?"

"I think you need to face this. You need to see those two together to get the Joe you met out of your mind. It's important to fill your thoughts with images of real life. He's not going to walk through that door, Holly. And you're putting on a good front, but I know you too well, and that's secretly what you're hoping for."

The ache that developed in her chest whenever she thought about him came back in full force. "Nana, you have a point, but I also need to make a clean break. If Joe's going to marry Katharine then he needs to get on with it and I need to let him." The idea had been going around in her head, but she hadn't made the firm decision until now. "Joe told me that all I have to do is get the wedding party in place at the beginning and the estate staff would take over. I'm going to tell Rhett to try to book our tickets for California the same day as the wedding—I'm not going to stay. I'll need something to take my mind off everything. With his touring schedule options already coming in, Rhett's been dying for a solid travel date; he'll be thrilled."

"That's two days away," Nana said, thinking. But it was clear that she was willing to let Holly deal with this however she felt she needed to. "I know you'll do the right thing. I'm proud of you, Holly."

Holly's phone pinged on the counter in the kitchen, interrupting the moment and, when she went over to it, curiosity and fear both consumed her at the sight of the email: "The Boy."

"Nana, can I just get this?" she said, waggling her phone, trying to stay low-key until she knew for sure what this was all about.

"Of course, dear." Nana went back to her chair and Holly abandoned the remaining laundry and opened the message.

Dear Holly,
  I can tell you that Joe's birthday is July 8, 1986. I hope that's sufficient for verification purposes…

Holly hadn't known Joe's birthday, so it could be anything… She stared at the date, happy to know it if it was true. He was a summer baby like her. July eighth… She ran the date in her head: Seven. Eight. Eighty-six. She paused, inspecting the email address again. 786@hb.com…786, meaning July of

1986? Then the letters of the address struck her. Harvey Barnes. Her post had been set to public and this could be anyone in the whole world, and there were lots of crazies out there. It could be a hoax—it all seemed too easy. She read the rest of the email.

I'm surprised Joe wants to meet Harvey. I've passed along the message. If Joe's serious about meeting him, he might consider it.

Again, no signature.

Holly needed to tread lightly. She didn't want to get Joe wrapped up in some kind of wild goose chase right before his wedding. It was clear by his behavior while planning it with her that he was already a little overwhelmed emotionally. Holly needed to be absolutely sure that this person knew Harvey before she got Joe involved.

She typed back:

I need something more to convince me that you really know Harvey before we go any further. I'm sorry, I'm just being very careful, because finding him is not something Joe takes lightly.

She hit send.

Her phone chimed with a text and she nearly jumped

out of her skin. With a steadying breath, she opened it. It was from Rhett. He told her the car was coming to get her tonight at seven thirty and he couldn't wait to see her. She texted back, *See you then!*

Rhett's text caused Holly's thoughts to move to tonight, thinking about how good it would feel to see Rhett play, to share in his moment with him. He'd been planning this for decades, and she'd been right by his side all the way. But she didn't have a lot of time to think about Rhett before another email came through with the message, "The Boy." Holly's heart pounded as she opened it.

Ask him about Rona's.

That was the name of the coffee shop in New York. The one Joe seemed to love but hadn't shared with Katharine. He'd also said he'd never spoken to his dad, so what did Harvey know about Rona's? Clearly, he and Joe had never been there together. But this person said to ask Joe about it.

Holly emailed back: *Ask him what?*

She set the phone down on the counter and waited.

"What time are you going to see Rhett?" Nana called.

"Seven thirty," she said back, her eyes on the empty screen of her phone.

"It's nearly six o'clock now. You should eat something before you get ready."

"Mm hm," she said absentmindedly. *Come on*, she willed her phone to ping. If this person would just tell her a little more, she might recognize what he was saying and not have to wait to tell Joe. They could go straight into planning a meeting. He'd be so excited to hear the news—she just knew it.

With nothing coming through on her phone after a few minutes, Holly made a quick sandwich. Then she went off to get ready, wondering what she could say to Joe to get the information from him without worrying him that someone had made contact. Would she have to tell him? Should she?

❄

The streets were already blocked off, every inch of them crowded with masses of people, filling in the gated-off sections of the road like herds of sheep, dressed in their hats and thick winter coats, ready to brace the cold to hold the unique distinction of having been on Broadway for New Year's.

Rhett had sent the car to pick up Holly right on time, the driver maneuvering through the chaos with relative ease. Holly considered the fact that, with the amount of people here, it was a real possibility that she may not run into Joe and Katharine in this crowd, which was just fine with her—she was still trying to figure out whether or not to ask him about Rona's and, since she didn't know if he'd told Katharine anything about Harvey, she had no idea how she'd get Joe alone to ask in the first place. This definitely wasn't the venue for that type of conversation.

The driver pulled up to one of the blocked-off areas, behind a large screen for projecting the concerts into the streets, and showed his ID to security, who radioed to someone and then let them through. The car bumped its way down an alley and came to a stop in back of the bar where Rhett was playing.

A lanyard with her pass swung in Holly's direction, hanging from the driver's forefinger. She took it and slipped it over her head, letting it fall onto her coat. Then she got out and her heels wobbled on the uneven pavement. As Holly was contemplating the best way to get into the building, the back door opened and another security guard ushered her inside.

"Holly McAdams?" he asked, rushed and all business, checking her tag for clarification rather than looking at her face. A band was playing, causing the man to have to shout over the sound of the music and the crowd, even in the back of the place, away from the stage. "Rhett's been waiting for you. I'll take you to his room." If this was anything like his usual concerts, no wonder he'd chosen to build a house in the quiet of the woods at home. Holly knew already that by the end of the night she'd be exhausted.

She remembered the little room where the security guard led her—it was the one she'd been in with Rhett the last time they were there. The door opened and seeing Rhett's familiar face in all this was so comforting. He grinned that crooked grin of his, thanked the security guard, and shut the door, which muffled the sound to a manageable level.

Holly shimmied off her coat, revealing the black dress she'd saved for a special occasion. Rhett's eyes immediately devoured it. "Wow," he said before meeting her eyes. "You look incredible."

"Thanks. So do you." He was wearing jeans and a fitted T-shirt, his old boots the only part of his attire she recognized.

He sat down on the sofa and patted the spot next to him. "Wild out there, right?" He was energized and buzzing with anticipation, totally in his element. Holly was glad to see him so content. This was what he'd dreamed of his whole life, and she couldn't fathom what it must be like to get up every day and do what she loved most. It had to be amazing for him.

"Yes. Crazy." In all the time she'd lived in the area, she'd never been to Broadway on New Year's. They'd always had parties at home or, better yet, popped a bowl of popcorn, opened a few beers, and watched the ball drop in New York on television and then went to bed early due to the time difference between Nashville and the East Coast. "I'm glad I didn't bring Nana. She'd never have made it to the end of the night."

"Ah, she'd have been just fine. I think she secretly likes the sticky floors full of sloshed drinks and obnoxious crowds. She's missing out."

Holly laughed.

"Will you stay on stage with me? There's an area behind the wall to the side where you can see out but the crowd can't see you. I'd love to have you with me," he said.

"If you want me to."

"I do. I want you right there the whole time." He put his arm around her.

"I was thinking," she said, twisting toward him. "Let's go to California sooner rather than later. I know your shows might not start for a while, but why don't we just go anyway?"

He perked up. "Like when?"

"Day after tomorrow?"

Rhett put his hands on her face, nearly bursting with excitement. He let out a low growl. "I want to kiss you right now!" He let go and rolled back onto the sofa. "But I'm trying to show you how much I respect your decision. Even though I think it's totally ridiculous!" He started to tickle her, making her squeal and jump to her feet.

"You're gonna mess up my dress," she said as she tried not to laugh.

"Fine by me!"

"Stop." She took a step back. "You promised, Rhett. Just friends. When you do that, it makes me have second thoughts about going. I want to spend time with *you*. I don't want this to be some sort of constant battle over what we are."

"It's not a battle," he reassured her. "It's a lifelong commitment to making you realize that I'm perfect for you!" He grinned, knowing he was pushing it. He stood up abruptly. "But I'll have to convince you later. I've got two minutes till my cue. Let's go."

He led her down the hallway, the noise like static in her ears, drowning out everything else. There was a chair just off stage with a view of the entire band. They'd taken their places to the roar of the crowd. The drummer was rapping on the center drum, raising the anticipation with every thump. Lights flashed in her eyes and then away as the guitars started in.

"Wish me luck," Rhett said and then kissed her cheek.

"Good luck," she said, but he'd already run to the front of the stage, the crowd in an uproar. Girls were pressed against the barriers in front, their hair swinging around their glittery "Happy New Year's" headbands as they waved their hands in the air; the mass of people turned into a sea of cell phone lights, all of them trying to get the best view as Rhett took his place in front of the microphone, the band revving up.

"How are we doing tonight, Nashville?" Rhett shouted into the microphone over the noise, and the crowd went wild. He looked so natural up there, like he'd been in front of crowds this size his whole life. "It's New Year's! Y'all ready for a good time?" he called. Another thunder of cheers came his way.

Holly took her seat on the small barstool by the wall that hid her from the crowd, thinking about how unrecognizable Rhett's life had become. It wasn't bad, just different, a sort of surreal existence. Just when she thought she'd seen a glimpse of what it was like in his shoes, she was surprised by something bigger, more massive, and his popularity stunned her.

Holly was so busy thinking about it that she almost missed the fact that Katharine and Joe were in the front row. They couldn't see her because of the angle, but she could see them. Katharine was smiling, nodding to the music, and Joe was still—that was how Holly noticed them. He was the only one not moving. His expression was pleasant, but his eyes were fixed on Rhett.

Katharine leaned over and said something into Joe's ear, and he nodded, his expression lifting into a polite smile. Just that small exchange sat like a bag of sand in Holly's stomach, and she let her eyes blur the image before turning back to Rhett.

But as Rhett went through his playlist, Holly stole tiny glances at Joe and Katharine against her will. Mostly, there was nothing to see, but occasionally, they'd share a chuckle or Katharine would look up at him, forcing Holly's eyes back to the stage. A few times, Rhett had taken breaks, allowing other bands to play, and he'd jogged over to her, occupying her attention. It was so loud that she and Rhett couldn't have any real conversation, but she liked to see how much fun he was having.

Joe went off through the crowd a few times and returned with drinks for him and Katharine, and after he'd had a little to drink, he started to sway to the music. It made Holly think about when they'd had all that champagne, the way he'd leaned back, how relaxed his expression had been. In the middle of her memory, before she knew what was going on, Rhett was pulling her to the front of the stage! The crowd started counting down in unison, the numbers blasting in her ears.

Just as she made eye contact with Joe, Katharine wrapped her arms around his neck, demanding his attention, and, coupled with the fact that the spotlight was on Holly, it was more than she could handle. She tore her eyes off them and focused on Rhett as he called into the microphone, "Five! Four! Three! Two…"

There was an eruption of cheering and just as the New Year arrived, Rhett clearly relented in his restraint, the atmosphere obviously giving him courage and hope in the new era that stretched out in front of them like a clean slate. He pulled Holly toward him one more time, his eyes meeting hers before he kissed her like he'd never kissed her before. At first, she wanted to resist—how many times had she told him not to? But then she wondered: why should she resist?

Holly had filled her night with thoughts about a man whom she could never have when she had someone right there who wanted to be her whole world. She tried to relax into Rhett's kiss to see if there was any possibility of her life being easier. She should feel lucky to have Rhett's affection. She kissed him back, giving it this one, real moment, their lips moving together, his hot breath in hers.

Fireworks cracked in her ears, the thousands of people in the streets cheering for the opportunity to start anew once more.

When Rhett pulled back, he looked down at her before leaning into her ear. "Happy New Year," he said. "And I won't kiss you again until you're the one to initiate it." He put his arms around her and pulled her close, and it was clear that he knew he'd given it everything he had for the last time. Rhett turned back to the crowd, and his soft demeanor that she knew so well morphed back into the stage-Rhett that she'd seen all night.

Holly couldn't help but think how wrong that kiss had felt. Rhett was like a brother to her. Why didn't he feel the same toward her? But then she thought back to the tobacco he'd said he should keep in his back pocket to remind him of the people who really knew him... She couldn't deny anymore that he might not be in love with her but rather in love with the familiarity of her and the fact that she'd never betray him. In time, she hoped that he'd see that she could still be there for him as a best friend. They didn't have to be a couple. She hoped that spending time together traveling would help him realize this.

Holly looked back at the crowd to find Joe, but when she scanned the faces, they were all unfamiliar. Then at the rear of the mass of concertgoers, she found him, facing away from her, heading out the door with Katharine.

Chapter Thirty-One

"Rhett kissed me *again*," Holly told Nana, shaking her head as they sat over coffee the next morning. She pulled her knees up in the kitchen chair, wrapping her arms around them while the coffee steamed in her new Leiper's Fork mug that Joe had gotten her. Holly turned the side that read "Someone's thinking of you in Leiper's Fork" away from view.

"He can be full of himself sometimes," Nana said, but her affection toward Rhett was clear. "He adores you, you know. He wants things to work between the two of you."

"I thought things *were* working. Why does he have to complicate everything by having those kinds of feelings for me?"

"We can't help who we fall for," Nana said, giving her a knowing look.

Her comment silenced Holly.

Nana leaned into view. "You don't have to have it all figured out. Go with Rhett to California and see where life takes you. You never know how your world might change."

Holly looked into her coffee in Joe's mug, contemplating

Nana's words. She was so wise, and Holly knew that she was probably right.

"Are you ready for the wedding rehearsal tonight?"

"As ready as I'll ever be."

"Just know that it takes the difficult times to appreciate the easy ones. This will pass, and you'll be stronger because of it. In the end, when you're my age, you'll look back and it will all make sense."

"I trust you, Nana."

"I'm glad." Nana set her coffee down. "Now let's play a game of cards and forget about it all for a little while."

"That's the best idea I've heard."

❄

Holly passed the time playing games with Nana and searching online to find furniture boutiques that might be interested in the dresser she refinished. She found a few strong leads and wrote them down, leaving them messages by phone. Afterward, she went out to the barn and took photos of the dresser, and loaded them onto her computer. She also looked up some ideas for website development just for fun. When she'd procrastinated long enough, she finally got ready for the rehearsal. She'd dressed up again, wearing a navy blue dress that fell just below the knee. Her hair was styled, and she'd added a little more eye makeup than usual.

"You look lovely," Nana said from her chair in the corner.

"Thank you, Nana. Will the fire last while I'm gone?"

"Yes, child. I wouldn't want you ruining your dress getting wood anyway. If I need something, I'll call Buddy over."

"Okay. I'll just be a few hours."

"Try to enjoy yourself."

"I will," Holly said, knowing it would be impossible to have a good time. She was torn between wanting to stay as far away from Joe as possible and needing to find time to be alone with him to ask about Rona's.

She grabbed her keys and headed out the door.

When Holly got to the Brentwood estate and went inside, the mansion was brimming with staff. The florists were busy creating the archway before tomorrow's eleven a.m. service, the beer and wine were being delivered, and the extra tables they'd needed for the entryway were going in. The wedding party had gathered together in the doorway to the grand hall where the ceremony was going to take place, and none of them had seen Joe and Katharine yet.

"I'm Holly, the wedding planner," she said to the group. "Let's go ahead and get started. If I could have the guys and ladies pair up, please?" she called.

Then she noticed the little boy with strawberry blond hair and a sprinkling of freckles on his nose. He was alternating between pulling on the collar of his button-up shirt and tapping his feet. "Hello," Holly said, coming over to him and squatting down to be on his level. "Are you the ring bearer?"

He looked to his mother for reassurance before answering Holly. His mother offered a doting smile and introduced him. "This is Toby," she said.

"Hello, Toby," Holly beamed.

"And I'm Sarah." A little girl with silver flats and a dress befitting the finest of ballerinas came bouncing over to Holly, her deep brown ringlets pulled into a clip. "I'm the flower girl." She took Holly's hand, grinning up at her, the little girl's innocent eyes framed with long, curling eyelashes.

Holly's face lifted for Sarah's benefit, and she held out Sarah's hand in hers. "I'll bet you are excellent at dropping rose petals. I can tell by your fingers. They're perfect for pinching those delicate flowers."

Sarah puffed out her chest in pride. "Yes, I'm very good at it."

Holly beckoned Toby over to join them. "Toby, you'll be here." She marked the spot for the young boy. "And Sarah, once you come down the aisle, you can stand in this spot." Sarah bounced over and stood where she'd asked.

"Sorry we're late," Katharine said, out of breath as she shuffled in. She shot a look over at Joe with some sort of silent message, but Holly couldn't decipher it. Joe, serious, stood beside Katharine, greeting the people in the wedding party quietly before glancing Holly's way.

Sarah broke her stance and went running over toward the wedding couple, calling, "Joe!" She nearly jumped into his arms, wrapping hers around his neck and his serious demeanor faltered.

"Hi there," he said, wrinkling his nose into a silly grin.

"Daddy said he's mad at you," she said with a giggle, twisting her sparkly fingernail-polished fingers behind Joe's neck as she looked into his eyes.

Joe held her easily with one arm. "He is?" He found Sarah's father and waved, and it was clear by the way they interacted that they were good friends.

"Yes. You always come over for the football game and you missed it last week."

Joe nodded. "I did. I'm so sorry about that."

"Well, I'm not mad at you," she said with a grin. Then she put her tiny lips to his ear and said, "And Daddy's not really mad at you either. He's only kidding."

Holly caught Joe's eye and smiled at him. He held her gaze for a moment and then lowered Sarah until her feet were back on the floor. There was something odd in his eyes, but Holly couldn't tell what it was.

"Okay," Holly continued, now that everyone was there,

"Joe, you're up by the musicians, centered at the end of the aisle. Toby and Sarah, follow me." She turned away from Joe and stepped in front of the children. "You two will come in slowly, walking down together."

Holly focused on the work at hand, the tasks coming easily for her. It was as if she had been designed for building things from the ground up, her ability to see what needed to be done coming so clearly and effortlessly that she couldn't believe she hadn't gone down a creative path sooner. All those wasted nights waitressing. She wouldn't let it happen again.

"First couple," she said from the front of the room. Holly beckoned the two people toward her and they began their march. "When they get to about the third set of chairs, the next couple can make their way to the front."

When everyone had walked down the aisle and assumed their positions, Holly walked to the back. She'd completely kicked into her business mode, blocking everything out but the job. "Katharine, you'll stay hidden until the wedding party is in place. Then, take your spot in front of the doors. I'll have ushers here to open both sets, and we'll have our money shot."

"Perfect." Katharine looked at Joe, but Holly noticed his gaze was somewhere in the distance.

"Any questions?" Holly asked. When no one responded with more than a polite shake of the head, she said, "Okay, then. Let's try this all the way through. If we get it first time, we'll break for dinner early!"

When they'd finished the run-through, Holly left Joe and Katharine smiling and chatting with their friends. She'd opted not to attend the rehearsal dinner. Sitting next to Joe while his best man toasted his new life with Katharine was about as comfortable for Holly as taking a stroll on hot coals. Plus, she had to head back to Nana's house in Nashville to get the things she needed to finish packing for California tomorrow.

She decided that she should probably call Joe to let him know her plan not to stay for the wedding ceremony. And after a lot of thought, she decided that it might also be a good time to mention the emails. He deserved to be a part of the conversation, and, at this point, it was pretty clear by the mention of Rona's that 786@hb.com was a credible source. She'd never forgive herself if she could've gotten Joe and his dad together and hadn't because she'd withheld the correspondence she'd received.

She hoped that Joe was okay with her leaving before the end of the ceremony. Rhett had got them a flight for one thirty tomorrow. Holly did a quick mental rundown of the timeline: she wanted to be at the airport a couple of hours early—to get a bite to eat and sit for a little while before the madness of travel across the country set in. Once the wedding started at eleven, she'd only stay for a half an hour before she had the perfect excuse to leave. With her duties done, she could allow the estate staff to take over, just as Joe had told her they would. It would give her just enough time to get the wedding going, and everyone would be too wrapped up in the ceremony to notice her leaving.

She'd told Rhett to pick her bags up at Nana's and to be outside the mansion by eleven fifteen—she'd give the guard his name to let him in once they closed the gates of the estate at the start of the ceremony. Then she'd be off to a whole new life, a new year ahead of her.

❄

Holly lay on the bed where Joe had stayed. She had changed the sheets earlier and dusted, not a single reminder of him remaining. With the rehearsal dinner probably over by now, she sent him a text, asking if he was free to call her. He texted her right back and told her to give him five minutes and he'd call.

While she waited, she went over different scenarios of how the conversation would play out. She didn't want to build up his hopes if this didn't amount to anything. The person contacting them might not have a clue where Harvey was right now. But something in her gut told Holly to tell Joe everything.

Her phone rang.

"Hello?" she answered.

"Hi." Joe's voice gave her a rush of comfort.

"Hey, I need to talk about the wedding, but first I have some news to share with you," she said, jumping right in.

"Oh?"

"Before I tell you, though, I need to ask you something."

"Okay."

She steadied herself and closed her eyes, nervous to bring it up. "Does Rona's have anything to do with your dad?"

Joe didn't answer at first, and Holly hung on every minute of silence. "Why?" he finally asked.

"Tell me first," she pressed gently.

He cleared his throat. "It's where my mother used to meet my father for coffee. It's where they fell in love."

"I think I found someone who knows your dad," she blurted, not wanting to think about the reasons he'd told her about the café but hadn't mentioned it to Katharine. If there was some sort of cosmic reason for him telling her, it was so that she could help him find his father. Holly could feel it in her bones.

"What?" he said, surprised. "How?"

"Someone responded to your Facebook post I shared. They sent me an email."

"What did it say?" He sounded breathless, and Holly could feel his need to know about his father coming through in his question. She was willing to bet it had eaten him up over the years and he hadn't let anyone know.

"Not a lot. It was cryptic...Is your birthday July eighth?"

"Yes."

"Nineteen eighty-six?"

"Yes, why? What did it say, Holly?" His voice was soft but urgent.

"Oh my gosh..." She clapped a hand over her mouth. "I think I might have been talking to your dad. His email was 786@hb.com. Think about it." When he didn't say anything, she added, "He told me to ask you about Rona's. That's how you'd know his message was legit."

She could hear his breathing—slow, deep breaths like he always did—and she cupped her phone against her ear with both hands, wishing she could hug him.

Finally, he said, "Send him a message. Tell him to come to the wedding tomorrow. I want him there."

"What if he's far away?"

"I haven't asked him for anything in my whole life. Except this. See what he says."

"Okay." She bit her lip. "I'll text you as soon as I get a response."

"What else were you going to tell me?"

"Hm?" She'd forgotten the other reason for the call, talking to Joe, their solidarity in this, the softness of his voice . . . She'd lost track of the rest of her thoughts.

"You wanted to tell me something about the wedding."

Oh! No . . . What if Harvey said he could come to the wedding? What if he actually showed up? How terrible would Holly look if she went sprinting out of the building without even a care about Joe's reunion with his father? That would be just awful. Joe had confided in her; they'd done this together. She couldn't just leave . . .

But she needed to be honest with him. As honest as she could be without ruining everything. "You'd said the staff will take over once the ceremony has started, right?"

"Yes. You won't have to do anything more once you've gotten us down the aisle."

"I wasn't planning to stay for the whole wedding. I'm leaving a little earlier than expected for California. But if Harvey does show up—"

"No, no, no," he cut her off. "Please. Don't change your plans for me." He said the words, but she could swear she heard disappointment in them and it made her feel terribly guilty. But how was she supposed to know he might need her?

Stop, she told herself. Joe had Katharine for support. Holly being at this wedding was only a favor she'd agreed to, and she had the rest of her life in front of her, starting with that plane ride with Rhett. Joe hadn't stopped his life for her and she needed to press on as well. But it didn't stop the way she felt...

"Joe," she said.

"Please," he said as if he knew her thoughts. "Go. Follow your heart."

Did he *want* her to go?

"All right," she said, resolving to make the most of things. That was what Joe wanted for her and she knew he was right.

Chapter Thirty-Two

Holly replied to the mystery emailer, inviting Harvey to the wedding. She gave the location, the time, and she even put his name on the guest list, but she hadn't heard back—nothing. When she texted Joe the update early this morning, he thanked her for trying and told her he'd see her in a few hours.

She was extra emotional telling Nana goodbye today when she was leaving to pick up Katharine's dress from Shimmer to take to the estate. With her bags packed and sitting by the door, the room seemed empty. Holly had never left her grandmother alone before. With the rental schedule clear for the foreseeable future, this would be the first time Nana had lived by herself, and Holly worried about her.

"Do you have enough here at the cabin to entertain yourself without me being here?" Holly asked.

"Of course I do. I haven't been able to just do what I want without consideration for anyone else in my entire life. I might blast the music and dance around the house for all you know."

Holly laughed, in spite of her intense fear of leaving Nana by herself.

"And worst case, I have *War and Peace*."

Nana seemed to be taking Holly's leaving very well, but Holly wasn't. Not sure if she'd suppressed her sadness over Joe's wedding, if she worried about him not connecting with his father, if she was concerned about traveling with Rhett, or if she still fretted over Nana—maybe it was all of it—but she'd sobbed on her grandmother's shoulder when she had to leave her for the wedding.

Holly was confident, though, that Nana would be taken care of. Kay said she'd stop by this evening, and Tammy was going to get groceries and bring them to the cabin weekly. Otis and Buddy both promised to visit every couple of days. She'd be okay.

With great strength, Holly stopped herself from blubbering and powdered her nose. Then, she headed out to go to Shimmer and then the wedding. It was the final time she'd face Joe before they parted ways for good, and she was ready.

When Holly arrived at the estate, she was the only one there. She delicately hung the dress up next to the full-length mirror in Katharine's bridal suite and then went to check that everything was in order. The portrait was on the easel already, and it was absolutely stunning. Holly honed in on Katharine's face, and her expression had been captured beautifully. She had a sort of tamed innocence to her smile in that moment, unlike any that Holly had seen from her, and it seemed she was as nervous and happy as any bride-to-be. Just lovely.

As the team entered, she was able to greet them with a confident smile, despite her state of mind. Katharine had flown in to the estate in a flurry of people, her bridesmaids all chatting around her, garment bags and shoe boxes in their hands, whisking her off to the bridal suite. Holly straightened the guestbook on the table in the entryway as she watched them go.

Not long after, the groomsmen came in with Joe, laughing at something and clapping his back. He was still in his plain clothes, the way she'd seen him at the cabin, and she felt a surge of fear at the idea that these were her final moments with Joe. She'd readied herself for it, she'd made plans to avoid most of it, but none of it prepared her for the way she felt right now, seeing him. Holly sank into the background to let him pass, her gaze on him. He was talking with one of the men, but then slowed and looked around. He found Holly with his eyes and broke into an enormous smile when he saw her, warm and friendly, simultaneously making her heart ache to have more time with him and giving her an overwhelming flow of emotion that he'd thought to look for her. He waved. She used all of her strength to smile back and then submerged herself in wedding details.

It took Holly a while to get herself to a point where she was confident she had her feelings in check. Once she'd finished the final preparations, and every last task was complete, the venue a picture of perfection, Holly went to the back room where the bridesmaids and bride were gathered. Katharine was in her dress, one of the bridesmaids finishing the buttons at the back. Holly was able to really notice her hair this time. It was swept into an up-do, but today it wasn't so perfect. It had a romantic, flowing quality to it, small wisps falling around her face, accentuating her eyes and milky complexion.

Katharine turned around to view her reflection in the mirror as her father came in, wearing a pressed tuxedo and shiny shoes, doting adoration on his face. Tears filled his eyes as he surveyed his daughter and the splendor of the white satin that cascaded to the floor in one perfect, seamless line. Katharine stared at the dress just long enough that Holly wondered if she was thinking back to the day they'd had the final fitting. Katharine noticed her in the mirror and snapped out of whatever her thoughts had been. She smiled at Holly, her eyebrows raised as if to say, "Here we are!"

"You look gorgeous," Holly said.

Katharine turned around. "Thank you." She fluffed her dress so she wouldn't step on it when she walked.

"Almost time," Holly said, putting on a good front. She kept thinking how she only had a few more minutes and then she could get on with her life. But right now, she felt like she'd been holding her breath all morning, and the minute she got into Rhett's truck, she'd gasp and pant for air.

Holly hadn't seen Joe in his tuxedo yet, and she thought she should peek in on him next to be sure he had everything he needed, like a regular wedding planner would do, but she'd been prolonging the moment. She also kept checking her phone, hoping she had a message, since no one had shown up on the guest list under the name Harvey Barnes. Her email had been silent. She wished things could've been different. Perhaps Harvey was somewhere across the world with spotty cell service, and he'd lost connection. Or maybe he just decided not to come…

She still wasn't ready to see Joe yet. He'd come get her if he needed her, she decided. "I'll do a quick sweep outside to make sure that everyone is in the grand hall now and ready to go," she told Katharine. "We don't want anyone coming in during the big two-door reveal, do we?"

"Great idea to check."

"Be right back." Holly turned on her cell phone to view the hour. "We'll start in just a sec." Then she left to do a final look around the grounds to ensure there weren't any stragglers.

The musicians were playing the instrumental seating music right on time, and the final arrivals were taking their seats, thanks to the ushers. Holly opened the double doors to outside and stepped under the portico, putting her hand on her forehead to shield her eyes from the light, making certain that everyone was inside prior to beginning the processional. The good news was that at eleven o'clock, they would close the gates to the property and no one but authorized personnel would be allowed to enter after that. The last thing they needed was someone clattering through those large hallways, echoing across them to their seats. Once the ceremony was over, the staff would reopen the gates for the reception.

She looked out at the clear blue sky above them, the sunlight nearly blinding. But then confusion snaked through her when she saw an elderly man sitting on the bench under the maple tree. Everyone else was inside. Had he lost his way? Wouldn't he have come with someone who could've helped him inside? Or...It couldn't be...Holly started walking toward him and he stood up, facing her. He wasn't senile or lost—it was clear by his expression that he was perfectly coherent. There was something undeniably recognizable about him, but she couldn't place it.

"Hello," she said, every inch of her on high alert.

The man dipped his head toward her once to acknowledge her greeting.

"Are you here for the Harrison-Barnes wedding?"

His mouth opened as if he was going to say something, but the words never came. Finally, he nodded. Holly stared at his face, and the more she looked at him, the more she could feel something different about this man. He wasn't just someone coming to the wedding. There was so much emotion in his face that he seemed like he might burst.

"Please, come inside. The ceremony is about to begin."

His gaze shifted from Holly to the doors, but when his eyes landed back on Holly, that was when she figured it out: that familiar thing...It was the same curiosity she'd seen before, and her blood ran cold because she knew now without a shadow of a doubt who he was. She searched the man's tanned face, that eye for detail of hers on overdrive, and the closer she got to him, the more she could tell exactly who he looked like. The man had a small birthmark on his upper right cheekbone, and Holly stared at it for the longest time before she remembered, her mouth nearly dropping open. That wasn't a watermark on Joe's photo.

Cautiously, she decided to try the name to see his reaction. "Harvey Barnes?"

The man's eyes grew round and he stiffened at the mention of it, and it was then that Holly knew a miracle was happening right in front of her.

"Come inside," she directed him.

The man shook his head and began to walk away.

Panic shot through Holly. She couldn't let him go. No one had been able to find him; they'd lose him again. "Wait!" Holly started after him, panicked, her heels wobbling against the uneven ground, her arms shivering with no coat. She chased after him across the lawn, finally grabbing his arm.

He turned around.

"Wait." She was quieter now, almost whispering, her breath coming out in exerted puffs. "Joe *wants* to see you. He asked you to attend his wedding. You're here. Why won't you come inside?"

That curiosity that she knew so well turned to intense interest, the old man's resolve nearly faltering before he regained composure and started to walk away again. "I've changed my mind," he mumbled, fear in his gaze as he looked over his shoulder at her.

"Don't go," Holly pleaded, her voice cracking, her eyes filling with tears, surprising her *and* him, but he kept going.

In that moment, she realized Joe had done so much for her. He taught her what she wanted in a partner, what it felt like to be with someone she truly cared about, he helped Nana through the pain of Christmas without Papa, and he gave Holly the opportunity to realize she could use her talents and change her future. This was her chance to give him something in return and she was going to fight to do that. All she wanted was to make Joe happy.

"Please!" she said, a sob welling up. She swallowed it down and took in a deep breath.

Harvey stopped, clearly to find out the reason for her emotion.

But right at that moment, Rhett pulled up and honked the horn lightly, waving to her.

Oh God. What time was it? The musicians were probably improvising by now. She had to get the wedding started. She waved at Rhett, but all her energy was going to Harvey Barnes. She walked up to him. "Please. Come in and sit in the back. Watch your son get married. He deserves to have his father at his wedding. I know how much he wants you there. He told me himself. That's the least you could do."

The old man seemed taken aback by her statement, but at the same time, the truth was evident on his face, and he dropped eye contact in shame. In that moment, he looked broken and sad.

"Don't go anywhere," she told him and then Holly ran over to Rhett.

Rhett put the window down, the truck purring.

"Can you just wait for me? This might take a little longer than I expected. I need to help this man inside."

"I have two hot coffees to get us through until we can

grab lunch together," he said with excitement, pointing his thumb in the direction of the cup holder in the center console. "Don't take so long they get cold!" Holly knew that as eager as he was to get the trip under way, he was going to be impatient.

"I'll try not to."

When she got back to the man, she was delighted to find he'd stayed put. Gently, she took him by the arm and led him inside. He followed hesitantly. She took him into the entryway and tugged the enormous door shut and led him across the shiny floors to the grand hall to find him a seat. As expected, the musicians were still playing, but their eyes, full of questions, found Holly. She nodded for them to keep going as she sat Harvey down.

"You can sit right here," she said. "Please stay. Joe can't wait to meet you." Then she quietly let herself out and sprinted down the hallway to the groom's quarters, bursting through the door.

Joe turned around and stopped Holly in her tracks. He looked incredible in his tuxedo. His hair was perfectly combed, his face clean-shaven. She'd never seen anyone so handsome in all her life, and just seeing him like that made the loop in her mind start again, tearing her heart out. He stood, alone in the room, his hands in his pockets, with a worried look. "What's going on?" he asked.

Holly muscled her way through her memories to answer. "Your dad's outside."

"What?" His face crumpled in disbelief.

"I'm not kidding." Holly stepped in front of him and looked up to meet his eyes, the intoxicating scent of him making her want to run right now and get into Rhett's truck before she completely fell apart, but she knew this was too important. She had to push past her feelings and make sure this meeting happened.

Joe put his hands on her arms tenderly and she almost crumpled to the floor. "Holly," he said sweetly. "How can you be sure?"

"He acknowledged that he was Harvey Barnes, but he didn't have to. He has your eyes," she said, tears starting to brim in her own. "He looks so much like you, Joe. He was sitting on a bench outside, planning to attend the wedding, in the freezing cold. I wonder if he's scared you won't forgive him."

Joe took in a breath, his chest filling with air. He began to pace the room. "Will you make an announcement and tell everyone the wedding will begin shortly? Tell Katharine...something. And then bring him to me? I can't wait until after the wedding."

"I'll have the ushers pass out glasses of wine and I'll tell the musicians to keep playing."

He nodded, his anxiety over seeing his father for the first time in his life evidently making him speechless.

"What do I tell Katharine?"

His jaw clenched in thought. "Uh. Tell her that I've had an unexpected arrival from out of town and we want to be sure he's comfortable before we start the wedding."

"You still haven't told her about your dad?"

"Holly," he said in that way of his, the word breathy and sweet, making the hair on her arms stand up.

"Okay. I'll think of something."

On the way down the hallway, Holly's phone pinged with a text. She looked down at it: *Hey! You coming?*

Rhett.

She tapped her screen, her feet moving at a record pace. *I'll be there soon. I promise. Just keep the car and the coffee warm for me.*

He responded: *I'm gonna drink your coffee if you don't hurry.*

Holly slipped her phone into her pocket. She found Katharine waiting with her bridesmaids in the room, an apprehensive look on her face.

"Sorry," Holly said, coming in. "A relative of Joe's is here from very far away—Joe never expected him to come. They haven't seen each other...Um. Anyway, Joe wants to be sure the man is comfortable before we start the wedding, and he's delighted that his...relative will be able to watch you two walk down the aisle."

Katharine assessed Holly skeptically, uncertainty filling those big eyes of hers, and Holly felt like she was in the center of a courtroom.

She walked over to Katharine. "It's a big deal," she said honestly. "I'm sure Joe will fill you in as soon as he can, and the wedding will go off as planned. I'm telling everyone we're just taking a bit to get started. The ushers are going to hand out drinks to keep them occupied."

Katharine pulled herself together and regained her poise. "Don't let him take too long," she said. "I'd hate to make everyone wait."

"Okay. Be back to get you."

Then Holly ran back down the hallway. There was a low buzz across the crowd when she made the announcement, and the ushers sprang into frenzied action the moment she offered everyone wine.

Relieved to find Harvey still there, she rushed over to him.

"Joe wants to see you," she said to him quietly as everyone began chatting and peering at their programs. Unwilling to wait for him to make a decision, Holly took him by the hand and headed toward Joe's room.

Chapter Thirty-Three

Holly didn't give Harvey any time to contemplate the situation before she opened the door to the room where Joe was waiting. The old man stared at his son from the doorway, unmoving. Holly felt Harvey trembling and just noticed that she was still holding his arm. Emotion had taken over his entire body and tears brimmed in his eyes as he took in the sight of his only family. Joe didn't move.

Slowly, Holly urged Harvey forward, walking him in and shutting the door.

"I've seen you," Joe said. "You spend time at the sandwich shop I go to on my lunch hour sometimes. You always say hello."

Harvey acknowledged him. "I wanted to be near you," he finally said, and Holly noted how much his voice sounded like Joe's.

Joe nodded as if he'd wondered before about the man he'd seen in the shop. "You're gone for long periods of time and then you just show up again, and I'll see you for a couple of weeks." Joe was cautious, not taking too large a step toward his father, his eyes intense. "Where do you go?"

"I live in a little fishing village on the coast of Mexico, but I come back to check on you, make sure you're doing okay."

Joe cut his eyes at Harvey. "Why?" His anger came out in the word. "You abandoned me and my mother."

Holly let go of Harvey and stood next to Joe, feeling the need to give him her emotional support like he'd done for her those times back at the cabin. While he was keeping himself in check and his exterior was calm, she could sense the years of frustration and resentment surfacing in his words. He'd brought it on himself by not telling anyone about his missing father, but this wasn't something he should face alone. He looked down at her before returning to his original question.

"I loved your mother," Harvey said.

"The hell you did."

Harvey wiped a tear away quickly. "Son." Harvey took a step toward him. "I didn't have the upbringing that you did. My parents weren't loving people; I hardly knew them. I spent most of my time with nannies, and a lot of them weren't very nice."

"None of that excuses what you did. You *left* us."

Harvey's eyes hit the floor and stayed there as he continued to try to explain. "When your mom told me she was pregnant, I panicked." He looked Joe in the eyes then. "I knew two things without a doubt: the first was that your mother would make the very best mom. I had no doubt in her ability to love, and in her kindness. But the second thing I knew was that I wasn't good enough to be a father to you. I'd never had anyone show me how. I envisioned that you would be this perfect infant when you were born, so pure and lovely—I didn't want to ruin you by screwing up your life the way my parents had done to me."

He sat down on a bench near the door, his knees trembling. "I sold everything and cashed out my accounts. I gave your mother money for herself and for you, and I took the rest to Mexico, as far as I could get, so I wouldn't interfere in your life. That was the best I could give you: my money. I have a friend I keep in touch with and, after I left, I made him swear not to tell your mother he knew where I was. When he told me your mom passed away three years ago, I came back to make sure you were okay..."

"I didn't need a perfect dad," Joe said. "I just needed someone to be there."

"I was—"

"Someone to count on."

"I know." Harvey hung his head. "When I got old enough to realize that, I thought it was too late, and you'd never forgive me."

Joe didn't speak. Holly knew that Harvey had said that in hopes Joe would actually forgive him, and she hoped he would. He didn't need to hold on to old anger. Harvey was trying to support Joe in the best way he knew how. Joe just needed to show him what to do.

Suddenly, Holly's phone rang in her pocket, slicing through the moment. She silenced it quickly. It was most certainly Rhett, waiting for her outside. Joe looked at her. Then finally he spoke to Harvey. "We don't have to do this now. Stay. We can talk later." And she could tell by his tone that forgiveness had begun to surface.

Holly looked at her watch: eleven thirty. "Joe's right. The guests have been waiting a half hour. We need to get started." She went over to Harvey. "I'll show you back to your seat. Joe, head to the ceremony and take your place."

But just as she was about to open the door, there was a knock. Carefully, in case it was Katharine, so Joe wouldn't see her before the wedding or it would be bad luck, Holly cracked the door and peered out of it. But it wasn't Katharine. Instead, she found Rhett, holding two coffee cups. "These are empty," he said, and she opened the door wider. "I drank them both. You're the one who told me to be here. Is everything okay? We have a plane to catch."

Holly turned protectively toward Joe, praying he didn't find her or Rhett insensitive. That was not at all the reason for her leaving now. She took in those intense eyes of Joe's, his broad shoulders, the way his lips were parted just so as he watched Rhett, and she knew that it would take her a very long time to get over him.

"I'll go now," Joe said, only half looking her in the eyes. "Just get Katharine to the doors and you can leave for your flight. We'll be fine." Then he leaned a little to view Rhett better. "I'm sorry I kept her," he said. Without another word, Joe left through the door at the back of the room, taking Holly's heart with him.

He didn't have to be sorry. It was his wedding and Rhett was being impetuous. Although, in Rhett's defense, he had no idea what was going on.

"Rhett, it's my fault," Holly said over her shoulder. She'd walked past him and was now hurrying down the hallway with Harvey, Rhett in tow. "Hang out to the side here and I'll be there as soon as I can. I'll explain everything on the way to the airport." She peeked into Katharine's room and gave her the thumbs up and the bride began to make her way to her place out of view. The bridesmaids started to take their spots along with the groomsmen who'd assembled with them. That was when Holly realized Joe had been alone when she'd found him.

"Why weren't you all with Joe?" she asked one of them.

"He had asked us to give him a minute," one of the

groomsmen said. "So we all came down here. Is everything all right?"

"Yes," Holly assured them. Perhaps he'd needed some time for reflection. And he didn't seem to be too big on crowds.

By the time she seated Harvey, the guests had already perked up because Joe had taken his spot. Katharine was waiting for her go-ahead and Holly cued the musicians and they began the intro for the wedding party. The parents of the ring bearer and the flower girl were there and waiting, and the children started down the aisle. Two by two, the bridal couples made their way until the ushers shut the doors, and it was time for Katharine's appearance. Holly ran quickly and signaled the staff to open the front doors of the estate.

"This is it," she said to Katharine, forcing a smile and handing Katharine her bouquet. *This was it* in so many ways…Holly fluffed out Katharine's train and straightened it along the floor. Katharine gave her a nervous but grateful nod.

The bridal music started, and the ushers opened the doors, the guests all gasping and getting to their feet at the sight of Katharine. Stepping perfectly in time to the bridal march, Katharine made her way down the aisle toward Joe, and Holly felt like the air was being sucked out of the room.

It all felt so wrong. Her heart broke. She turned away, unable to handle it, not wanting that image in her memory.

While all eyes were on Katharine, Holly quickly grabbed Rhett's hand and rushed toward the front door away from Joe.

✳

After a sprint through the Nashville Airport, the race to the gate had been a blur. They had to stop quite a few times for Rhett to have pictures taken and sign autographs, and if Holly looked past him across the aisle, she was nearly certain a profile shot of him was being uploaded on Instagram at this very moment.

"We're third in line for takeoff, folks," the captain's voice came through the speakers of the plane. "This flight has service to Denver with continuation to Los Angeles. Hope to have you in the air shortly. Looks like a smooth ride today; the weather is clear, so we should have you on the ground in Denver in two hours and fifty-five minutes. We'll get the beverage service going once we're in the air. Thank you for flying with us today."

Holly pushed her carry-on bag under her seat with her foot as the plane began its journey down the runway. With the holiday, options had been limited and, on such short notice, Rhett had only been able to get them business class seats. He didn't seem to mind, though. He wriggled excitedly next to her, completely oblivious to the gawkers, his eyebrows raised and a goofy grin on his face, making her laugh—she was happy for that. She explained about Joe's father on the way, and apologized for making Rhett wait, but he'd been over it before they'd even hit the road, offering to get her another coffee at the airport. Holly didn't want to prolong the conversation anyway, because it was time to start a fresh chapter of her life.

But it must have been on his mind longer than she'd thought because, once they were in the air, he said, "Tell me seriously, you really didn't have the hots for that guy?"

For a second, Holly battled the urge to hide the truth, but then it occurred to her that Rhett had been very honest with her the whole holiday. Now, with no way to ruin anything for Joe, she finally admitted it. "I really liked him."

"I knew it." He looked past her through the window, over the wing of the plane. "You're so easy to read."

Following that comment, she wondered now if Joe had also known her feelings. "It hurt to see him marry Katharine," she confessed. After all, Rhett had been the one person she'd told these kinds of things to, growing up.

"You'll get over it," he said, and she was surprisingly annoyed by the way he brushed it off as if her feelings for Joe meant nothing. But she knew that it was because his jealousy was surfacing.

"How do you know?" she asked, irritated, and her eyes met his. "You've probably never been hurt like that, and you never will, given who you are."

"What's that supposed to mean?" he asked quietly.

"You're Rhett Burton, Mr. Nice Guy, the sensitive song-writer. Who would want to hurt you?"

"That's not true. You act like being a singer entitles me to some kind of perfect life. Well, it doesn't. Why do you think I came back home?"

"Why *did* you come back?" she asked, her interest over-powering her frustration over his lack of sensitivity.

"I met someone after I left. She lives in Nashville—a singer, struggling to make it in the business. We dated seri-ously, and it ended badly. She cheated on me," he said in almost an inaudible whisper. Holly could see the shock still there as he said it. Rhett could be a handful at times, but one thing that was always true about him was his honesty. He'd never cheat on someone, so Holly could only imagine the complete disbelief he probably had when someone had betrayed him that way.

"That was when I knew that the price I pay for fame is not being able to trust anyone. I feared it before I even left, and that just sealed the deal. She was with me for my name and my face, not for who I am. It was terrifying." He looked out at the clouds as they billowed past them through the window. "After that, I bought the land in Leiper's Fork. I didn't want to live anywhere but home. Home is where the real people are, the ones who know me best. Right before I went out on the road, I started to have feelings for you. But after that breakup, that was when I *knew* that you were the one for me."

Holly let this new information sink in, processing it. "So I'm the one for you because some woman in Nashville cheated on you? I don't follow."

"That's not it, Holly. All I'm saying is if you and I were together, I'd know that you were with me because you love *me*, not the guy on stage every night. I know I can trust it."

The flight attendant came and took their drink orders. Still thinking about what Rhett had said, Holly ordered a Coke. The attendant handed her a small bag of peanuts, but they sat unopened on Holly's tray. All her energy and focus was on Rhett right now, her skin prickling with unease. She shook her head, everything becoming clear. "Rhett, we had an almost-kiss right before you left and you keep trying... But it isn't right and you know it." She twisted toward him, taking his hand, looking around to make sure she wouldn't be on the headlines tomorrow. Instagram Girl was reading her book, thank goodness.

"I *don't* know it... I have no idea why you think it isn't right," he said.

"Yes, I think you do. You just don't want to admit it."

The attendant returned and held out a white napkin with a small cup of Coke, the fizz popping against the ice cubes. Holly took it and set it down, only half acknowledging the attendant with a smile, still engrossed in her conversation with Rhett.

"We're best friends," she reminded him. "But you're not in love with me...You're just scared to take another chance. Because it hurts to be let down." She knew that from experience. "But you can't hold on to the past and run away from life just so you won't get hurt again."

Rhett leaned his head back against the seat, thinking. She wasn't entirely sure he believed what she said. But Holly knew she was right. And in that moment, Holly realized she was ready to live life as if she'd never suffered a broken heart before. The only way to do anything was to go into it full steam ahead without any reservations. She wanted to have stories to tell Papa when they met again— he'd be asking.

It was time to make herself a life with no regrets, and she was going to start right now.

Chapter Thirty-Four

One Year Later, Christmas

New York was so different from where Holly had lived most of her life. She'd spent the last twelve months traveling, only a week of those twelve months with Rhett. It had only taken that week for him to see that they were better as friends. On their last night traveling together, they'd had a long talk about it, and she'd never forget what he said.

"I think the closeness you and I had confused me for a while there," he told her. "I love you so much." He flashed that contagious smile. "It's unlike any love I've ever had. It's different than the way I love Mama or your papa or even old ex-girlfriends. When I find the words to describe it, I'm gonna write a song about it."

She reached across the table and took his hand, never feeling closer to him than she had in that moment.

"Our week together, away from all the noise from people, our past, expectations, everything that surrounded us, brought a lot of clarity for me; it gave me a chance to sift through what I want from you and me together. And I know now that the two of us are better off as friends. I just want you to be happy."

Before she left for her flight the next day, he'd given her another kiss, but this time it was on the top of her head. Then he put two fingers to his eyes and then pointed at hers. "My world," he said. "It's good."

As she headed out the door, she turned around one last time. "Hey," she called to him before tossing a tin through the air. Rhett caught it and looked down at the tobacco container in his hand. "I checked with Buddy. That's his kind."

That was when Rhett ran over and hugged her.

Holly decided to use some of the money Papa left her and go out on her own, traveling all over the US and Europe. But she'd saved the one place she'd always wanted to go for last.

She still thought about Joe. She hadn't heard from him at all, but she hadn't reached out either. It would just be too hard to stay in touch. And she'd considered going home to be around family, but Holly wanted to be isolated for a while to find herself, so she could ponder her true desires in life. She hadn't even told Nana about traveling solo during their weekly calls.

While traveling, Holly decided to start her own design firm, specializing in restoration and upcycling of family heirlooms. She thought about wedding planning, but decided she'd like to use her talents in a quieter line of work. She'd done a few decorating jobs already across the country. She met with the client to get a feel for how they wanted the pieces incorporated in her design of the room.

One of her customers in Seattle asked her to completely repurpose an old trunk as the shell of a farmhouse-style kitchen sink. They'd built rustic legs on it, drilled holes for piping and the sink itself, and refinished it to a distressed but highly clear-lacquered shine. Then they dropped a porcelain sink into it and finished it with brush nickel taps and a granite counter on top. With a jar of wildflowers next to the tap, it was magazine photo material. That had been her most favorite project so far.

There wasn't anything quite like Holly's business in Nashville, and she knew that there would be a market for it. She planned to start small, with a clean and simple website, only doing a few choice projects that really inspired her. She put the photos of the jobs she'd done so far on her page and her new email address she'd opened was already filling up with requests, so she made a questionnaire to send out to help her choose which project to do. The first question was, "Is there a particular piece you'd like to incorporate? Tell me its story and how it inspires you." That was what she'd finally understood about Papa. He hadn't ever chased the money or The Big Deal because in the small things, he was inspired, and that was what life was all about. As he said, he'd never worked a day in his life. That was because he'd spent his whole professional life in a dream, just like she was now. She couldn't imagine anything better.

She also wanted to share all that wonderful furniture from her childhood. Memories like that shouldn't be piled up in a barn. She planned to refinish a few more pieces of Papa's furniture when she got home, presenting them as one-of-a-kind design options, and she was going to offer free one-room furniture placement consultations in the Nashville area to ensure their best placement. She couldn't wait to see Papa's furniture in their new homes be a part of another generation making family memories.

Holly couldn't wait to tell Nana about it all, but not from New York. She'd postpone the news until they were together.

"Rhett called," Nana said through the phone as Holly sipped her White Chocolate Peppermint latte and took in the view of the New York City street outside from Rona's. People bustled by with their holiday packages, their boots and winter shoes clipping along at a hurried pace, while the snow fell around them.

"I figured Rhett would call you for Christmas," she said to Nana, holding her warm cup in one hand and her phone in the other.

"He says you two went your separate ways."

"Yes." Holly peered down at her coffee. The bells on the door jingled, announcing another patron's entrance. She didn't look up, her mind on the call. "We'll always be best friends, Nana, but I needed some time to myself."

"I know, child."

"He knows I love him, and he promised he'd call me after the tour."

"I'm sure he will." Holly could almost feel Nana's smile coming through the line. "When are you flying in?"

"This afternoon. My flight's at three o'clock." She pulled her phone from her ear to view the time and then came back to the call. "That's four hours. I'll be back at the cabin for Christmas, just like I promised."

"Ah, my girl's coming back home. Finally. I can't wait to see you."

"I can't wait to see you either! Is everyone coming—the whole family?"

"Yes. They should be arriving any minute. I've got the house full of food!"

"I'm so excited! I'll call you once I land in Nashville, okay?"

"All right, dear."

It would be nice to see a familiar face. Holly had spent a whole week alone in New York, seeing the sights, but this morning, she'd wavered in her resolve and found Rona's café near Times Square, the one that Joe mentioned all those nights ago. She still had the print that he'd gotten at the gallery—she packed it before leaving with Rhett, and she carried it in her suitcase the whole time.

The café was a cozy little spot, tucked away just enough from the busy street that she could warm herself by the small fire, sip her coffee, and read a book but still have quite a view through the large picture window framed in thick Christmas garlands. The inviting and relaxed ambiance was right up her alley, and she knew why Joe had thought she'd enjoy it. It was like a little slice of home right in the center of the city. She could just imagine his parents talking over steaming mugs, their eyes having silent conversations, the two of them lingering because neither wanted to leave . . . It was that kind of atmosphere.

Perhaps one day she'd be lucky enough to find a second person that could light up her day the way Joe could—that was the thought that kept her warm on those cold nights, even though she didn't always believe it could happen. Joe was uniquely wonderful, and chances of finding someone who could even come close to the way he made her feel seemed impossible.

If life were like the movies, he'd come bursting through the door, wrap her in his arms and walk with her into their happy ending, but, as she looked around at all the unfamiliar faces, she knew that wasn't how things really went. And that was okay. She wished nothing but happiness for Joe and hoped he'd found his soul mate in Katharine. And she wondered how things were going with Harvey. Had they come to terms with the past and started to build a future as father and son? She hoped so.

Being alone for this long had taught Holly to cherish her time with family, and she was so excited to get back to Nana. Nana told her that Otis was having his usual gathering for Christmas Eve tomorrow. Holly would get to see Tammy and Kay, Buddy, and all their other friends who were like family to her, and her own family was coming, thanks to Nana's invite. Her mom, dad, sister Alicia, her husband Carlos, and little Emma would all be there.

Holly was ready to get back to the life she knew so well. She'd miss having Rhett there this year, but she was sure that he'd return home, and in a matter of time, he'd be with them again on Christmas like he always had. They'd grown so close—their friendship was so much stronger with all their thoughts now out in the open. They were better than they'd ever been. She wished he could be there this year. But he was following his heart, living his dream, and he was where he was meant to be.

With the New York City snow starting to fall more heavily, Holly finished her coffee, tucked her book back into her bag, and walked out into the beautiful Christmas chaos that only a city like that could provide. She meandered down side streets until she got to Rockefeller Center where she took her last look at the Christmas tree as it dazzled passers-by. Then, when she felt like she was finally ready to leave, Holly hailed a taxi for the airport.

❄

The flight into Nashville had been relatively uneventful, but Holly felt the sleepiness that travel caused washing over her. It had been a long year. She dropped her bags off at the cabin. The smell of Nana's cooking, all her family's bags tucked in every free spot, and Emma's toys nearly bringing her to tears. She took a quick shower to get the airport exhaustion off her. Then she dressed herself in a new outfit she'd bought in New York and headed to Otis's barn to see Nana and her family.

With everyone from town in attendance this year, it was quite a crowd at Otis's. She scanned the faces for Nana, waving to people as she searched. Kay hugged her, and little Hattie, the kitten, ran by with a jingle bell around her neck.

"Looking for me?" Nana said from behind.

Holly turned and threw her arms around her grandmother, breathing in the scent of her, the comfort of home so strong that she didn't know if she could ever leave again. It had taken time away to really appreciate what Holly had there and she knew now that this was exactly where she belonged. While it wasn't the happy ending of movies, it was real and it was wonderful. And it was hers.

"Everyone's been waiting for you," Nana said, pulling back to offer Holly the most gorgeous smile she'd seen Nana produce in years. "Turn around."

Holly followed Nana's gaze and squealed at the sight of Alicia, Carlos, Emma, and Holly's parents all grinning at her. Emma ran over to her and embraced her middle. "You're getting tall, Emma!" she said, fighting back the tears. Holly greeted each of her family members with a giant hug, so thrilled they were all there.

"Want to head over to a table?" Nana suggested. "My feet are killing me."

They all settled in, and Holly noticed the quiet that descended upon them.

"I have a surprise for you," Nana said.

And then, when she thought she couldn't be any happier, a familiar first chord rang out on the stage, demanding her attention. Holly threw her hands up to her gaping mouth just as Kay grabbed an empty seat beside her, Hattie in her lap.

"He got himself two days off just to come." Kay put her arm around Holly's shoulder.

Rhett had changed the words to the song they'd started last Christmas, the one with the lyrics "she's gone." This time, he sang, "*She's gone but she's with me everywhere I go. On the road, in those cold hotels, her smile lingers. My best friend, my girl.*" He winked at her. She used his old gesture and pointed two fingers at her eyes and then at his as a sign of their unity as friends and his new promise to always be there for her.

When everyone had settled into quiet chatter, Rhett started to play a new song about love and soul mates. "Holly, come up here," he called into the microphone between lyrics. She wondered what he was doing. It was all a little reminiscent of the last time he'd professed his love to her, and she hesitated, not sure of his motives. But this was different than last time. Waving his arm in a beckoning fashion between chords, he urged her with his smile to join him.

She crinkled her eyebrows together, trying to show her confusion, but he just hooked his finger in the come-up-here gesture. A tingling sensation snaked down her limbs and her heart sped up. He did understand, right? She had gotten it through to him that they were just friends … Surely, he wasn't going to tell her he'd changed his mind and he still had feelings for her, was he? He kept singing lyrics about love, his eyes on her, making her stomach start to swirl with unease. She looked to her family but they all just seemed to be swapping glances, their faces giving her nothing.

Everyone had stopped what they were doing, conversations ceased. Tammy's eyes were glued on the two of them as were many others'. They were probably all wondering if it would be a replay of last year too. Slowly, she climbed the few steps to join him. Otis had installed more lighting just for occasions like these and beams of white light blinded her. She squinted at Rhett, his face obscured by the glowing dots that had formed in her vision.

He finished the song.

"Delivery for you," Rhett said, his voice booming through the microphone in the silence that followed once she got up there with him. From a stool behind him, he took a box that looked like it had a pie inside. "Open it," he insisted with a crooked grin.

Hesitantly, Holly lifted the lid to find a sweet potato pie, and, in icing, it said, "I think I could fall in love with you." Fear flooded her as she looked at Rhett for answers. Hadn't they settled this? Now all these people were looking on. This was awful.

"What does it say?" someone called from the crowd.

Holly's heart thumping like a snare drum, she searched Rhett's face for understanding, but he kept that maddening smile. She felt sick, woozy.

Then, Rhett's face softened as if to tell her that she was okay. "When you went out on your own, I told you that I just wanted you to be happy. Remember?"

"Yes."

But Rhett had to know that he wasn't the one who could make her happy. How many times did she have to tell him that? *Papa*, she said to herself, *send some Christmas magic my way. Make this be something wonderful and not something terrifying.*

"As your best friend, I wanted to be here to give you my blessing," Rhett told her, and he nodded to the floor at the front of the stage. The spotlight disappeared leaving larger spots in Holly's eyes as she tried to focus on the person standing in front of them below. At first it was just a shadow, but when her vision cleared, she made out those square shoulders, that perfect hairline, that navy blue trench coat, and then, suddenly, the whole picture became sharp, and there he was.

Joe.

She scanned all the faces in front of her to be sure that she wasn't dreaming, Tammy swooning in the center of the crowd, Nana grinning as big as day. She looked for Katharine, frantically searching for her, but she came up empty. What was going on?

Joe walked up the steps to join her on the stage, their gaze now locked, and Holly felt like she hadn't missed a single day with him. She was just as happy to see him now as she had been when they were together last.

"You got married..." she said, her words barely audible through her surprise.

He shook his head. "Katharine and I called it off together." He took a step toward her, everyone looking on. "You didn't stick around to see."

She let out a quiet gasp, putting her nervous hand to her mouth. "But the wedding?" she said through her fingers.

He allowed a smile. "We'd had an argument before the rehearsal. When you first met me, I was at the cabin alone because we'd been arguing a lot over seemingly nothing, and I didn't know if I should be getting married, so I'd wanted some time to think. I realized that I felt a duty to do right by her because of how my father had treated my mother." The lights were on him, the entire stage theirs, Rhett off to the side, but Joe didn't seem to care. "I'd made a promise to Katharine, and I was ready to carry it out, but as we stood facing each other at the altar, it was as if both of us came to our senses. She and I decided together that we didn't love one another anymore. And we both knew that marrying each other wasn't the right thing to do."

Joe put his hands on Holly's waist and looked into her eyes. "I hadn't loved Katharine in a long time, and Katharine felt the same way about me. She told me that she felt pressured too."

"Is she okay?"

"She's great. I think she's dating an intellectual property lawyer now." He grinned down at her.

Holly was glad to hear that Katharine had moved on. But that thought brought her back to Joe and what he clearly still had to tell her. "And you? How are you doing?"

"I'm really good." His eyes said more than just that, his hands tenderly resting on her hips. "Holly, I didn't know what true love was until I met you," he said. "What made me realize it was that I couldn't get over my feelings for you, watching you leave the wedding that day. But I wanted to be sure that when I came to tell you how I feel about you that both of us were in the right place for that sort of admission." He pulled her close. "I completely fell for you last Christmas. It blindsided me. And I spent the last year trying to get over it. But I couldn't."

"He called me nearly every day to see how you were, Holly," Nana said from her seat. "I knew he felt the same when he was at the cabin—I could tell! But I kept quiet."

It was absolutely silent in Otis's barn as everyone looked on. Holly blinked away her tears.

By the look on Joe's face, he challenged her to tell him what she was thinking, but the lump in her throat was so big that she couldn't talk.

"I just noticed that I'm the second person to profess his feelings for you on this stage." He and Rhett shared a sort of comradery just then, making Holly smile through her tears. He held up a finger. "And I can't sing. But I *am* the first to do it with pie." He shrugged off his coat and draped it on a stool. Then he took her into his arms.

Holly sniffled and laughed at the same time. When she'd finally managed to form words, she said, "I thought about you all the time. I couldn't get you off my mind."

Joe brushed away a tear on her cheek. "Think you could fall in love with me too?"

"I already have."

That curiosity consuming his eyes disappeared from view as he cupped her face in his hands, and pressed his lips to hers. Her blood pulsed through her body like fireworks, the rhythms of their lips moving against one another, the most perfect thing she'd ever felt. Everyone in the barn went wild, cheering, but all Holly noticed was the absolute perfection of him. That movie reel came back in full force—the feel of his arms around her, the way they'd felt tangled up together on the sofa that morning...But this time, she didn't have to push it out of her mind. This time, his arms were around her now and she knew that it was only the beginning...

When they both finally realized where they were and slowed to a more respectable pace, Joe pulled back and grinned at her.

"Aw, Joey and Holly!" Tammy said from the crowd, her hand on her heart. "Y'all are so cute together."

They both laughed.

"I'm definitely more Joey than Joseph," he said. "And this is the closest to home that I've ever known."

Holly got up on her tiptoes and kissed him again.

"Guess what," Joe said, a sparkle in his eye. "I'm here all Christmas. And look who's with me."

Joe pointed to the table with Holly's family, and she had to force her vision past the light to see, but sitting between her mother and Nana was Harvey. He waved happily. Holly sucked in a breath of surprise, delighted for the both of them. She couldn't wait to catch up on everything Joe and Harvey had talked about. Holly let her mind wander to the big Christmas they'd have this year with everyone there—her family and his.

"Merry Christmas," Joe said into her ear.

"Merry Christmas." Then Holly stopped. "Oh! You don't have any gifts under the tree again."

Joe laughed. "Well, there's always Puckett's." He reached into his pocket and pulled out his keys, dangling them in front of her, the "Joey" keychain on the end.

"Y'all ready to dance?" Rhett said, cutting in. "Holly, you and Joe start us off." With his guitar in his hands, Rhett began Chuck Berry's "Run Rudolph Run."

Joe's eyes grew round. "This is fast. Does that mean I have to line dance?"

"Sure does!" she said, pulling him down the steps to the dance floor.

Harvey ran over to them and handed Joe the camouflage hat Holly bought him last year, and went back over to the table. Joe put it on his head, making Holly double over laughing. She grabbed him by the arm and took him across the dance floor where he stopped still.

Holly looked into his eyes to find the reason for the abrupt halt and his gaze swallowed her. "I have to confess something," he said.

She waited.

"I think I finally believe in magic."

Holly tipped her head back and laughed before Joe took her into his arms and pressed his lips to hers. In that moment he made her feel it too. She thought about how just the mention of his name made her heart flutter, the explosion of nervous energy that came from an unintentional touch, the way every hair stood up on her arms in response to the way he said, "Holly." That was nothing short of magic. Christmas magic was all around her tonight.

Suddenly, the music screeched to a halt, causing Holly to pull away from Joe and look over at Rhett.

"You have to stop kissing to dance!" Rhett teased them from the stage, making the whole barn burst into laughter. "Will y'all please help them?" he called to the crowd. Little by little, they all started to filter onto the dance floor and Rhett resumed his song, the thumping rhythm of it swirling around them.

"Here, you two," Otis said, tapping his feet with Nana holding his hands. "We'll show you how it's done."

With a big smile, Holly leaned in toward Joe and stole one more kiss before dancing into the night.

A Letter from Jenny

Thank you so much for reading *It Started with Christmas*! I hope you enjoyed Holly's story and found it to be a heart-warming Christmas escape.

While you're making a warm cup of hot cocoa, if you'd like me to drop you a line when my next book is out, you can sign up here:

www.itsjennyhale.com/email-signup

I won't share your email with anyone else, and I'll only email you when a new book is released.

If you did enjoy *It Started with Christmas,* I'd love it if you'd write a review. As an author, hearing feedback from readers is as exciting as unwrapping a giant Christmas gift, and it also helps other readers to pick up one of my books for the first time.

Still craving a little more holiday cheer? Check out my other Christmas novels: *Coming Home for Christmas, A Christmas to Remember, Christmas Wishes and Mistletoe*

Kisses, All I Want for Christmas, and *We'll Always Have Christmas.*

Until next time!

Jenny x

        7201437.Jenny_Hale

        jennyhaleauthor

        @jhaleauthor

        jhaleauthor

        www.itsjennyhale.com

Acknowledgments

A warm thank-you must go to Oliver Rhodes for his guidance and direction over the years. He is the one who first breathed life into this career of mine, and keeps me going strong, book after book. I will be forever grateful.

To the wonderful Natasha Harding, who gets to hear my one thousand questions every time something new pops up. She answers them all with grace and kindness, and I am so lucky to have her on my side.

The team at Bookouture is second to none. I am thankful every day that I found this amazing publisher and that I've been able to grow with it. A big thank-you to the team for all the behind-the-scenes action that is required to get my books into the hands of readers.

And I couldn't do any of it without my family. To Justin, for all the household chores he's finished (or done all on his own), the nights out to celebrate the big days and to relax after the tough ones, and the listening ear through it all, I am so grateful. To my kids who get to have firsthand knowledge of every single thing that comes my way as I drag my computer to parks, skating rinks, and trampoline arenas, I thank you too!

I'm blessed every day to be in this field and I couldn't do it without prayer and faith. What a ride!

About the Author

Jenny Hale is a *USA Today* bestselling author of romantic women's fiction. Her novels *Coming Home for Christmas* and *Christmas Wishes and Mistletoe Kisses* have been adapted for television on the Hallmark Channel. Her stories are chock-full of feel-good romance and overflowing with warm settings, great friends, and family. Grab a cup of coffee, settle in, and join the fun!

You can learn more at:
ItsJennyHale.com
Twitter @jhaleauthor
Facebook.com/JennyHaleAuthor
Instagram @jhaleauthor